Calpurnia

Calpurnia

Anne Scott Beller

Alfred A. Knopf   *New York*   2003

This Is a Borzoi Book
Published by Alfred A. Knopf

Copyright © 2003 by Anne Scott Beller

All rights reserved under International and Pan-American
Copyright Conventions. Published in the United States by
Alfred A. Knopf, a division of Random House, Inc., New
York, and simultaneously in Canada by Random House
of Canada, Limited, Toronto.
Distributed by Random House, Inc., New York.

www.aaknopf.com

Knopf, Borzoi Books, and the colophon are registered
trademarks of Random House, Inc.

Library of Congress Cataloging-in-Publication Data
Scott, Anne.
Calpurnia / Anne Scott.
p.   cm.
ISBN 0-375-41380-4 (alk. paper)
1. Philadelphia (Pa.)—Fiction.   2. Inheritance and
succession—Fiction.   3. Historic buildings—Fiction.
4. Appraisers—Fiction.   5. Aged women—Fiction.
6. Mansions—Fiction.   I. Title.

PS3602.E646 C35 2003
813'.6—dc21   2002030096

Manufactured in the United States of America
First Edition

To Ave

Calpurnia

1

ELIZABETH turns her back to the sun between two urns planted with ivy so dark it's almost black. The house sits broadside to the street in its own little false forest of rhododendrons and Irish yews: Villa Calpurnia, faced with yellowing plaster scored to look like stone, its name in unembarrassed italics above the tall double doors. It's three-thirty, the hottest hour of the hottest day so far this June. From the cracked flagstone terrace six tall windows divide the front façade, lined up like mirrors to outstare the southern sun.

Entering a new house for the first time there's always a moment when you begin to wonder whether you've really come to the right door, whether the borrowed key will actually fit the unfamiliar lock, whether the pins will ever line up, the barrel will ever turn. Elizabeth has no aptitude for locks and keys, and this lock has a mind of its own: there's no play in it, no give and take. Leaning in on the doorknob for one last try she's conscious of a silence so deep she can hear the sound of her own breath and supposes she must look like a burglar standing here in broad daylight fiddling with the cranky lock.

But nobody's watching. The street at her back is empty, stuck in its formal parquetry of clipped privet and straight slate walks, and it's only as she's about to give up and go back to her car, admit defeat (this far and no farther; a principled last stand), that she feels a split second's shift somewhere deep inside the barrel of the lock: a skipped heartbeat, some kind of grudging second thought. On her next try the key turns, the door swings open, and the hall widens out ahead of her like a book opening to someone's favorite passage on its best-read page.

ELIZABETH puts her handbag on the telephone table and digs out her clipboard, then loads it with paper and roots in her pocket for a pen. The hall is alive with watchful pictures: dogs and cats with human faces, bewigged burghers and Roman senators, nineteenth-century poets and forgotten queens. Stepping in out of the sunlight and closing the door behind you, there's a sense of suspended argument and the half-stunned silence of party-goers turning to face a new arrival at the door. Elizabeth starts to count them, and gives up. Even from here you can see that Calpurnia's going to be an embarrassment of riches. Just classifying everything, let alone inventorying it and putting a price on things, will take her days, or even weeks.

Elizabeth uncaps her pen and writes: 6/5/84: Villa Calpurnia, parlor floor, Entrance hall: wall art and fixtures; furnishings; (smalls?), then looks for a window to open, overwhelmed and out of breath before she's even begun. The indoor air is heavy with the smell of paint thinner and dried bergamot, a perfume she thinks of as Edwardian. From the hall there's a wedge of red-walled dining room visible, and, beyond it, a corner of glass-faced pantry cabinets. The library has Persian airs, the sunroom is Japoniste; if she's lucky there will be eighteenth-century silver in the sideboard and hallmarked china in the butler's pantry. Nothing spectacular, probably, but nothing undistinguished either, once it's had a decent cleaning and taken a nice high shine. Which doesn't mean the sale won't be profitable or the turnout won't be good. Because Calpurnia comes with its own folklore (the uncle who helped invent Mentholatum and endowed a chair at Penn; the grandmother who danced all night with the Prince of Wales), not to mention the whiff of scandal attaching to the lady of the house, dead in March, and the tennis-playing heir apparent, her only son. Or the fashionable niece; or the dowager bridge-playing aunt. By the same token every scrap of table linen and chipped china will have its own provenance and its own little story to tell. People will come to see the sights and leave with something to show for it. Even the pots and pans will bring a decent price.

ELIZABETH has been in this business for seven years, much longer than she ever originally set out to be. It started as a sideline, something to tide her over until she got her life together and a real job came along, but a real job never did, and by now it's her major souce of income: a living, if she's lucky, and sometimes something more. And though she pretends otherwise, even to herself, the truth is that she has never really been in it entirely for the money or, on a grander scale, the art and artifacts. What keeps her going, she supposes, is the history and prehistory, the secrets, a trespasser's sense of lost and found. People think that when they die the whole world dies with them: they hide things in safe places and forget about them for years or even generations at a time, while their bibelots go out of fashion and become invisible to the undereducated eye; copies of old deeds go yellow and tear in the creases; rings roll under the radiators or into the depths of the upholstery and simply disappear. Elizabeth would feel cheated if there were no mysteries to unravel except the biographical ones, no surprises except the bottom line.

The family's due at four (Peachy Carmichael has briefed her): there's a niece, Nina English, the estate's executor, owner of a shop in Clover Hill that sells hand-painted sportswear and patchworked imports from Japan; a brother from Cleveland, with or without his wife; the deceased's unmarried son; and probably an attorney or two, because in Elizabeth's experience people like that never go anywhere without their lawyers in tow. Maribel Davies was buried three months ago and the property taxes are due in August; the heirs have been advised to put the house up for sale in plenty of time for the back-to-school market in the fall.

Villa Calpurnia may show well from the street but isn't expected to bring what it's worth at resale. It's too hard to heat, too deed-restricted, and too big: you'd need a staff of two or three to run it, and deep pockets to pay the bills. "Everything's falling apart, but she still had some lovely pieces," said Peachy, who had landed the listing through Nina. Peachy's connections in the real estate business are legendary, and she never throws an old Rolodex card away. "You'll make out like gangbusters on the sale," she said, handing Elizabeth the key.

Seen in close-up like this the lovely pieces are a bit shabby and somewhat few and far between, but Elizabeth always tries to sound grateful when she talks to Peachy; they've known each other since high school, they were in love with the same English teacher, they sat next to each other in French, and what would Elizabeth do without Peachy's little leads? It was Peachy's conviction that there was a good living in estate sales if you kept your social bridges mended and knew the right way to talk to well-heeled heirs and sorrowing widowers. "You're artistic," Peachy said. "Don't deny it. You know your Victoriana backwards and forwards. You're going to be an absolute natural at this stuff."

Elizabeth glances at her watch (where to begin?) and wonders what makes anyone a natural at anything, other than good or bad luck, and fear of the wolf at the door. She's got ten or fifteen minutes before the family gets here, time for a quick look around, at least downstairs, and a hasty trip to the john. She double-checks the lock on the front door and sets off in search of the powder room, past silvery etchings and commemorative mezzotints with titles in a lacy cursive almost too beautiful to read. By artistic she supposes Peachy means impractical, easily dazzled, seducible by every passing fad: guilty as charged? On a hexagonal tabletop there's a chased brass tray full of junk mail and unlabeled keys, and, flanking the table, a pair of caned Hepplewhite chairs with deeply sagging seats. The mirror, early nineteenth century and possibly French (she may have to get Ellios in on that), runs to within a few inches of the ceiling, a good seven feet. Coming in for a closer look at the foxed edges of the glass (not worth replacing, but saleable just the same), she sees herself fuzzily in its depths—blond, fortyish, wide-eyed, overwhelmed—and gives herself a little scare.

In the living room three windows with thick entablatures and green dime-store roller shades exaggerate the room's haphazard classicism, but whole sections of the egg-and-dart chair rail are missing and the plaster Beaux Arts medallion in the middle of the ceiling sports a brassy new department-store chandelier. There's a white marble mantelpiece on the left wall and a dark red sofa on the right and above it hangs a handsomely framed painting of what must have been the woman of the house: Maribel Archibald Davies, presumably in her youth, together with an unhappy little boy in a Prince Charles haircut under a rakish dandelion wreath.

The painting guards the living room like a dog. Except for the face with its dated, too red lipstick and tented eyebrows, it's not your standard family portrait: the subject, in full dress costume (something neoclassical, diaphanous but otherwise unrevealing), wears a single strand of overlarge pearls around her neck; she has a headful of barbed black hair and a cinematic, mid-twentieth-century smile. With her left hand the sitter balances the corner of a huge heraldic shield angled into the bare earth like a shovel, reflecting a wavy monochrome version of her head and her sulky off-center Cupid in his crown of yellow weeds. The face in the portrait is almost but not quite beautiful: the nose is too long and the jaw too narrow, but from the look in her eye you're meant to know that she's aware of her imperfections and may even be challenging the painter to spell them out. Elizabeth kneels on the couch for a better look at the painting and the title on the plaque (*Aphrodite the Gravedigger*). A tough sell, probably: just old enough to be old-fashioned but not quite old enough to pass for an antique. And, more important, too personal: a riddle; a cartoon without a caption; a kind of inside joke.

ELIZABETH checks her watch again and circles the hall from left to right (the Persian library, brown but charming; a sunroom shuttered tightly against the sun; the deep red dining room) and, last but not least, the powder room—an architectural afterthought wedged into a boxy hexagon four steps below the central stairs.

Inside, green tiles bounce a thin underwater daylight from wall to wall. There's a pedestal sink on a fancy fluted base with a basket of dried yellow flowers beside it and, in the marble soap dish, an ancient potpourri that smells of slightly rancid oranges and turn-of-the-century cloves. Elizabeth ducks her bag behind the flowers and flushes the toilet to make sure it works. Above the sink there's a Venetian mirror with articulated candlesticks and, to its left, a pair of delft sconces on the stair wall; with, opposite them, three dime-store towel holders and an ascending series of engravings hung stepwise, one to a stair. The pictures are cheaply framed and matted—Italian, probably (Parla Mercurio a Glauros; Parla Vulcan a Ceres), and late Renaissance or possibly early baroque: a series of mythological couples in suggestive poses, sloe-eyed and unsmiling, with banners modestly unfurled from left to right across their private parts. The banners appear to have been drawn on years if not whole centuries after the fact, in dark blue India ink, though if you get up close enough you can still see the ghost of the bowdlerized couplings underneath—Vulcan's larger-than-life erection, the outlines of Deianira's hand as she guides Hercules into place under the thick sculptural folds of her skirts.

If Elizabeth had to make a guess she'd say they're worth a few hundred dollars as a set to the right buyer, but she could be off by a hundred or a hundred and fifty on either side: you'd have to take them out of their frames and pry off the backings to be sure. Hardly what you'd call her area of expertise, though of course the real art in this line of work is knowing what you don't know and keeping an open mind about everything you think you do. He's not a personal favorite of hers, but you can't help thinking of people like Ellios at a time like this. Ellios is an unapologetic realist. He's seen everything and knows how to market everything he's seen: behind the scenes, if need be, and without embarrassment to all concerned.

ELIZABETH pulls the powder-room door shut behind her, then heads for the kitchen to run herself a glass of water and have a quick look at the crystal and tableware before the heirs arrive. Because there's always a moment at the beginning of a new job, let's be honest, when you feel like a miner without a lamp, a dowser without a wand. You get over it, of course, because you have to; by tomorrow, knock wood, she'll roll up her sleeves, get to work, and make the best of her own ignorance and anxiety as she goes along. If she's lucky she'll find the long-lost jewel, the hidden love letter, the unexecuted will, exercising an archaeologist's tricks (dig deep before you dig wide; take nothing at face value; leave no stone unturned). It's her art, her craft; her bread and butter; she's done it a hundred times before; she could do it in her sleep. Slowly but surely she'll get the hang of the house, its locked drawers and hidden bolt-holes, its geological sequences, all its little twists and turns. She'll unbury the buried treasure and learn the cast of characters by heart (which colors they favored for their sheets and towels, what music they played till the record cracked, what pills they took to put themselves to sleep) until she gets to know these perfect strangers as well as she knows her own next of kin. Or maybe, if the truth be told (an outsider looking in), as well and in some ways just a little bit better than she has any right to assume she's ever even really known herself.

2

EG KEEPS watch from the cutting garden as the first cars arrive: the butcher, the baker, the candlestick maker: she knows all of Maribel's faithful and their cars by heart (except Conrad's rental, picked up at the airport whenever he comes in, dark red this time around). Otherwise they're all black, including the first one to arrive, who, having pulled her square black Buick only halfway under the porte cochere, has made it difficult for the others to squeeze themselves into position on the turnaround. A tall blonde, from what Peg can see of her, maybe just a little past her prime, in a well-cut blazer and moderately high heels: another real estate agent, probably. There have been quite a few of those lately. But, thank God, no more visitations from the Lower Merion police.

"Just a formality," Nina kept telling her, "because you were the one who put in the call; I mean what was there to hide? Nothing to worry about," she said. "Dr. Giles has explained everything to them; they have to fill out their reports, it's only natural. That's their job." Nina talks to Peg as if she were ninety years old and inattentive instead of seventy-six and moderately deaf. "Look, I know this has been trying for you," she'd said.

Peg slows down to a snail's pace and keeps her head low; she's given herself the job of dead-heading the peonies today and watering the impatiens at either side of the bed. Her cutting garden is on the side of the house that faces Maribel's and, weather permitting, she's always out in her garden; or was always out in her garden in the days when she could still spend five hours at a stretch down on her hands and knees; and wasn't it Nina herself who asked her to keep watch on things across the way? Peg's bedroom is catty-corner from Maribel's and the studio runs the length of the house; for the last six months, at least, she's made it a point to check the lights over there before she goes to bed. As requested. (As requested by Nina personally, she might add.) Maribel was a sick woman but she didn't want nurses, or visitors, or company of any kind: a party girl turned loner in her declining years. "I'm not that far gone yet," she said, and still went on saying when she was very far gone indeed.

Coby's the last to arrive, in that awful truck of his; he'll have to park on the street. And just as well; his bright blue pickup wouldn't look right in the driveway over there cheek by jowl with all the expensive cars. Not Peg's fault; if she'd had her way he'd still be driving Joey's Citroen, brand-new: pneumatic, it went up and down whenever you got in or out. It's years since Peg has driven it but she refuses to sell it even so; after Justin died the damn thing just sat there, going to rack and ruin, taking up space in her garage, and what would it have cost her to turn the papers over to him? But Maribel said no. Couldn't come up with the cash to buy him a decent car herself but she didn't want anyone else doing the honors either; no indeed. Peg shrugged it off. Good hedges make good neighbors, though

Coby lost out both ways. When the young policeman asked her who'd been around to the house the day she died Peg never hesitated to give her answer: No one that I recall.

Peg collects the spent flower heads in a plastic supermarket bag and cuts seven fresh ones to add to the vase in the hall. It's come to the point where she has no tolerance for bought perfume, even the expensive kinds; she wants her perfume the way God made it, natural as the lilies of the field, straight from mother earth, and at this time of year the whole house smells of flowers, real ones, with peonies in the lead. Unlike Calpurnia, where no matter how many windows you opened or doors you closed, you could never get rid of the stench of paint and turpentine. Sick as she was, didn't it turn Maribel's stomach, day in, day out? "Oh, you get used to it," she said. "It's just like air to me. It's already in my blood."

Not a great thing to have in your blood, along with all the other stuff they made her take at the end, Peg thinks as she wipes fern scum from the pruner blades (the last few blooms are only half-opened; you want to encourage the new growth, yes; but shouldn't there be some show left over for the neighbors and the envious passerby?). Maribel never took the painkillers that people like Peg suggested to her, and Giles himself wasn't much of a man for pills. "I suppose he's saving it for when the pain is really bad," said Maribel.

Peg pulls herself to her feet by her own wisteria vine, hand over hand, daring it to snap or break away; and exactly who was supposed to say when the pain was bad enough for painkillers, you had to ask yourself? The wisteria holds, but barely. (She'd be happy to see the end of it; it's only bloomed once for her in fourteen years, not a great batting average for something so well dug in.) Upright now, even standing on tiptoe, she can barely see over the top of the hedge these days, and wouldn't want to be caught looking anyway. Not by that crew of smart young and not so young know-it-alls, dressed like party-goers in their Sunday best, alighting from their big black cars. Still, it's like old times at Calpurnia over there with all those cars in the drive; life, music, action, and strangers from out of town. It takes you back. At Maribel's funeral the flowers were knee-deep on the coffin but Peg was the only one to cry.

"I'm just glad it's all over," said Nina, "for her sake. I'm just glad it went so fast."

Peg nodded and blew her nose. Everyone who knows her knows how easily she tears up at the movies, at weddings, watching the evening news: she's famous for it, she weeps at the drop of a hat. "I know, you're right, a blessing," she said, and went out of her way, afterward, to make sure Coby knew where to come if he ever wanted a nice cup of tea and a friendly shoulder to cry on.

Because one of these days Peg and Coby really need to have a little talk. If and when he ever finally breaks down. If and when he ever finally feels the need.

3

"**T**HAT's Maribel, yes, aged—oh, thirty-eight or thirty-nine," says Nina English. "Portrait by Lipscomb, *the* number-one portrait painter of the day: well, locally, anyway, I suppose. Her father commissioned it when he retired from the bank; he said he wanted something classical, and this is what he got: Maribel's little joke. It's a takeoff on some famous Greek bas-relief; that's Coby in the corner, holding up the shield, aged four—maybe five. His grandfather was not amused, but he paid up. Maribel was the apple of his eye." She looks at Coby, the portrait's grown-up four-year-old slouched in a velvet armchair in dusty tennis whites, who refuses to return her smile.

"I suppose that means someone in the family will be taking it, then," says Elizabeth.

Nina raises an eyebrow. "Well, it's been discussed," she says. "Is that going to be a problem?" The smile she flashes is hostessy and off-putting, full of unnecessarily white and perfect teeth. She's a woman in her late thirties or early forties with a mane of fuzzy Pre-Raphaelite hair in various shades of gray, dressed in a floaty caftan hand-painted with giant paisleys and other abstract shapes.

"Oh no, no problem at all," says Elizabeth.

"It's a fabulous likeness, actually: I used to sit in on the sittings; she was a terrible model. Oh, the worst—the painter painted, wouldn't stop talking; couldn't sit still, you know the type. I was madly in love with that costume; old-fashioned China silk—you never see it nowadays; the real McCoy. Are you interested in fabrics, Mrs.—is it Miss? Oliver? because Maribel never threw anything away."

Elizabeth doesn't wear silk if she can help it (too hot in summer, too cold in winter), but she's happy to hear that Maribel never threw anything away. "Oh, I answer to everything," she says.

Nina English puts her hands together in the classical gesture of *namaste.* She's her own masterpiece, mannered and polished; her jewelry is famous; her dress shop has been featured in *Interior Design* and *Vogue.* "Peachy Carmichael speaks so highly of you," she says.

Elizabeth nods and smiles. Peachy would speak highly of her, of course, as Elizabeth would and does of Peachy when the tables are turned. "Peachy and I have known each other for ages," she says. "We went to school together, actually. That's how far back we go."

Nina uncouples her hands and waves them at the men behind her on the couch. "We all trust Peachy implicitly, don't we?" she says.

There are five of them; Elizabeth has been carefully introduced but is finding it hard to keep their names and faces straight. Starting from the left there's Maribel's brother Conrad (or Conwell?), a red-skinned man in his late sixties or early seventies with a small confrontational beard; then Maribel's son

Coby (thin and dark, dressed like a cartoon undergraduate in a soiled white varsity sweater and not quite matching pants), as well as three much older men, at first glance almost undistinguishable in their almost identical gray suits, lined up at exactly equal arm's length on the couch. Nina has done the honors: her husband Hugh, fiftyish, a man with a permanent and perhaps congenitally curled upper lip, and next to him in ascending order of both size and (probably) age, the family lawyer, Jaxheimer, and the elderly doctor, Giles. "We were so thrilled when she suggested you," says Nina. "We would simply have had no idea where to turn. The whole thing happened so unexpectedly," she says. "I mean, didn't it, Dr. Giles?"

At the sound of his name the elderly doctor nods briefly and looks carefully at his shoes. The oldest and smallest of the three gray suits lined up together on the couch, he has the look of a man who's much too polite to keep checking his wristwatch but wishes you would just get on with things, and the others are even more visibly ill at ease. These are the kinds of men, Elizabeth thinks, who are always overdue for another meeting, who always have bigger fish to fry, and in the meantime haven't quite made up their minds exactly where they want to be found standing if and when the flashbulbs start to pop.

Nina waves her hands and one of her rings flashes blue like a short circuit in an electric line. "Maribel was the kind of person who had never been sick a single day in her life," she says. "I think it was that generation, all those wars: you have to be brought up that way. It was blood poisoning, wasn't it, Dr. Giles? Maribel was just like a mother to me. People said we looked alike and I suppose we did. Maribel taught me everything I knew."

Elizabeth waits for Conrad to settle down and for Dr. Giles to stop fiddling with the stem-winder of his watch before she makes her presentation. "Please believe me when I say that I know how hard it can be deciding what to do at a time like this," she says. "A person's belongings are so much a part of them." She takes a quick look at the portrait; there is a certain likeness to Nina there, but it goes in and out of focus in the fading light; the shape of the face is the same but Maribel's nose is longer, and there's a deep cleft in Nina's tight, round, and childlike chin.

Nina says, "Oh, dear God, isn't that the truth?" though the most valuable of Maribel's belongings have already gone to Sotheby's or Freeman's, and from what Elizabeth can see there's no obvious fortune to be made on anything that's left. Which doesn't mean that everyone in this room doesn't have his or her eye on some little something too inconsequential for the auction block: and, she hopes, some sense of who gets what already worked out between them, because she doesn't believe in leaving these agonizing decisions till the bitter end. "Then of course you're always faced with the usual dilemma," she says. "I mean whether to opt for the memorabilia or the cash."

On the couch Maribel's son puts his hands in his pockets and closes his eyes so tightly it's as if a light had been turned off in his face. It's her standard speech to the bereaved; but has she put things too bluntly, said too much too soon? From the looks of it Elizabeth guesses Coby is too recently bereaved to have given much thought to what he wants or doesn't want from his mother's house; years later he'll wake up one morning and wonder why he didn't speak out for this or that treasure, these old photographs or those old books. Nina looks at her cousin and looks away. "You're an absolute mind reader," she says.

Maribel's brother, the man with the beard, gets to his feet and starts passing a little damask pillow back and forth from one hand to another like a football or a catcher's mitt. "I understand you're an art historian," he says.

For a moment Elizabeth thinks she hears the edge of a sneer in his voice, but if so his square-cornered smile disowns it. "Oh, nothing quite so grand," she says. Peachy always makes the most of her to prospective clients, and she understands the brother's need to check her out, but labels make her nervous. "I suppose I set out in life to be an archaeologist," she says, "but this is as far as I got." The brother nods, but Coby's gray eyes stay closed, and something in his clenched face reminds Elizabeth of a child refusing to watch the sight of his own blood.

Maribel's brother puts the cushion back on the couch. "Nina tells me we're to go through the house from top to bottom and make lists of anything that we particularly want," he says. "Is that the drill? I like to do things by the book." He's tall, he has Maribel's nose and chin without her sardonic eye, and there's something self-indulgent in the way he fondles his perfect beard.

"Well, don't we all?" says Nina, then turns, startled, toward the hall, where there's the sound of a key scratching, furtive and mouselike, in the lock. They all stop talking and their collective silence, ears tuned to invasion, reminds Elizabeth of her own recent struggle on the other side of the door.

"Oh, my God, Roberto," says Nina. "Of course; better late than never, but how wonderful he could come." She heads into the hall to help. "Roberto, how wonderful," she says. "We're so glad you could make it. Did you have a terrible trip?"

The newcomer is a man on the far side of middle age with black hair and a neat, gray, Italianate mustache. He pockets his key and makes the rounds of the room shaking each hand carefully, and, when he finally reaches Elizabeth, raises hers to chin level, then lowers it again, as if he had originally meant to kiss it and then had second thoughts. The Latin lover, Elizabeth thinks; but whose?

Nina makes the introductions. "Miss Oliver is an art historian," she says. "No, an archaeologist—have I got that right? You two will have so much in common. Mrs. (Ms.) Oliver is going to handle the sale for us locally, all the dealers and appraisers and so on; we're putting ourselves in her hands." And to Elizabeth she says, "Roberto is our in-house adviser. He knows Robert Woolley at Sotheby's." She's putting Elizabeth on notice in the nicest way: Roberto's the family curator; there will be no unexpected windfalls here, no veins of unmined gold.

Coby opens his eyes. "Lloyd George knows my father, Father knows Lloyd George," he sings, in a surprisingly crisp and tuneful baritone.

"Ah, Coby," says the man who knows Robert Woolley at Sotheby's. "I didn't see you there; I hope you're well." He finishes his rounds of the room, then turns back to Elizabeth and shakes her hand again. "I'm delighted to meet you, Miss Oliver; delighted to see all of you again. I hope everyone is well."

Nina claps her hands. "I think this calls for drinks," she says, "don't you? All those in favor say aye."

No one says aye, but Nina heads off to the kitchen anyway and comes back to serve crème de menthe and Armagnac, apologetically, in little juice glasses, including Maribel's portrait, for a minute, in the toast. "To Roberto," she says. "And I think I speak for all of us when I say that Mrs. Oliver has our full cooperation, doesn't she? If there's anything we can do, I mean anything you need at all, please feel perfectly free to ask." She puts her hand on Coby's arm, giving him a quarter turn in Elizabeth's direction, as if setting him back on course. "And vice versa," she says, "I would certainly hope, naturally."

"Oh, naturally," says Elizabeth. "And, please: Elizabeth is fine."

Outside the afternoon sky has darkened, erasing some previously fine line between light and shade. Downhill there's the sound of thunder, and the leaves of two matching dogwoods turn inside out in a sudden breeze. Any moment now there's going to be a storm.

Nina stands between Coby and his mother's portrait as she hands him his little glass of Armagnac ("What *is* this stuff?" says Conrad), and when he ducks to drink it there's something in the weight of his neck inside the not quite white collar of his shirt that reminds Elizabeth of her own son, Pen. But nobody else takes more than a token sip, and, one by one, at Nina's suggestion and under her fussy supervision, the family sets off in search of keepsakes, carrying handfuls of the little colored stickers she has thoughtfully provided for them (red for Conrad, blue for Coby, green for Roberto, yellow for herself and Hugh) before everything is ticketed for sale and it's understood to be too late. Left behind in the living room as the rest of them set off on their treasure hunt are Giles, the doctor, and Coby, the son, immobilized in his velvet armchair, pasting his little stickers uselessly to his wrists.

"I grew up in this house, you know," he says.

Elizabeth says, "This must be so hard for you."

Coby looks right and left like someone searching, jokily, for evidence of hardship; from the circles under his eyes Elizabeth guesses that he hasn't slept in days and wonders if he's grief stricken or merely strange. He pulls a pair of sunglasses from his shirt pocket and puts them on. "I've been through worse, believe it or not," he says. "I mean, haven't you? Hasn't everyone?"

It's a small child's question, irritating though otherwise

probably innocent, but Elizabeth has never had to fake a sympathy she doesn't feel; she's about to disassemble the scenes of his childhood, dismantle his oldest memories and sell them off to the highest bidder for whatever the market will bear. She knows from bitter experience that even the most amicable divorce is plunder, and death is obviously even worse: no one can ever tell how much they really love the familiar heirlooms and hand-me-downs until they're under the gavel, going, going, gone.

"Well, yes and no," she says.

Waiting for the rest of them to come back downstairs Nina has already started rounding up glasses and Elizabeth pitches in, collecting napkins and coasters from the tabletops. "Coby," says Nina, bossy and maternal, "be an angel; give us a helping hand." The son of the house reaches for a glass on the mantelpiece and misses; it shatters on the spiked finial of a black iron andiron and splinters on the hearth. Less than a second later there's another drumroll of thunder from the garden, much closer this time than the first, like a sonic boom: a seeming inversion of cause and effect. Coby turns to Elizabeth empty-handed. "Do you believe in ghosts?" he says.

Elizabeth laughs, and bends over the hearth to pick up the pieces, happy for something practical to do. Outside there's a zigzag of lightning in the western sky, reflected like tracer fire in the opened French door, and Nina's husband appears in the hall like something sucked downstairs by the sudden wind. He hands Nina a fistful of the bright yellow stickers he has not seen fit to put on anything. "Did you ever get the alarm system fixed?" he asks his wife. From the garden there's a smell of boxwood as strong as brimstone.

"But I thought you said you were going to take care of it!" Nina says. She drops his unused stickers into a large glass ashtray on the coffee table like the petals of some improbably yellow flower, as Conrad returns, empty-handed, from the top of the stairs. Behind them Elizabeth stands in the door to the garden with a handful of broken glass; the party's definitely over now, though nobody wants to be the last one out of the house. Jaxheimer, a busy man with places to go and things to do, gets up and bows formally to Elizabeth. They'll meet downtown later this week and draw up a contract, he says; spell out the appropriate terms for the sale. He's concerned about the tax implications and hopes she'll be sensitive to the neighborhood parking restrictions, not to mention Calpurnia's status as a local tourist attraction, so to speak, ha ha. He feels sure she understands the fine line they all mean to walk between appropriate accessibility on the one hand and some kind of ghastly neighborhood extravaganza on the other; but he's sure they're in good hands.

Elizabeth adds her handful of glass shards to the stickers in the ashtray and shakes his hand. It seems to her that she must have passed the test; she's been deemed appropriate; Jaxheimer presumably speaks for all of them. Later there will be papers to sign and details to be ironed out, deadlines to set and percentages to nail down, but the worst is probably over: it dawns on her that they must have had some meeting of the minds about her suitability while they were all upstairs. Elizabeth nods and tries not to look relieved. The sale will pay her co-op costs for the next three months and her share of her daughter Robin's doctors' bills. She'll be able to put something aside for her son Pen's birthday in the fall. She can get her carpets cleaned and buy new tires for the car.

The men close their briefcases and Nina goes from window to window lowering sashes and locking locks, while Coby stands empty-handed in the door to the sunroom, a wing of dark hair on his forehead, prepared to wait out the storm. In the curtain of all but tropical heat at the front door Dr. Giles steps aside for Elizabeth with a kind of stylized gallantry. From the looks of it he must be in his eighties, and she supposes it's a wonder he's still practicing; on their way out the door he puts his hand on her sleeve so lightly that for a moment she thinks a leaf has fallen on her wrist or a strand of ivy has cut loose from the wall. There's something he wants to tell her and she can see that he's been practicing his speech in advance: she knows the signs. "I don't want you to leave with the wrong impression," he says. "Mrs. English is not a physician; she doesn't have all the facts. Mrs. Davies didn't die of blood poisoning, she died of breast cancer; it's no mystery: she'd been sick for many years."

Elizabeth nods and tries to look open-minded, someone who minds her own business and doesn't need all the facts and figures to be convinced.

But Giles isn't finished. "This was not a sudden death," he says. "The disease had been in remission for several years and six months ago it began to affect the bones. Once that happens all kinds of things can start going wrong, and often do."

Elizabeth nods again.

Dr. Giles is of the generation of men who still tip their hats to women and, hatless, his gesture takes the form of a slight, not quite military salute. His car is the last one left in the turn-around, but he has his umbrella under his arm; if there's anything life has taught him it's to be prepared, always, for unexpected rain. "It's a matter of record," he says. "I don't want to leave you with any misunderstanding; Maribel Archibald Davies was a very sick woman. It's no secret at all to anyone that she'd been fighting for her life for years."

4

ONRAD kicks off his shoes and stretches out on the huge hotel bed, groping for the remote, locating himself by his beard in the mirror opposite the bed. Well, that's over, he thinks; everyone's happy, including, hopefully, Dee. The gold-rimmed glasses and champagne flutes are spoken for, ditto the silver which Nina can hopefully be trusted to divide equitably when the time comes—or, if not Nina, then the blond estate sale agent, whatever her name is, who hopefully has no axes to grind, but certainly no family ones. Well, at least they'd presented a united front this afternoon. A real production, stage managed by Nina as usual; God knows how she kept Coby in line. But she did, he has to hand it to her. The loving family: united we stand.

Nina's right; nobody knows which way Giles is going to jump, although once he signed the damned death certificate you wouldn't think there's much more he can do, would you? And that restorer of hers, that art historian, the Spaniard or whatever he is: he's obviously got his own key to the house, a nice touch, the lover of record fumbling at the door: trust

Maribel. Which leaves Peg, the neighborhood Greek chorus and Maribel's devoted fan; though Conrad guesses she's probably too dim to make trouble. And of course the maid, but she hadn't been paid for weeks anyway, and if Nina gives her the price of her plane ticket back to Peru, that ought to take care of that.

Conrad scans the face of the remote, looking for the off-on switch, the sequencer, the options: twelve cable channels, three networks, CNN, and a quartet of dirty movies, at least two of which he thinks he may have seen before. He should call his aunt Ibby while the night's still young, but surely that can wait. The old girl drinks herself to sleep and, everything else being equal, she'll be easier to handle the further along she is. He yanks at the knot in his tie until it comes loose enough for easy breathing and unbuttons the collar of his shirt. One more night in Philadelphia, then home to Shaker Heights, to Deedee, then a week's worth of sales meetings and phone calls to return. There are people he should call before he leaves, but he won't. Conrad no longer knows everyone who is anyone in Philadelphia, or even anyone who is no one in particular, and pretends to himself that he therefore no longer knows anyone at all.

Even though he could return to the various scenes of his childhood without apology now, if he were so inclined. Because Conrad has done well for himself in the dried-egg-white business, a process his father-in-law patented before the war; the market has doubled every eight years, more or less dependably, since then, and Conrad's end of it is sales. He still has two accounts in Philadelphia, friends of his father's, old men whose hearts died with Alf Landon; there used to be five of them. It was never a market he personally tried to develop, anyway; he was hardly looking for excuses to come home. If he'd needed to, he could always have stayed at the Fox, or with his nephew in Saint Davids, or his deaf aunt Ibby in Chestnut Hill; but with the expense account, why bother? His nephew is an investment trust underwriter without any small talk at all, while Ibby chatters on a mile a minute and won't let you go upstairs to bed before midnight or one o'clock. He keeps in touch, he goes to all the weddings and funerals, but the fewer opportunities he has to return to the land of his ancestors the better, as far as Conrad's concerned.

And hopefully this is the last time ever for any of them at Calpurnia—this famous pile of stones built by his grandfather Aubrey in the eighties as his gift to his Italophile wife, the fabled Villa Calpurnia, modeled after some mansion in Frascati and named for Caesar's two-timing wife. Left to Maribel in her grandmother's will—lock, stock, and barrel—as if Conrad hadn't grown up there too; while Conrad inherited his grandfather's antique sextant and azimuth compass, and a small trust fund set up to expire when he reached the age of thirty-one.

Not that he cares, at this late date: why should he? Conrad's a happy Philistine; they left out the aesthetic gene when they made him. He's color-blind; he hasn't set foot in a single museum since he left school. Not only does Conrad not know thing one about art but he can honestly say he doesn't even know what he likes. And to make matters worse, doesn't care who knows he doesn't: including Maribel.

Maribel was her grandmother's favorite, arty, artful—no, *artistic:* but she knew which side her bread was buttered on, though Conrad guesses that if she ever cleared a thousand dollars a year on her paintings even in a good year it was a lot. Gerald professed to be an art lover himself—at least until Maribel started sleeping with every self-elected Rembrandt in Montgomery County, presumably; and did he still count himself an art lover when she ran away to Cuba with the paint maker, that summer right after the war? Or the winter she made him go sleep in the den? Did he still go all starry-eyed over Rubens and Velázquez after that? Did he buy that tripe about artists being different, above it all, finer tuned than the rest of us poor Philistines?

Conrad gives his ex-brother-in-law the benefit of the doubt; Maribel wasn't a great beauty, but she had a way with men. Maribel talked about sex as if she were talking about the weather and knew the French translation for all the major four-letter words; half the boys on Conrad's high-school football team would have given their eyeteeth for a date with Maribel. Who for her part hated athletes and musclemen, despised organized sports, and couldn't be bribed for love or money to play the simplest games, not even as a child. "Leave her alone," said Father. "Maribel has other fish to fry."

Artistic fish, presumably. But she had Father's number: the face that sank the thousand ships—their mother's face, to be exact. Including the long Aubrey nose and the Medusa hair, those famous smoked-out eyes; and just lucky for all concerned that she could draw. Drawing her own self-portrait she drew their mother's Greco-Roman profile and downcast eye, the face on the piano top in its Edwardian bridal finery. Father took her least little pencil sketch and had it shellacked and framed: in silver (nothing but the best!). It was the only likeness she ever even tried to get, but it was the only one their father cared about. She was her mother's spitting image and that was all it took: he let her walk all over him.

Well, all that's ancient history now. Maribel's dead, Father's dead, and Calpurnia's a dying beast; all that's left are the champagne flutes and the silver and whatever the paintings manage to bring at auction in New York. Conrad reaches for his address book, though he used to know Ibby's number by heart. Let them make a goddamn museum of it, he thinks. Why not? Nina's dead set against it, but Conrad rather likes the idea himself, and there may be something in it for him if he uses his influence with Coby, such as it is. Not to mention the famous tax write-off, which God knows he could use this year and/or next. Though Jaxheimer refuses to take a stand on the museum issue, pro or con, invoking conflict of interest, as usual; but you can never pin the bastard down on anything. Whereas Conrad looks at it this way: at worst it'll cost them all a few dollars on the sale of the house, and even that's merely hypothetical. Because why shouldn't the museum committee pay fair market share? Ibby's friends are demon fund-raisers; they can squeeze blood out of a stone and their money's as good as anyone else's, as far as Conrad's concerned.

The only problem, of course, will be getting Coby to go along. Understandably, because Coby has no income to write taxes off of anyway. Odd that Hugh is still on the fence on this, but maybe he doesn't need the write-off as badly as Conrad does. Which is to say that maybe that shop of Nina's isn't doing quite such a land office business as they all pretend it is, over there in Clover Hill among the chic cafés and old curiosity shops.

Which in turn all goes to prove that you can't take it with you when you go; *n'est-ce pas?* None of it: not the lovers, the paintings, the favors, the favoritism, the villa, the tennis courts. And even if you could, exactly how much was there left of any of it all anyway, by the time Maribel went to her reward? Conrad happens to know for a fact that she died dirt poor, because Jaxheimer's filled him in. She sold the last parcel of pasture land in seventy-two, and she's been living on capital ever since.

Calpurnia may be a white elephant, but in the end it was really all she had, because love isn't money, and none of those gentlemen callers of hers ever had a dime. Conrad saw the look in her eye when she called him a self-made man, but what if he is? By the time Father died there was nothing left and Conrad had no choice but to invent himself out of whole cloth, de novo, from the ground up. So yes, he's a self-made man, and proud of it. Self-made in spades; because just who the hell else was ever going to make a man of him if he didn't step up to the mat and do the job himself?

Conrad finds Ibby's number and places the call. It's a little past eight, she'll be mellow but not incoherent yet; he'll mend his bridges, pay his respects, tell her his car broke down. Ibby's of the old school; she doesn't mind being lied to so long as the major amenities are preserved. Waiting for her to pick up the phone in Chestnut Hill he imagines her in the garden room, drinking champagne, searching blindly for the white telephone under the couch. People don't call Ibby anymore; she's retired from the social scene she used to dominate and it's years since she's played any kind of bridge. It's too much bother getting her hair done and finding the keys to the car, she can't read the street signs at night anymore, and everything considered, she'd probably rather do her drinking alone at home in her favorite easy chair anyway. For which Conrad doesn't blame her. He's her favorite nephew; he gives her the benefit of the doubt.

She picks up, finally, on the seventh ring, not even a record for that matter. "Conrad darling," Ibby says. "Where are you? How are you? How's Dee? How are the girls?" Her voice is thin and a little out of breath, as if she's been climbing stairs. She always asks about his daughters, but can never remember to ask about his son.

Conrad makes his usual excuses for not coming by: a staff meeting tomorrow that he can't get out of, the family gathering at Calpurnia, and an iffy rental car; and Ibby doesn't call him on any of them. "But how did it go this afternoon?" she says.

"I thought it went well," says Conrad. "Coby behaved himself. Nina's hired someone to sell the furniture and prints. Some art historian. She seems to know her stuff."

Ibby sputters and coughs, but at this end of the phone it's hard to tell whether she's angry or simply swallowing the wrong way. "I begged her not to do that," she says finally. "I got down on my hands and knees; not till she's spoken to Julia Romaine. You know Julia; her brother went to St. Paul's with you. Julia says she's been leaving messages for Nina all over town."

"Look, Ibby, I had no say in the matter whatsoever," says Conrad; "Nina's the sole executor. I think the general idea is to convert some of the paintings and knickknacks and furniture to cash for Coby. Mine not to reason why."

"Oh, no?" says Ibby. "Then I'll tell *you* the reason why."

But Conrad doesn't want to hear Ibby's reasons. "Please, Aunt Ib, not over the phone," he says. "Loose lips sink ships."

"Don't be ridiculous," says Ibby. "It's common knowledge, and Giles is in on it too, that old fool. He could lose his license if it ever came out, assuming he still even practices, except for Maribel."

"Ibby, darling, united we stand, divided we fall. Giles is a respected member of the medical community, and Coby's on the wagon, at least for now. Let's let sleeping dogs lie."

Ibby clicks her tongue, an antique, censorious sound. "Giles is even older than I am, believe it or not," she says. "He must be ninety if he's a day."

"And speaking of sleeping dogs," says Conrad, "I don't

know about your neck of the woods, but down here in the big city it's beginning to get kind of late; and yours truly has a plane to catch tomorrow morning at five o'clock."

Ibby laughs her tipsy laugh; at the other end of the line there's a tattoo of clicks, and the sound of glass on glass. "Oh, you and your planes," she says. "Far be it from me to keep you up." Conrad can see her as clearly as if she were there in front of him: the papery face with its brown dog's eyes and sunken chin; her tissue-thin hands with the knuckles shining through the skin. "Give my love to Deedee and the girls," she says. "If they get to see you before I do, ha ha." She pauses to take a drink without putting down the phone, her face so close to the receiver that Conrad can hear the wine sloshing in the glass. "You know me, I don't bear grudges," she says. "Even though just between the two of us Coby hasn't been by to see me in years. Six years, to be exact, and he only came then because he needed five hundred dollars. Which I gave him. Which I might add have never been repaid." There's a pause while she ducks the phone to cough her anguished smoker's cough. "And don't worry; you know perfectly well I'm not about to sink any damn ships," she says.

CONRAD jabs at the on button and the television screen three feet from the end of the bed comes to sudden glaring life. Ibby's a loose cannon, but that's Nina's business, not his: if she wants to protect Coby, what skin is that off Conrad's pearly white teeth? He was fifteen hundred miles away the night that Maribel died, and he can prove it five ways to Christmas, which is probably more than any of the rest of them can.

Virtuously he flips through the cable selections for CNN

and watches some double-breasted hack in London expatiate on the failure of the French to support the franc against the mark in the recent interest rate standoff. Conrad's business is strictly national, they buy their eggs in seventeen states, the packaging comes from Kansas, and their payroll has held steady without major layoffs for the last thirty years; you can't say it hasn't been a good life. The house, the healthy kids in the good schools, the vacations: he wouldn't trade it for Maribel's, dollar for dollar or year for year. Would anyone? Coby's been nothing but trouble since the day he was born; but what does any of them stand to gain by saying so?

Enough of the European bond market, though; enough of the balance of trade. Conrad's not into emerging markets, overseas markets, foreign trade; he's into the great old American equities himself, stick with what you know. Ibby may have inherited the lion's share of the Aubrey money but she didn't inherit a shred of the ancestral common sense, and Conrad knows for a fact that the reason Coby hasn't been by to see her is that she's told him never to darken her door again. If Ibby's got a single brain in her head she'll keep her mouth shut, and so will all the rest of them, including Giles.

It's getting late—too late to call his nephew in Saint Davids, and much too late to call home; and he'll have more than enough time to say good-bye to Nina and Hugh and Coby tomorrow at Jaxheimer's. With a little luck and a small vodka and chaser from the minibar the buzz should last him through the better part of the evening news. He reaches for the little cardboard tripod that tells you how to program the TV and makes himself a watery drink. Most of these so-called adult movies are total farce anyway, trash only a seventeen-year-old could get worked up about; though would someone please tell

him what the hell else there is to do between now and dinnertime here in Philadelphia, the hometown he left without regrets or brotherly love some forty-odd years ago this August to
go into business in Cleveland, and make a man of himself, and
marry the blond and bossy Deedee, and live happily ever after,
if he does say so himself?

5

NINA SAYS, "Well, that's over. What a relief. I thought
she was quite all right, didn't you? A little bit starchy
at first but better that than the kind that's all over
you, telling you the story of their lives. Peachy Carmichael
swears by her, and they say she knows her art. I mean I thought
it went well, didn't you? Coby seems to have pulled himself
together for the time being, and, let's face it, I find Conrad
without Deedee always so much easier to take. You were a darling to come and sit through it all, I know how busy you are,
but I did want her to see that we're all together in this, that
there's going to be someone looking over her shoulder, keeping
a close eye on things. I mean giving someone the run of the
house like that, I don't care what anyone says, but you have to
take a lot on faith. Especially with those museum people of
Conrad's breathing down everyone's necks. I'm going to go
over there tomorrow and offer to help her with the books; I
think we owe it to Maribel, don't you?"

Hugh doesn't answer; Hugh rarely answers her questions
except to disagree. Instead he goes on hanging up his clothes on

the little wooden valet stand she got him for a joke the first Christmas they were married: pants first, then the shirt, the jacket one step higher, and last the tie: a headless mannequin that leans ever so slightly forward, as its owner does, and smells exactly like the living Hugh.

"You know my position," he says. "They should have brought someone in from Freeman's. There could be a gold mine in there. This way none of us will ever know."

They've had this argument before, but Nina refuses to take him up on it. If there's a gold mine in Calpurnia she thinks she would have been the first to know, and someone from Freeman's might turn up more than any of them wants to deal with in the long run. As Hugh hardly needs to be reminded. Nina's been over there more days than she wants to think about in this heat, looking everywhere, picking at baseboards and loose paneling with her bare fingernails, playing a kind of posthumous hide-and-seek with Maribel. She'll give it one more week, or two, and see what Peachy's friend turns up, if anything, then call it a day. Because all these weeks since Maribel's death the shop has been going to hell in a handbasket. The accounts receivables are two months old, the sales figures are slipping, and when she calls in from outside no one ever answers the phone. Anyway, you can only do so much. It's conceivable that Maribel burned the damn things, or sold them, or gave them away; it's conceivable that they aren't at Calpurnia at all.

Nina has no intention of driving herself crazy over this: there's only so much time she can spend on Weavers Way without losing her self-control, getting the weepies, hearing things and seeing things that she knows perfectly well are all in her mind. After all these months, years really, of waiting for Maribel to die (let's be realistic), when the ax finally fell it had perversely come as a total surprise to everyone. Well, almost everyone, but Nina knows better than to let her mind wander down that particular garden path. The point is to get the house on the market, isn't it? Get the furniture and personal effects out of there, search every nook and cranny for what's left, and break Coby of the habit of returning to his mother's doorstep like a dog to a bone before he embarrasses them all; or worse. Then leave the estate to the lawyers to figure out, including Hugh: because, let's call a spade a spade, isn't that what lawyers are for?

Coby's too much. Grief is one thing, Coby's got more than his fair share of grieving to do, whichever way you look at it—but so do all the rest of them, don't they? And God knows no one could be more devastated than Nina is herself, because in some ways, if you want to be brutally honest, Maribel was more of a mother to her than she ever was to poor Coby, her only child. Even so, this homecoming compulsion of his has got to be nipped in the bud; it's for his own good, really, isn't it? Because, look, what's the fatal attraction to Villa Calpurnia, now that Maribel's gone? Especially considering how hard it was for him to get over there when she really needed him, while she was still alive. Either way it doesn't sit right, and either way tongues will wag. Nina can't for the life of her imagine what ails him now; at least she hopes she can't. Is it the Oedipus complex in reverse, or some other Freudian thing Nina doesn't even know the name of? Is he looking for something in the ruins too? Or is he back on the sauce again and simply out of control, as Conrad seems to think?

Nina took the opportunity of looking him over carefully this afternoon at Calpurnia, and while it's true he seemed a bit under the weather, for the most part he was perfectly coherent and more or less wide awake—or as wide awake as Coby ever gets. Coby weighs heavily on Nina's conscience, whether he realizes it or not—he was her child as much as Maribel's in some weird way, her little brother—but this isn't something she can talk to Hugh about.

Nina turns out the light on her side of the bed and moves as far to the center as she thinks prudent. Hugh is a subtler reader of signs and portents than most people give him credit for, and Nina doesn't want to go on record as having been unwilling or unreachable, but since Maribel's death, let's be painfully frank, she's been deep in the deep freeze. She can't explain it; it's not like her (well, not really); she didn't go into a tailspin when she lost her own mother six years ago, did she? But you have to be careful with Hugh. He claims to be a team player, he pretends he always has the family's interests at heart, but Nina knows better, and she remembers everything: including the time that Hugh actually called the police on Coby seven years ago when he first hit the skids. Nina didn't exactly catch him in the act of placing the call but she's done some sleuthing of her own and all signs point to Hugh. Though she's never called him on it: what would be the point? But in her heart she knows it's true.

Maribel was wrong to trust Hugh; she was in awe of his arithmetic and his bank account and that long-lipped English cavalry officer's face; and it didn't hurt that he was wide in the shoulders and six foot three. Maribel had no use for ugly men.

On the other side of the bed the mattress sinks as Hugh sits down to remove his socks; he puts them in his shoes for Lorella to retrieve in the morning. Neat as he is, Nina has never been able to get him to throw his socks in the hamper at the end of the day; or for that matter to hang up his suits in the closet instead of arranging them on that stupid wooden stand, from which Lorella will simply have to remove them and rehang them when she makes the bed and cleans the room. Hugh thinks Lorella owes him that. It's part of the job description, isn't it? He pays her salary, doesn't he?

Nina listens to the socks going into the shoes, the pajama pants unknotting, the legs unfolding, the watch unbuckling from his wrist. She sighs and closes her eyes; she's forgotten the exact number of times she's turned her back to him this week and last. Not counting the two weeks after Maribel died, when she slept in the guest room to spare him her weeping and her profoundly sleepless nights. Six weeks has it been—or maybe even seven? There's a period after someone dies when time seems suspended, you're stuck in the same endless present, there's no going forward and no going back. The day Maribel died Nina forgot her weekly touch-up at the hairdresser's for the first time in years. A week later it was as if her hair had turned gray overnight: the fulfillment of an old wives' tale.

Maribel died the last week in March, and spring has come and gone since then, but Hugh hates it when she dissolves in tears, and what would she do without Hugh? How else could she run the shop? Who else would keep her books and make sure that the IRS doesn't darken her door when she loses track of her foreign expense receipts? Who else would have stayed so faithful to her all these years, or put up with the sloppy way she keeps her books, her admitted shortcomings as a cook and housekeeper? And (let's be gruesomely honest) the money that never materialized from her father's estate after her mother finally had the grace to die?

Nina closes her eyes and thinks of Maribel's nudes. Maribel belonged to a generation that put a certain premium on being good in bed: the first post-Victorian generation, the one that had so much riding on free love and Sigmund Freud, and the last that still thought men were wonderful. Including Hugh, whom she admired for his stiff upper lip, and for his senatorial head and neck, which she would have painted if she could. "I can see why you married him," she said. "Good-looking men don't grow on trees."

Nina moves one inch, then another, in Hugh's direction across the undivided bed. Because there's no time like the present, and life goes on. The funeral's over; the will goes to probate as soon as they can all agree what to do about the house, including the paintings, and, if she ever finds them, those god-awful drawings; and sooner or later she was going to have to make it up to him anyway (wasn't she?) for all the nights she's turned her back on him since Maribel's death, without apology and without recourse.

6

ELIZABETH wakes at the sound of the first bird calls, unable to hang on to her last dream, then makes herself a cup of tea and goes out to the terrace to drink it, hemmed in by the tops of weeping hemlocks in this morning world two stories above the real one. She bought the apartment with the proceeds from her divorce settlement; it was more than she could afford but the timing was right and she liked the sudden sense she had of living dangerously, without a house, without a husband, one child away at college and the other in California with his father, suddenly unanchored by bureaucracies and good habits or urgent family ties. Three and a half years later the apartment is still excitingly strange to her, like a kind of hotel suite, or, as she pretends when she conducts her business there, a private gallery. A scattering of familiar objects left over from the scenes of her sixteen-year marriage to Douglas are like artifacts from an ancient culture: she's tempted to trade up to something cozier but so far she hasn't had the money or the time. As one of several sidelines to the estate sales and appraisals that help to pay her rent, Elizabeth buys things and sells them from her own white living room, and it's therefore important, or so she tells herself, to keep things colorless, impersonal, and spare. It's by her own choice that the place has never quite taken on the feel of home.

With no one awake in the world, seemingly, but herself, Elizabeth puts her bare feet up on the terrace railing and faces the creamy dawn. The tea is just a gesture; she's already wide awake and making mental lists: equipment to order, staff to hire, ads to compose and place. Last night she spoke to Clemmie, the retired gift shop manager who likes to pick up a bit of extra cash now and then on sales and who knows exactly how to price the residual kitchen junk; and for the heavy lifting she'll have to call Henry, her daughter Robin's ex-boyfriend, a would-be flute player who has never quite made his way into the non-flute-playing world. Then somebody else to help with the books: the sort of person who knows the difference between a first edition and an umpteenth printing of some forgotten bestseller, and can be trusted not to throw the wrong things out.

Ordinarily Elizabeth would do the books herself; old libraries have become a specialty of hers, and, if you happen to know what you're looking for, a good place to make a modest profit without attracting too much attention from either the family or the estate. Because the expenses at Calpurnia are going to be brutal, let's face it. All those windows and doors to police; all those rooms to be inventoried and silver to be cleaned, all those pots and pans. Clemmie has connections among local retirees and ex-alcoholics, people with pickup trucks and flexible hours, but she'll have to hire professionals for the garden, and line up a team of drivers to do the carting, both before and after the sale.

It's the old story: either there's not enough in the house to make an honest dollar, or there's so much of it that you end up spending all your money on staffing the sale. Added to which, everyone's always in a hurry. The executors are waiting for the estate to be valued so that they can get on with their work; the relatives want to put their grief behind them so that they can get on with their lives; the buyers want to nail their bargains; and Elizabeth herself wants to get in and get out, make her money, and pay the most pressing of her long list of pressing bills. It's something she's come to think she may have had in common with Maribel, who probably never had to worry about where her next meal was coming from but, from the evidence, may no longer have had the kind of wealth that lets you go out and buy exactly what your heart desires for years.

ELIZABETH finishes her tea, makes the white bed in the white bedroom, wrestles with her hair and gets carefully and thoughtfully dressed, then goes downstairs and heads the car toward Weavers Way. By the end of the week the Buick will know its own way to Calpurnia and she'll know the floor plan of the house by heart, starting at the top and working her way down from there, getting a jump on things in the studio in broad daylight without the risk of unexplained noises and things going bump in the night. She's trained herself to expect the worst (anything that can go wrong probably will go wrong), but the front door lock is in a good mood today, the unrepaired alarm chooses not to go off, and the studio door opens mercifully on her first try. Then and only then does she allow herself the luxury of gratitude for a day well begun.

The enormous room runs the length of the house, reclaimed from the original third-floor ballroom with attic space sandwiched into the eaves on either side and identical Palladian windows at both ends. The architect was famous for his suburban adaptations of Beaux Arts mansions in the eighties and built five of them before the crash; Calpurnia may be the only one still left standing now, if Peachy's facts are right. Cut into the sloping north roof there's an expanse of skylight with what looks like chicken wire embedded in the glass: a thin layer of grime has bent the incoming light toward blue, a timeless and stale true north. On the west side of the room there's an old divan with a fringed cover, two easy chairs draped in cheap 1960s Indian bedspreads, and, opposite it, an enormous oak easel and a complicated hi-fi system with trailing wires and outsize loudspeakers left over from an earlier and clunkier electronic era. The large piece of plastic kitchen cutting board that Maribel used for her palette is still awash in pale grays and marbled wipeouts. Canvases lean against other canvases in orderly ranks, face to the wall, on all four sides of the room.

Peachy's judgment on her notwithstanding, Elizabeth tells herself she isn't interested in art as such; she can go through a museum in an hour and she's stood unmoved in front of some of the greatest statues in the world, while it's the rare painting that stops her dead in her tracks; but when it does it's like unrequited love, not something anyone in their right mind can stand to live with for very long. Either way, though, you have to be professional about it, not let yourself get bowled over by mere beauty and astonishment, or when would you ever have enough money to pay the bills? Elizabeth thinks of herself as a historian or a spy, but a realist first and last, and the idea of sitting in judgment on Maribel's paintings makes her uneasy in advance. It's therefore with a kind of trepidation that she reaches for the first of the canvases that comes to hand and turns it around to face the light; then another; and then a third, overcoming her shyness as she works her way down the wall, turning the canvases back to front like someone opening doors and windows, airing out a house.

On the evidence Maribel had only two or three subjects: strange long-waisted nudes with their backs to you at the windows of dusk-colored rooms, compositions of things on tabletops, or, in by far the greatest numbers, scene after scene of empty rooms with lifeless draperies and spills of white bedding or white underwear trailing from empty chairs. At first glance these rooms with their tall French windows and unmade beds appear to be all one color, a pearly gray one shade too blue for true grisaille; there's an impression of smoke and stale perfume in the air above the furniture, something astir psychologically in the spaces between the tables and chairs. If you had to find a word for the range of Maribel's palette it would be somewhere between monochrome and antichrome. Her paintings are the color of introspection and second thoughts.

Elizabeth sits down on the rose-colored divan at the end of the room and starts to make notes on her clipboard in her square back-slanting script. Third-floor studio, she writes; contact Freeman's; research local galleries. Maribel may or may not have painted for a living but she clearly painted for dear life; at a quick count there must be close to a hundred pictures here. Which means that the studio will almost have to be handled as a separate collection, a project in its own right, and billed accordingly. Meanwhile she'll have to research the tax implications of discounting the paintings in block to an auction house against the pros and cons of putting them up for sale at a single gallery. If Maribel's had any success as a living painter she'll be in the standard directories; if not, the possibilities are limited.

Elizabeth caps her pen and puts it back under the clip, and the morning closes in on her with its tropical heat and its hundreds of issues to be resolved; but you can't let yourself be over-whelmed. The furniture's a jumble of good and bad; she'll need to do some serious research on the etchings and she can't even stop to think about the china or the rugs, not to mention the erotic prints in the downstairs powder room: and up here in the studio she's going to need all the help she can get.

Elizabeth starts at the north end of the room and works her way back to the door, counterclockwise, turning the paintings front to back again; they switch off like lights going out but the mood they leave behind is hard to shake. Maribel's surfaces are as refractive as mirrors; you have the illusion that if you were to look at them long enough and from enough different points of the compass you might actually end up seeing yourself in them. And there's something unfinished about them that invites rethinking and remorse. Even Ellios may have a hard time putting a price on them.

Ellios buys cheap in New York and sells dear in Zurich and vice versa; he remembers the knockdown prices of paintings auctioned years before Elizabeth first entered the business ("that Van Gogh *Glass with Hellebores* sold for twelve thousand dollars in 1960," he said, "although there were people who didn't think it was worth even that much then, believe it or not") and he knows the price of everything in deutsche marks and Swiss francs. Or did; because in all honesty Elizabeth hasn't seen him in years. ("But collectors are voting for the nineteenth century now," he said. "It's the counter-revolution, they'll pay anything; though I hope I'm not trampling on some favorite enthusiasm of yours?" until Elizabeth had turned away: "Oh, enthusiasm's not my thing," she said. "It's all really just a job to me.")

No, let's face facts: she hasn't seen him in ages, but business is business, and anyway, how much choice does she have?

The dealer she'd been resorting to in Chestnut Hill has moved to Florida, while the local academics don't come cheap and couldn't be trusted to keep their mouths shut about those prints in the powder room even if they did. Ellios may be hard to take, but he knows everyone who is anyone in New York and he doesn't charge a small fortune for his services. On the contrary, if she's lucky something at Calpurnia will catch his eye and he'll be glad to take it out in trade. If all goes well no money need ever change hands, no record need ever go on the books.

Elizabeth sticks her clipboard under her arm and closes the studio door behind her. She hasn't seen Ellios for years and it's months since she's returned his phone calls, but there's a statute of limitations on everything. She's a big girl now; she keeps her own books and does her own taxes; she has a reputation for sterling connections and fair dealing that's probably worth its weight in gold. Besides, in this business it isn't what you know but who you know; and Elizabeth, thank God, knows Ellios. You can't possibly be an expert on everything and two heads are almost always better than one: that way, whatever you give up in the short run you're bound to make up for on the final deal. In the long run both you and the client almost always come out ahead.

ELIZABETH hasn't seen Ellios in years. Her fault, probably, because you can't take anything personally in this business or you'd never live to tell the tale. Elizabeth has been on her own for six years now; she meets her married lover David at his convenience four or five times a year; she keeps her own books and handles her own investments, such as they are. And Ellios has powerful connections here and abroad; it's clear from the importance of the deals he makes and the markets he deals in that there's major money behind him, not all of it necessarily his own.

Elizabeth remembers her first meeting with Ellios at a suburban dinner party. "Are you an art lover, Miss Oliver?" he'd asked. She said, "I suppose so. Isn't everyone?" He raised his eyebrows at her like a fencer raising his mask and turned back to the woman on his right: "But of course in a way all art is expressionism, abstract or otherwise, isn't it?" he said. "Even the old masters, the cave painters, the Greeks: they all had that same need to turn themselves inside out, express themselves, bare their souls. Isn't that what art is all about?" Two years later (they'd had lunch together twice by then and she'd bid against him at two rare book auctions in New York), at an otherwise deserted intersection on their way home from an exhibit of English manuscripts, he expressed himself by putting his hand into the top of her dress and drawing a line from the top of her jugular notch to the end of her right nipple with his forefinger like a carpenter sinking a line. If seduction is an art form, then it was either the act of a rank amateur, she thought, or a master so sure of his skill that he had no compunction about breaking all the rules. It took her months to get over her outrage, and by the time she did she had already hung up on him twice and left at least four of his calls on her answering machine unreturned. But since that night she's replayed the scene in her mind at least a dozen times, trying to repeal the shame and edit out the guilt, until there's nothing left of it but the memory of his hand, and the elegiac smell of mock orange flowering uncontrollably behind them in somebody's hemlock hedge.

On her way downstairs Elizabeth collects the silver-backed mirror from Maribel's dressing table and the matching hairbrush from her bathroom windowsill (the monogram's a lucky coup; doctors' wives and mothers will fight over the set and bid it up, then pay a hefty premium for the elaborate MD.) Never say you don't like so and so, her mother used to say, invoking the lofty etiquette of her own high-minded childhood; just say he's not my favorite person and let it go at that. Well, Ellios is not Elizabeth's favorite person, but he knows everyone and everything. Ellios buys Dutch salt safes in Malaysia and sells them for twice his cost in Leyden. He can convert dollars without a calculator into currencies you've never even heard of and remembers what famous dealer sold his entire stock to which famous rock star years before Elizabeth ever turned her hand to art.

Besides, once bitten, twice shy. She's older and wiser now; she knows how to take care of herself. She's met her fair share of men like Ellios since that night in the car and has mastered the trick of putting them off without quite putting them out of her life for good. Elizabeth's a pragmatist; in a business like this, where you make all your money on the gap between what you know and the buyer doesn't, what other choice do you have? Downstairs, in the kitchen, she puts Maribel's mirror and hairbrush down beside the big silver tray she's set aside for Clemmie to clean before she calls the dealers in to bid, and heads for the powder room to brush the smell of Maribel's studio out of her hair. Because let's be realistic: outside the big cities and the major markets of the world men like Ellios are few and far between. And under the circumstances you could easily make the case, couldn't you, that she owes it to the family to bring him in on the sale?

7

C OBY CIRCLES the block, looking for a parking space (here goes nothing), then circles again. He's going to be late for his appointment as usual, but what else is bloody new? It's a miracle that he's here at all, really. He overslept; the Benadryl he took at two didn't kick in till three, but there's no such thing as a good night's sleep without a pill, and you pay the price in the morning, assuming you wake up at all. Not that you'd be likely to die of an overdose of Benadryl, even supposing you wanted to: and Coby doesn't want to. All he wants is a good night's sleep, maybe two in a row; is that so much to ask?

Or a good round of tennis, like the opening game at Wimbledon on Channel 5, watching Ivan Lendl destroy the twelfth-ranked player in the world, a Slav with an unpronounceable name and what looks like the same clunky racquet that Coby has played with all his life, a Wilson T200 that Peg gave him when he was twenty-two; they probably don't even make them anymore. Of course Littlefield doesn't believe in tennis, doesn't play, doesn't watch, and thinks Coby's passive aggressive, or anal retentive, or who knows what, and gives him no credit for keeping his weekly appointment, at whatever cost to his sanity and a good night's sleep.

HE KEEPS these appointments for Maribel, not for Littlefield, and least of all for himself: it was the deal he had with her, the condition she set for continuing to pay his rent. It was either Littlefield or back to school, and Coby chose Littlefield. She must have known she'd made a bad bargain but, to her credit, she didn't say so, and it doesn't matter now. Anyway, this is it, the grand finale, his next to last time at bat. The bill is prepaid till the end of the month, Maribel's idea of what a good mother will do for an otherwise undeserving and only son (hell, only anything). The real money was scheduled to run out when she died, of course; it was her trust fund, what was left of it anyway, or so she said. The last of the money, good as gold and just as scarce: his grandfather had tied it up in a million knots so that no one would ever marry her for her money again. She laughed it off. "Let Daddy pay for all the trouble he's caused," she said.

Now that it isn't an option anymore, ironically, Coby has begun to see the point of Littlefield, i.e., the uses of confession, the professional purging of the soul: his single Catholic grand-mother's genes finally coming out in him. Because don't shrinks have to keep their patients' darkest secrets? Isn't that the law? Unfortunately, now that he finally has a secret of his own to keep, there's suddenly no more money to pay for the luxury of confiding it. Just my bloody fucking luck, Coby thinks; ridicu-lous to even spend the money on the gas to drive to Littlefield's office and back again. Not to mention the hazard of going on the road with a headful of cotton and a liverful of over-the-counter bliss, driving half blind and more than half asleep.

Well, he doesn't do it for himself, he does it for Maribel. It's one of the few promises he ever made to her, or made to her and kept; and he'll keep it till Littlefield turns him out. Just on the very off chance that there's anything left of her out there somewhere: watching, keeping track.

Coby's down to his last eighty dollars; he's ready to dig ditches or trim trees, assuming he still has the muscle for it. Because if they turn off the phone on the twenty-sixth, he's dead. Nina keeps saying to hang on till they sell the house, but that could be months. Let's face it, that could be years. Or never, if they give Calpurnia to Ibby's friends to turn into a museum. Though Coby hasn't got years to wait and Hugh knows it. Of course he does. Hugh knows everything.

Coby mourns Maribel in his own way—watching Wimbledon as if it were the story of his life, taking pills in his own hit-or-miss rotation and catching those late-night reruns, movies that only women are supposed to weep at, under the cover of a sudden allergic conjunctivitis, only half trumped-up. He's saving the strong stuff for last; for the moment of truth when it all either comes together or falls apart and some small still voice pipes up to announce the last stop on the train to nowhere, the end of an endless line. Well, he mourns both Maribel and her trust fund, equally, let's be honest—her trust fund, that self-renewing resource that was always good for the current doctor's bill, the ultimatum from the gas and electric company, the bench warrant for his parking tickets at the shrink's. He mourns her by showing up at Littlefield's religiously two days a week, drunk on Benadryl and Cosanyl (but still technically perfectly clean), his mother's favorite and only son, hanging on to the lifeline of a promise he made her two years ago. Because what else does he have to hang on to; what other promises does he have to keep?

Still, even Coby knows he can't go on like this. Once unemployment turns you down you're finished: and where's the famous safety net that's supposed to be out there for everyone? Where are the good old old-boy networks; where's the social security? Conrad's connections in the incentive and fulfillment business are both at least ten years old by now, very ancient history, let's face it, and there isn't a club within a hundred miles of here that would take Coby on as a pro. Meanwhile Nina blows hot and cold about his request for some advance on the will. Not to mention knocking him off the list of speakers at the funeral and changing the locks at Calpurnia the minute his mother was in the ground.

He knows what they think, all of them. Well, let them. Not that he'd wanted to get up there in front of everyone and talk about Maribel anyway. And not that he wouldn't have begged off himself of his own accord, when push came to shove. Because what exactly are they so afraid he would have said if they'd let him have his say? My mother loved me but she died, as in the classic Thurber cartoon? Or: my mother offered to pay my way through the Academy and give me the sports car of my dreams if I agreed to devote my life to art? Or (more likely): my mother would be turning over in her grave if she knew you fucks had gone and changed the locks on me and left me without a key to my own house?

Coby slows the car to a crawl. Half a block ahead of him a man in a Trans Am has just turned on the gas; a plume of blue exhaust sends cones of brown leaves and yellow pollen skittering out behind him into the street and Coby feels his luck turn from bad to good. He'll head for Calpurnia as soon as his session with Littlefield is over, and talk that blonde they hired to do the tag sale into letting him in, with or without an appointment, key or no key. She'll answer the door; she's a local girl,

Emily Post and Robert's Rules; not bad-looking but nothing special either, and if he plays his cards right she may even give him the new front door key to copy. Or, if she doesn't, let's face it (nothing ventured nothing gained), he may just take it and copy it anyway. Although he hopes it doesn't come to that; and with any luck (knock wood) it won't.

You and your blondes, said Maribel, admiring her tense athletic son for whatever she could manage to (your God-given talent, she said; your way with women; your amazing eye), trying to make a working artist out of this weighty albatross around her neck, good for nothing else in life but mother love, her one and only and living work of art. He parks the truck behind the little red Honda as if it were as maneuverable as a sports car or a Coupe de Ville, and puts his last four quarters in the meter: a law-abiding citizen about to cut long-lasting ties from his law-abiding shrink. But no regrets, because Coby knows as well as anyone, or maybe better, that money can no more buy absolution than love. And once his luck has truly turned, once that lunar shift has raised all ships and the riptide is fully under way, who really needs Littlefield anymore anyway?

8

ELLIOS sits sideways on an unmade sofabed in the maid's room of the apartment he has lived in for the last seventeen years of his life, and waits for his call to go through to his agent in Thailand. It's almost twenty-four hours since he first got Elizabeth's message from his answering service, and late daytime of a totally different day in Bangkok, but he's been on the phone all day, back and forth between the chip designers in Brussels and the antiquities dealers in Bangkok. Watching the lights click off across the street through a crack in the closed blinds, waiting for the phone to ring at the other end of the world, Ellios wonders what finally moved her to pick up the phone and call him after all these years, and how long it would be politic to wait before he calls her back.

His ex-wife's maid has left her mark on the room in which he conducts more and more of his business these days, in ways that he can't be bothered to erase; Selena was partial to pictures of dogs and cats and the artifacts of his ongoing work are increasingly incongruous alongside her leaping Scotties and kittens at play among balls of yellow yarn. Beside the copying and fax machines lined up next to each other on the bureau top Ellios's old-fashioned Rolodex is propped open to the letter *o;* but although his good Swiss watch never keeps the right time and the notes he writes to himself on ruled index cards frequently tear at the edges or go astray, Ellios remains unimpressed by the complicated technology that patches his calls through to the tropical time zone where his agent warehouses his goods and his shippers punch up their daily inventory figures on Japanese computers with bright blue screens. Here on his own home ground Ellios still keeps his balance sheets cross-referenced to his inventory the old-fashioned way, discreetly, and inaccessible to third parties, in his head.

Ellios unloads the second of two briefcases and uncaps his fountain pen so that he can jot down the Thai figures when he gets them on the line. It's been a long day; he wants to get off the phone, unwrap the Freeman's catalog he picked up on his lunch hour, and check his answering service one last time before he goes to bed. He's a man who draws no fine lines between night and day. You can't in this business, once you go international, but every once in a while even someone like Ellios needs a good night's sleep. "You work too hard," the service operator tells him; and Ellios is flattered; for as long as he can remember people have been telling him to slow down, relax, give himself a break. "I work hard so that people like you can eat," he says.

At the other end of the line the invisible operator laughs her girlish laugh.

"Oh, go on, Mr. Ellios," she says. "The way I eat you'd have to work right around the clock."

Ellios twines his fingers through the phone cord. "Good; I like a woman with a healthy appetite," he says, and jots down the last of the three numbers she gives him.

Elizabeth hasn't seen him face-to-face in years, still nursing a grudge, he supposes, for a pass he made at her one night in the front seat of his idling car: bad timing on his part and perhaps a little crude, but hardly an actionable offense. Hemmed in on three sides by old filing cabinets full of dead files and yellowing instruction booklets on the care of vanished manual typewriters and Addressograph machines, he watches the phone and tries to remember how long it's been since they last spoke. Nine months? A year? Maybe even more? The desk is improvised, a plank of oak shelving balanced on an open bureau drawer, but the handsome tooled leather desk accessories are new and so is the black-and-silver telephone with its three outside lines, and the nightly call to the answering service institutionalizes the procrastinations of a constitutionally sleepless man. She had not left a message, strictly speaking, just her name, and word that she would call him back; and so far Ellios has resisted the urge to ask the service operator for further data: the length of her call, the tone of her voice: details, markers, clues. He drums his fingers on the phone. He sleeps (or doesn't sleep, more accurately) in the maid's room now, because it's handy to the brand-new fax machine and you can't get those fellows in Baole to respect the off-hours rates of American standard time. He's got two seventeenth-century screens and a tansu chest waiting for transshipment to London as soon as his insurance agent gives the word: beautiful pieces bought at rock-bottom prices and slated for the September auction at Christie's; but the paperwork has been snarled for weeks and he can't afford to miss the go-ahead call if and when it finally comes through.

From where he sits Ellios can only see the back of the framed eight-by-ten portrait of his still beautiful ex-wife Dorothy, newly married, surrounded by climbing roses and some kind of vine. He is and has always been a connoisseur of women's faces; he studies them minutely in paintings, in sculpture, and in the flesh. ("Stop looking at me like that," Dorothy said. "I'm not one of your goddamned Cambodian figurines." But would she have been any happier in the long run if he'd looked at her like some Chinese singsong girl instead?)

At the far side of the open sofabed Ellios straightens his spine and lifts his head a second before the phone gives the short half-ring that means the international long distance operator has finally spliced his call through indirectly from Bangkok. Instantly upright and wide awake, he turns the volume control to high and settles the phone securely on his pelvis, with his legs stretched out at a narrow angle to each other like crossed bayonets. Ellios doesn't think as fast as he used to anymore, but he still has the habit of command. It's a zoo out there: people are always either at your feet or at your throat. "Options—what options?" he says, and lets his voice rise dangerously like the needle on a pressure gauge. "There aren't any options except to renegotiate the terms. We're not shipping sweaters and table linens here." He's got to get these goods to London in time for the next auction if he wants to make a serious offer on Chin's head of Siva and that extraordinary pair of Bencharong bowls. You have to let those Chinamen know you're still out there, still in the game; and you have to keep the packers on their toes.

DONE. With the nightly phone call behind him Ellios unfolds his legs and swings them over the side of the bed; he hates to sleep alone, but what are the alternatives? Ellios knows from experience how easily a well-intended amiability can turn to lechery, affection to the sticky warmth of something like true love; then before you know it they want to move in with you and settle down. Ellios keeps the memory of his ex-wife in reserve for these occasions; they were divorced thirteen years ago but he made it a point not to tell anyone when the final decree went through, because an extant wife is always the best excuse. He thinks of Elizabeth Oliver, a woman with one of those English faces that never quite go out of style, as compared to Dorothy's, a Romney or a Reynolds compared to a Gibson girl: soft, distant, and mysteriously calm, but with eyes that give much more away than they mean to if and when she lets you get close enough to look.

But Dorothy had it wrong: why shouldn't a man love a woman for her face? What's wrong with being beautiful? What else is there, really, in a woman (or anything else in the world, when you get right down to it) to love? He tells people, women especially, that his wants are few and far between and on the whole it's true: wasn't it enough for Dorothy that after twelve years of marriage he still found her beautiful, that he still couldn't get enough of the sight of her sunstruck and rosy face? And would she think more or less kindly of him at this late date if she knew that he still kept all those photographs of her, lined up on the untuned piano, on the dining-room walls, the bedroom chest of drawers?

Night reduces Selena's room to the size and shape of the sofabed as Ellios puts on his pajamas, pulls down the blanket, takes his place in the darkness, and goes through the motions of putting himself to sleep. The Scotties and kittens subside into invisibility all around him and from where he lies there's nothing left to see but a corner of Dorothy's picture reflected in one of the double-glass doors to the dining room, generic and unreadable from here. The face of a woman, seductive and half-toned, though at this distance and in this light it could be hers; it could be Elizabeth's; it could be anyone's. But isn't that the point? Ellios knows from experience that no woman is really irreplaceable, and neither is a piece of ceramic or a work of art: including even Chin's amazing Siva and his incredible Bencharong bowls. Ellios unties his pajama pants and peels back his memory of Elizabeth's face from the layers of images in his head. A good day, by and large, and now that it's over it's one that he can't help seeing as a kind of watershed. Elizabeth isn't Dorothy (too tight-lipped and stiff-chinned, with none of Dorothy's windblown charm) but then neither is Dorothy, probably, after all these years. And Ellios is older and wiser now too, and ready to trade up. Amazing, under the circumstances, isn't it, that Elizabeth should finally have called him again after that stupid gaffe in the car, today of all days, after all these years?

9

BUYING flowers for Oscar is like carrying coals to New-castle, as Elizabeth can see the moment he leads her into the garden, roses in hand. It's been a mild winter and now everything has come into bloom at once. The sweet-smelling mock orange hems in the garden on all sides above the fading azaleas, and towering powder-pink rhododendrons are about to take turns blooming at the property line. Oscar is a fanatical, almost religious gardener, and it's not every year that he gets to see his works spread out before him like God, all at once and side by side. She's been invited to officiate at this splendor like someone invited to witness a miracle, a bleeding statue or water becoming wine.

"You look wonderful," says Elizabeth, and he does, but she would say it anyway; the ritual greeting has less to do with the way he looks than the fact that he's still there to be seen at all.

"Do I?" he asks. "As Tetrazzini once said, I'm old, I'm fat, and I'm ugly, but I'm still Tetrazzini: or still Oscar, as the case may be. Dinner on the terrace, I hope you don't mind?" He takes the store-bought flowers and kisses her perfunctorily on the forehead. Oscar looks his age, but the effect is rosy and game; he's small, beautifully dressed, and wears a cockscomb of starchy white hair, an advertisement for a happy and profitable old age. On the cracked brick terrace the table is already set; there are citronella tapers in buckets of beige sand, wine cooling in a silver pail.

"You're a sight for sore eyes," he says. "You must be in love. I can tell from the color of your cheeks."

"The color comes in a little pot, but thanks just the same," says Elizabeth. "It must be the sleepless nights."

She sits down facing the lineup of rhododendrons that wall Oscar off from his neighbors to the south; Oscar's little dinners on the terrace are one of the few luxuries left to her since she and Douglas came to the parting of the ways. Oscar is her mentor in this sideline that has so slowly but surely turned into a career; it was as his consultant for the Americana at a pricey Rosemont redecorating project gone bad that she originally learned the trade. Retired now and in failing health (though you'd never know it from the table he sets and the garden he keeps), Oscar still keeps his hand in by buying and selling the odd antique, and continues to have a proprietary interest in everything she does. He counts on her to keep her share of the gossip fresh, the stories up-to-date.

Elizabeth says, "Sorry I'm late; I haven't had a minute to call my own in days; unless you count playing phone tag with Ellios over a bunch of naughty prints."

Oscar laughs. "Naughty prints? How delicious. You must tell me more. And how is dear Ellios?" he says. He pours her a glass of wine and the flares at the ends of the citronella candles bend in a sudden breeze, flashing their spicy detergent scent on the darkening scene. Elizabeth feels an instant and indelible happiness, mysteriously content in Oscar's garden, about to eat his wonderful food, spinning her own version of the foolish yarns that keep him happy in his old age.

"As ever, I suppose," says Elizabeth. "I'm doing a sale in Merion and I just happened on these prints: gods and goddesses in flagrante, not my sort of thing at all. One of the Carraccis or Piero del Viego, probably. Do you know the genre? I felt a little out of my depth."

"Poor Elizabeth," says Oscar, "and who wouldn't?" He puts one fatherly hand on her wrist and shelters a guttering candle with the other. "Tell me about your prints," he says, "in your own inimitable fashion. I promise not to blush. Where did you find them and who actually owns them, anyway?"

"The estate still owns them, I suppose," says Elizabeth. "A painter named Maribel Archibald Davies. She died of cancer in April."

"Oh, good Lord: Maribel," says Oscar.

"Don't tell me you've heard of her?" says Elizabeth.

Oscar says, "My goodness, yes. Who hasn't? Well, I mean, you were just a schoolgirl, but it was in all the papers for months, oh years and years ago." Oscar has heard all the stories and has a prodigious memory for scandal, bankruptcies, and fraud. "Peter Flemming did her sister-in-law's house—horrendous; pink and blue. Her mother was very big at the flower show, hybrid azaleas; she had this wonderful plantation, masses and masses of them every spring, but I don't think Maribel was ever all that interested in flowers. She was supposed to be having an affair with Lipscomb, the portrait painter. Do you know the name? And no, you may not quote me on that; it never got into the papers. Everyone used to close ranks like little tin soldiers in those days: this isn't New York or Hollywood, you know. Well, not yet, at least, thank God."

Elizabeth hears herself saying, "Oh, Lipscomb, of course,"

as if the painter is someone she runs into regularly at cocktail parties and openings and benefit balls. "He painted her portrait; you'd love it, six-by-four in a lovely gilt frame, sort of forties neoclassical, if you know what I mean. Aphrodite at her toilette, using Ares' shield for a mirror. The Cupid was her little boy; well, at least he was little at the time. It's still hanging in her living room right over the couch, in the place of honor, for all to see."

"In her living room, front and center?" asks Oscar. "How extraordinary, how echt Main Line. Good-looking woman, as I recall, but wasn't she rather dark? It's funny; people think art is supposed to confer immortality on the painter, but isn't it the sitter who really lasts the longest in the end? There was Spanish blood in there somewhere as I recall, I think on her mother's side. The father moved to Maryland with his second wife; yours truly was consulted on their carriage house once upon a time, but it was an all-day drive; in the end I had to respectfully decline. The old man thought the sun rose and set on Maribel but the second Mrs. Davies simply would not receive her; this was before things became so racy and go-go, in the sixties, and Maribel was always ahead of her times. But *well* ahead of her times: the illustrated *Kama Sutra*, after all? And I don't speak metaphorically; it came up at the divorce proceedings; or was it *The Perfumed Garden*? Well, either way."

Oscar disappears into the kitchen and comes back with the first course, an orange-colored soup; he doesn't have a mean bone in his body but gossip is the staff of life, and Elizabeth, getting into the swing of it, fights a mild embarrassment on Maribel's behalf. "Not that the portrait isn't perfectly respectable," she says. "It's some sort of takeoff on a famous Greek bas-relief: not quite what you'd expect to come across in the average suburban living room, probably, but then it isn't really the average suburban house. There seems to be some talk of turning it into a minimuseum: a kind of period piece. Edwardian—you know the type. Not that I'm sure I see the point, since all the good paintings have already gone to Sotheby's for sale. But there may still be letters and interesting ephemera in some bureau drawer somewhere. They say she knew Tamara de Lempicka in Paris in the thirties, and God knows who all else." She lowers her voice; the garden is smaller than it looks. "Actually, there seems to be some lingering question about the way she died."

"Really?" says Oscar. "How delicious!" He pulls his chair closer to hers and passes her the bread. "Well, you can certainly rule out suicide, can't you? Painters never commit suicide, everybody knows that. They're much too egotistical to do themselves in. It's all about immortality, my dear." He wags his hands airily above his head. "And the work, of course, lives on."

The air is heavy with the smell of citronella, and boxwood so tall it must have been planted at or before the turn of the century, decades before the Russian revolution and the graduated income tax. Oscar's garden is thick with shrubs that people don't plant anymore, and nostalgia for a world he either was or wishes he had been born into, once upon a time: another kind of immortality. "You must tell me all about Ellios," he says. "Is he bidding on your prints? Does he still have a terrible crush on you?"

Elizabeth pretends to laugh; Oscar thinks the whole world has a crush on her. "He's going to take a look at them this week," she says. "We've been leaving messages on each other's answering machines. Ellios knows someone in New York, in case the family decides to sell."

"Plenty of time for a second opinion, then," says Oscar. "Because Ellios doesn't know everything, a word to the wise: he isn't the last word. Ellios was a dentist in another life; that's where he gets that pontifical pose of his: doctor knows best! No, I kid you not; it's common knowledge. He used to invest all his earnings in art. Then one day someone gave him a fake Picasso drawing to settle a bill and he was so incensed that he set out to learn everything he could: and the rest, as they say, is history." Oscar pauses for effect, pouring her a second glass of wine. "Once a dentist, always a dentist, though," he says.

Elizabeth tries to imagine Ellios as a suburban dentist, and his clinical gravitas as he promises you that you will feel no pain. "Dr. Ellios," she says, and laughs. "I can't quite picture it. Can you?"

"Dr. Elliosoff," says Oscar, "if you really want to dot all the i's. His father was a white Russian with a trade in seventeenth-century icons; but that's probably not the whole story either, not by a long shot, as you can well imagine."

"Icons," Elizabeth say. "Good Lord."

Oscar twirls a tongful of pale spaghetti toward her plate, then passes her the silver sauceboat and the cheese. "I know," he says, "incongruous, isn't it? They came to Argentina on one of those Nansen passports and I suppose in those days pulling teeth must have seemed like a perfectly marvelous port in a storm."

"I've never really understood all the fuss about icons," says Elizabeth. "It must be my low church upbringing—no saints, no graven images." It's true, as she discovers only in the act of saying so—religious art embarrasses her even more than Maribel's Carraccis, when you get right down to it; but it goes without saying that painters will paint women's faces wherever and however they find them, whether sacred or profane. "Do you

think portrait painters always fall in love with their subjects?"
she says.

Oscar grates cheese for the pasta. "Good God, no. In love
with the commission is much more like it, isn't it?" he says. He
threads the last of the spaghetti onto his serving fork and loads
it on her plate. "Though they say that Rodin, for one, could
never keep his hands off his models; couldn't tell where the clay
left off, so to speak, and the living flesh began." He spoons
grated cheese over both their plates in little clouds of aromatic
pollen as white as the flowering mock orange on either side
of them. "Just try telling that to the abstract expressionists,
though."

At the edge of the property line a row of lacy hemlocks
scratches black lines onto the dark blue sky like script in an
unknown language, and Elizabeth wonders if her secrets are as
safe with Oscar as his have always been with her. "What about
the collector, though?" she says. "Doesn't the collector have
to be in love with the things he collects? Isn't that what eggs
him on?"

"Ah, the collector, that's a bit more complicated," says Oscar,
and, Elizabeth supposes, somewhat closer to home. "A collector doesn't want a painting," says Oscar. "He wants a whole
collection. There's a difference. Not to mention the people
like Ellios, who basically collect out of revenge and wounded
pride." He pushes himself to his feet and shakes off her help as
he collects their empty dishes. "And who cares, just so long
as he doesn't add *you* to his collection?" he says. Elizabeth holds
the kitchen door for him and wonders how much he remembers about her version of things with Ellios. "The lives and
loves of Elizabeth," says Oscar. "And speaking of which, by the
way, how is the great romance?"

Elizabeth lets the door swing safely shut behind them. "Do

you mean David?" she says. She's on thin ice here: loose talk about Ellios is one thing, but David's a married man. "Oh, David's fine," she says. "He's coming in August, I think."

Oscar arches his old man's thick and disbelieving eyebrows at her. "August!" he says. "But when's the last time you saw him? December? January? And while we're on the subject of icons, my dear, has anyone ever told you that you have the patience of a saint?"

"It isn't patience," says Elizabeth. "It's the rules of the game. It's not as if anybody had ever made any promises to anyone."

Oscar looks at her piercingly as he squirts soap into the sink and runs hot water into it. "Well, you might at least tell him he'd better step up the tempo a bit," he says. "Does he know he's got competition? Does he know he's not the only man out there in love with your big blue eyes?"

Elizabeth goes back to the terrace for whatever's left of the napkins, knives, and forks, and tells herself not to worry: whatever she may have told Oscar about David in the past, she's always been scrupulously careful about naming names. "I don't think so, but I'll be glad to give him the message," she says; and doesn't add that it was March, not January, when she saw David last.

"Coffee, anyone?" says Oscar, but it's just a formality: he's a bad sleeper and Elizabeth's an early riser, especially when she's in the middle of preparing for a sale, and they've had a long-standing agreement anyway for years: no dessert, no after-dinner coffee, ever, anywhere. Inside the swinging door he takes the dirty cutlery out of her hands and shoos her away from the sink; in Oscar's kitchen no one is allowed to do the dishes but himself. Elizabeth waits till he's stacked the plates to his satisfaction, then puts her arms around him and breathes in his wonderful, soapy, nursery smell. " 'And her heart was a hummingbird,' " Oscar says softly, somewhere over her shoulder, " 'and flew from art to art.' " She hangs on to him tightly for a minute more to remind herself that she's not alone in the world, that all men are mortal, and that nothing lasts forever anyway. But Oscar has always made much more of her love life than it deserves, spinning gold out of flax according to some wishful formula of his own; and he must surely know after all these years that her eyes are gray, not blue.

ELIZABETH drives home the long way, along the river, playing *Tosca* on the cassette deck to keep herself alert. Another long day, but she's still making steady progress; tomorrow she'll go through thirty years' worth of Maribel's daybooks, unearthed by Clemmie at the top of a derelict bookcase in the upstairs hall, then make a final tally of Maribel's trousseau lingerie and buy some for her own account, at fair market price, of course. Her twenty-year-old daughter Robin has a birthday coming up in July; just once Elizabeth would like to give her something completely frivolous, useless, unimagined, and unearned.

It's later than she thought and the half-dreaded meeting with Ellios is scheduled for tomorrow, though with the sale pending and profits to be earned she's pretty sure she can depend on him to observe all the obvious proprieties. Because if there's one thing she's sure of, it's that Ellios will always put business ahead of pleasure. Some things you can count on, at least till the deal is done and the money's on the way to the bank.

Elizabeth drives as slowly as the road allows, thinking of the men in her life (Douglas, settled in California in some midlife fantasy of strong sunlight and easy living, full of rattan porch furniture and lemon trees in tubs; and her married lover David, miles away in Colorado, saving the world from famine but due to come east for a symposium on Asian flood relief in August) and wonders, as she always does on her way to or from Oscar's house, whether there will ever be another dinner, whether this one or the next will be the last. Elizabeth's father left her mother when she was still a baby and, of the two men her mother subsequently married, one ran off with her beautiful best friend and the other made strange, clumsy, and finally unmistakable overtures to Elizabeth whenever he'd had too much to drink; but with Oscar in her life Elizabeth has never wanted for a father. It's a fact of her life by now that Oscar adores her. She sends him flowers on his birthday and eccentric gifts at Christmastime; she talks to him at least once a week and takes him to the doctor when he's sick; she wants him to live forever, just like all the artists he pretends to be so scornful of.

Tosca is just finishing her famous second-act aria by the time she turns off Lincoln Drive. It's time for the showdown in Scarpia's chambers; she's lived for love, she's lived for art, but now she's face-to-face with him, terrified either of losing her virtue or of failing gloriously in its defense, and waiting for the light to change at the corner Elizabeth wonders what would really be so terrible about having it both ways. She wants love and fidelity to triumph, yes—but in all honesty maybe only after the villain has actually had his way. Elizabeth understands the ambiguities and contrarieties that the libretto leaves out: yes and no, advance, retreat, and a perverse desire for the object of your most profound ambivalence and the triumph of sexual curiosity over the meat-and-potato certainties of true love. Puccini's women are more complicated than they look, and Elizabeth wishes she'd had the nerve to pump Oscar more thoroughly on the subject of Ellios while she could. Or maybe not. She knows herself; some things are probably always better left unsaid.

Elizabeth turns off Montgomery onto Whitaker, the home stretch. Left over from everyone's childhood is the mysterious joy of early summer and its long, hot, empty days, with the smell of honeysuckle rising from the hedgerows like invisible steam. On the cassette deck virtue triumphs at last and Scarpia goes to his noisy death just as Elizabeth makes her turn into the parking lot. The fountain in the driveway turnaround purls on and on in the summer night, its lily pads glassy with moonlight, as she pulls the key from the ignition, wishing that her life to date had entitled her to say, like Tosca, that she had lived for art; because at the end of the day it's art or nothing, isn't it? What else is there left in the record, that is, when all the chips are down, considering how rarely any real woman (herself included, God knows) can ever truthfully say that she has lived for love?

10

PEG WATCHES Coby's truck pull out of the drive but leaves the curtains undrawn, if only for auld lang syne. With Maribel dead Peg considers herself the last of the original settlers on Weavers Way and the last link to the street's suburban history; wouldn't you think he could at least stop in and have a chat? But he's keeping his distance these days; probably afraid of her, rightly or wrongly. Because Coby knows better than anyone that Peg's got eyes in the back of her head.

The vigil Peg keeps is just a reflex now; she got in the habit of it years ago when Maribel first took sick, gauging the forward march of her illness by the hours of electric lights left burning in the bedroom over the arborvitae hedge through night after silent night. Her bathroom window is almost directly opposite Maribel's bedroom and Peg's up two and three times a night to pee anyway, so she can honestly say she's kept tabs on things without even trying to all these months. Once or twice, before the cancer went to her bones, Maribel had asked her to come over and listen to old French music-hall records with her until she fell asleep; other times they sat up together drinking premixed daiquiris and looking at black-and-white movies on the late-night television stations, until things got bad and she finally had to cave in and take a pill. And not much of a pill at that, if Peg's any judge. Because Giles didn't believe in narcotics, and neither, when you got right down to it, did Maribel. I want to stay clear for my work, she said. All those paintings up there in the studio that nobody ever looked at anyway; but, of course, to each his own. And, as she said once, so that she'd be clear enough to go quickly, if and when she decided to pull the plug. Well, Peg can relate to that.

Peg's no longer a practicing Catholic, she hasn't been to confession since she was twenty-three and the first of the three dead babies was born, but she'd found it hard to ask the obvious question, which is, and where would you get the pills? Even though that's the $64,000 question, isn't it? Because where *would* you get the pills when you had to—an old woman with a young know-it-all ex–altar boy for a doctor, let alone a mean old Presbyterian bully boy like Giles? No, let's be practical. Is there some possible way of interviewing your starchy Gyn and henpecked proctologist in advance for their views on an easy death before you sign on for what's left of your life with them? Some way to smoke out their secret thoughts about mercy killing without giving your own secret purposes away? Or, better yet, a way to simply present them with some standard questionnaire right up front, to make them spell out exactly where they stand on pain and painkillers, the dignity of the naked, the rights of the dying, the innocence of the uninformed?

Watching Maribel die (and not just Maribel, but Mikey before her, and Justin before that), Peg has had occasion to ask herself these questions. Till now she's been lucky, knock wood. She has to watch what she eats but her blood pressure's not that bad, and maybe her eyesight isn't exactly what it used to be either, but whose is? In the last analysis it's like the tough guy in that old movie, who walks into the bar and says, Nobody here gets out alive: to which Peg says, amen. It isn't really death that worries her, though; it's pain. She knows herself; she keeps what stiff upper lip she has for her gardening, her last and only physical pleasure, if you can still call it that, considering her knees. Whereas a spoiled stomach puts her out of commission for days on end and a sick headache has her running to the medicine chest in search of the strongest stuff she can find.

"ANY IDEA what medicines she took?" the young cop had asked her that week after Maribel died. He had a headful of bristling red hair and large disingenuous eyes; she told him to check it out with Giles, but he pressed on. He had caught her at the cocktail hour, alone in the sunroom, having her first martini of the day. "Was she much of a drinker?" he said, looking sideways, she noticed, at Peg's glass, "or more like a social drinker, say, knocked back the odd glass of wine in company— or maybe something stronger, cocktails before dinner, that sort of thing?"

Peg put down her glass and resisted the urge to edge it out of sight behind the African violet under the lamp. "Are you trying to say Maribel had been drinking when she died?" she said.

He cleared his throat. "I'm not trying to say anything, ma'am, we're just covering all the bases here." He stood a little to the left of the couch with his pen and his opened notebook at the ready, waiting for her to ask him to sit down. "Any history of drug abuse you might know of, for example? Or prescription pills? Any over-the-counter medicines?"

Peg reached for her glass to steady her hand. The Lower Merion police must know all about Coby. Did they think: like mother, like son? The young cop looked at his notebook. "Because when a person dies alone like that we have to cover all the angles," he said loudly, patiently.

Peg's martini, when she raised it to her lips, had a cold medicinal smell. "Look, Maribel was a sick woman," she said, grateful to the gin to cover whatever tricks her voice might want to play on her. "She didn't have long to live whatever way you want to look at it; she'd been sick as a dog for years. Cancer, you know. Of course she took pills; who wouldn't? Wouldn't you? Why make such a big issue of it? Wouldn't anyone?"

The cop wrote something down. "I'm just doing my job here, ma'am," he said, "seeing that you were the deceased's nearest neighbor. By your own say-so you looked in on her every day." He shifted from one foot to another; you could see him struggling to keep his feelings under wraps. He capped his pen and tried again. "Can you tell me what she was wearing, maybe, when you saw her last?" he said.

Peg had begun, at long last, to feel her gin. It was true, she had looked in on Maribel every day, but that might not be much help because Maribel always wore the same clothes, day in, day out. Probably that old black canvas coolie coat she clung to through thick and thin, though Peg would hate to have to swear to it in court. (Don't you ever get hot in that thing? she used to ask; but Maribel was cold-blooded by nature: even before she got so sick she'd never been one to feel the heat.)

"Something black," said Peg. Black or gray was always a safe bet with Maribel. Something that you could throw in the wash and hang up on a hanger to dry, something that didn't show the dirt. Peg was sorry but that was the best she could do.

He wrote that down, then closed his notebook with a snap as if anything he asked her now would be off the record, just between the two of them. "And speaking of pills, I mean not to change the subject," he said, "but did the deceased ever talk to you about, ah, I mean, you know, making an end of things?"

Peg closed her eyes, almost glad in a way that he had stopped beating around the bush. But how can you explain to someone as young as this wet-behind-the-ears red-haired moralist that suicide is something everybody talks about, quite realistically, after a certain age?

"I don't think so," she said, "no more than anyone else her age." Let him put that in his pipe and smoke it till he suffered the first grown-up tragedy of his life. Wait till his mother died, or his dog. Or (God help him) wait till he lost a child.

The young cop nodded, as if she had given the right answer on a test, and moved on down his list. "You've said that the lights were on," he said. "Can you tell me when you first noticed this?" He wiped dust and ink from the end of his pen, then clipped it to his notebook; they were back on the record again.

Peg opened her eyes, but it was a while before she got him back into reasonably good focus again. She doesn't hold her liquor as well as she used to in the good old days; or is it that the drinks are getting taller and she's got into the habit of drinking them faster nowadays? "Well, let's see," she said, and reminded herself to pick her words with care. "I woke up at midnight, or thereabouts, and then again at three." No need to spell things out in any great detail, was there? The drink was making her thick-headed and thick-tongued; she had to home in on her consonants more carefully than she normally would. "Probably about three-thirty or quarter to four I tried to get her on the phone. I made a little mental note to wait half an hour, then check again; but then I dozed off, and by the time I woke up the lights were still on, and that's when I called Nina, Mrs. English. And of course Nina called Dr. Giles."

"You're saying it was Dr. Giles who found her?"

"Yes, I suppose so; it must have been. Well, at least I know I had to get up to let him in."

The cop said, "I take that to mean you had the key?"

He looked so serious standing there taking his little notes in his little book that Peg felt sorry for him. "Yes, I did," she said. "Of course I did. Good Lord, who didn't? Look, everyone and their grandfather had Maribel's key, not to mention the one she kept under the urn."

The young cop looked at her wide-eyed; she had succeeded in amazing him at last. Were there really still people left alive out there who didn't believe in serial killers and burglars, rapists, muggers, foreign terrorists? Peg loves young people and makes allowances for their self-certainty, but sometimes it makes her positively tired to think of all the rude awakenings still lying in store for them. She for one never leaves her front door unlocked and never has, but Maribel had always hated coming all the way down from her studio to answer the door, and passed out her door key like penny candy, one to a customer. She'd grown up on Weavers Way when Villa Calpurnia was the only house on the block, and the burly chauffeur or either of the two gardeners would have made mincemeat of any tramp who came to the door. "Well, I know it's hard to believe," she says, "in this day and age; but that was Maribel."

The young cop went away to file his report, presumably, and that's the last Peg ever heard of him; she told Nina about the interview later that week but didn't go into any more detail than she had to. Why borrow trouble? Nina has her hands full, and that lantern-jawed husband of hers has always had it in for

Coby, so the less said the better all around. And anyway, as far as Peg knows (thank God), nothing ever came of it. Meanwhile she thanks her lucky stars that she didn't make a serious hash of it, all things considered, and so much for *in vino veritas.*

PEG WATCHES a black car pull up under Maribel's porte cochere, then reverse a few inches, backing itself into the shade. A blonde in a navy blue blazer works her way out of the car, her arms full of nested packing boxes in a precarious tower; the same one who was here last week, Peg thinks: some Realtor friend of Nina's, probably. It's amazing how much more traffic there is over there on the other side of the hedge since Maribel died. In the old days (as opposed to the good old days, before Gerald left, before things got squalid, before the money ran out) she'd have been lucky if Coby had stopped in to see her once or twice a week, or Nina had come by to check on her after she closed up the shop at night. Leaving it to Peg to take up the slack, drive Maribel to the radiologist, pick up the odd prescription at the pharmacy, make the necessary supermarket run. Not that Peg ever really minded. Because the Peruvian cleaning lady never learned how to drive, so who else was there? And who else did Peg have to dance attendance on by then?

On the other side of the hedge the blonde in the blue blazer stands outside her car, checking through the contents of her bag. Peg remembers that hedge when it was waist high, planted by Maribel's mother to make sure no one crossed the line. Slow-growing, it took the arborvitae twenty years to do the job of blocking out the view; nowadays you have to climb all the way to the second floor to see over the top of it.

There's something crisp and almost industrially methodical in the way the woman in the blazer switches things from her right hand to her left, then back again. These professional women of Nina's are a new and to Peg an exotic breed, all dressed like airline hostesses or television anchorwomen, their faces inscrutably cordial, their sleek professional hair, and they all have lovely legs. Women in Peg's generation didn't have legs like that, and when they smiled at you it was to disarm you and make you feel at home, not keep you at arm's length; this far and no farther, hold the line.

"Can you tell me if the deceased had any outstanding insurance policies?" the young cop had asked. "Would you happen to know whether she might have left anything of value, other than the house itself?"

Peg can't remember what she answered; maybe this sort of thing is standard operating procedure in a police investigation but all she can remember is her own surprise that he should bother to ask her at all. You should talk to the relatives, she should have said, or the Realtors. Maribel wouldn't mind telling you the most bizarre and intimate details of her sex life if you happened to want to listen—how she put herself in the mood, whether to wear skirts or pants, which positions to take, what perfume to wear—but money was the great taboo. Peg knows more about Roberto's libido and the size of his you-know-what than she does about Maribel's finances. Other than the inescapably obvious: that unpaid oil bill last winter, the repossessed air conditioner, the unrepaired washing machine.

Well, at least she died in the spring—too warm for the heating season, but not hot enough to expire from the heat. And Peg knew better than to play lady bountiful with Maribel: not after that fiasco with Coby and the car. People who have lost all their money come in two basic versions: the kind that will take any handout that comes along, and the kind that would rather starve before they admit they're down to their last dollar in the bank. That woman down there in the blue blazer probably knows more about Maribel's net worth than Peg does, believe it or not. And that's all right with Peg.

The house, she has to assume, will go to Coby: unless they double-cross him and turn it into a museum. Which they'll have to do over Peg's dead body, incidentally—though she's been approached, ever so graciously, of course, by Isobel Aubrey, acting on the family's behalf: Maribel's famous aunt Ibby, the ex–bridge champion, playing grande dame from that little fake castle of hers in Chestnut Hill. It was the first time Ibby had called Peg in a hundred years; did she really think all she had to do was pick up the phone and everyone would fall swooning at her feet? "Let me think about it," said Peg, knowing as well as Ibby did that they can't go ahead with that museum scheme of theirs without her say-so and goodwill. Because what about the parking? What about the zoning variances and rights of way? What about the crowds?

The blond woman on the other side of the hedge gives up on whatever it is she's looking for in the bottom of her purse and slides halfway into the car to check the glove compartment. Her perfect legs hang comically out the other side; she wears beige stockings and plain dark pumps with the dignified sheen of old books—not a hair out of place, not a button loose anywhere. Maribel wouldn't have given a woman like that the time of day. Miss America, she called them, because they never wore anything but red, white, or navy blue. Grown-up Barbie dolls, so much blond wood.

Maribel would have laughed at the idea of the museum— the pomposity of it, the la-di-dah. Or would she? Sometimes Peg isn't quite so sure. For all her contempt for family bloodlines, the pictures meant a lot to her: her own, not to mention the ones she inherited and bought. To Maribel the house wasn't so much a roof over her head as a series of walls to hang the paintings on; and when you get right down to it, isn't that the whole point of a museum? Not that Peg cares about Maribel's last wishes, really: why should she; why should anyone? Peg's never been a museum-goer herself and, even if she were, what matters isn't Maribel, now that she's gone; it's Coby, isn't it? Peg may be Catholic but she doesn't believe in the afterlife, never did; even as a child she had a hard time with the idea of heaven and hell, devils with pitchforks, angels fluttering. What matters to Peg is the here and now: hordes of tourists trampling the verges and cars parked bumper to bumper in the street; candy wrappers on the sidewalk; cigarette butts in the pachysandra. What matters now is what's to become of Coby. Maribel wasn't as bad a mother as she's made out to be, as who would know better than Peg? Or as unmercenary as she tried to look. What matters is the living, not the dead.

The young cop was right. When a person dies alone like that (as Peg will die someday herself, getting out of bed, working in the garden, stepping in or out of the tub), you have to cover all the angles: interview all the friends and neighbors, track down all the leads. Anything less and you might miss a clue or overlook the obvious; anything less and you wouldn't pay your dues to the majesty of death. Or (what was it he kept saying that day, taking notes in that fat little black book of his?) anything else, and you wouldn't really be doing your job.

11

Mrs. Bright, the naval attaché's daughter, is eighty-two but well preserved; her father had served in the navy under Maribel's grandfather and there are ship prints everywhere, some of them eighteenth-century, hung close to the acoustical ceiling and out of scale for the boxy three-room suite in the retirement community where she has come to end her days. Elizabeth would take a closer look but she's not sure the prints are on the list of heirlooms she has been invited to appraise. On the fake Chippendale coffee table in front of the couch there are pimento-stuffed olives and celery sticks on an impressive Georgian silver tray, and double-strength martinis in monogrammed glasses with matching coasters underneath.

Mrs. Bright is one of those women who have been ageless for so long that it's become second nature by now: a small-boned beauty who must have gone gray in her thirties and stayed that way for the rest of her life, as women did in those days. She was born three months earlier than Maribel, she says, and Elizabeth tries to imagine Maribel in this room, gray-haired, sipping martinis and eating canapés with the age-defying friend of her youth.

"One grandfather was what we used to call a hard-shell Baptist," says Mrs. Bright, "and the admiral was true-blue Episcopalian, though I believe the mother was a Catholic of some sort, but Maribel had no use for religion, none at all. Her grandfather on her mother's side owned a houseboat on one of the Jersey tide-creeks. We used to have picnics there in July—it was right on the way to Bay Head. My mother had conniptions because there were reports of nude swimming: coeducational, if you know what I mean. Not that I ever saw any of that, but I wouldn't have put it past Maribel. No, indeed! Maribel was always a hell-raiser, if you'll pardon the expression, even before she went to France and turned bohemian; the mothers were all in abject fear of her, and rightly so."

Elizabeth accepts one of the canapés and its accompanying little monogrammed paper napkin with fluted edges. She takes the small, well-thought-out bites of a good child at a grown-ups' party; it's the kind of public graciousness that can make or break you with the generation represented by Mrs. Bright. The request to look at her father's naval memorabilia and a pair of Japanese screens has come couched in the form of an invitation to Sunday cocktails, and presumably took some engineering on Peachy's part. But Elizabeth's in her element; she has always had good luck with people like Mrs. Bright—widows and maiden ladies of limited means but unlimited memories and social graces. They sense her respect for their antecedents, her willingness to be charmed by their perfect manners and Jazz Age cocktail snacks.

Mrs. Bright hadn't kept up the connection to Maribel in later years, she says, but she lived close by as a child and went to Agnes Irwin with Maribel; there's a sketch of the adolescent

Mrs. Bright in a dress with a middy collar signed MARIBEL in big block letters on Mrs. Bright's dressing table to prove it. The drawing is tentative and sweet, like nothing else of Maribel's that Elizabeth has ever seen, and they take turns admiring the strong likeness to the living Mrs. Bright today.

The old lady is a conversationalist of the old school, trained to keep up a pleasant patter and fill all social silences to the brim. Elizabeth is already half in love with the photograph of her uniformed father on the mantelpiece: a slender man in full dress regalia, posed with four other dignitaries at Warren Harding's inaugural ball. As a little girl Mrs. Bright had gone to Maribel's birthday parties and played croquet on the Calpurnia lawns with her two brothers (Conrad and Win, the handsome one, who died in Italy during the war), and when they grew up the Archibalds' chauffeur drove them to the Assemblies, until they were old enough to have beaux with cars of their own: whereupon Maribel went off to Paris alone to paint. "I am sorry to say that when I saw the obituary in the paper I honestly hadn't seen or probably even thought of Maribel in years," she says.

"I keep trying to imagine what she was like as a little girl," says Elizabeth. She doesn't want to push, but Mrs. Bright is the first person she's run into, not counting the bearded brother, who could possibly have known Maribel as a child. Scanning Maribel's daybooks, memorizing old photos, reading old letters, she's had a harder and harder time getting a fix on her subject. The paper-thin little girl with the grudging party-goer's smile and the enormous hair bow at a sunny summer lawn party seems otherwise unrelated to the grinning gypsy waving good-bye from the deck of the *Queen Mary* in 1936; and the unsmiling bridesmaid with the unruly hair in the receiving line at Win's wedding is hard to match up with the hilarious bride vamping through her own veil at her own wedding in 1939. Trying to put these pieces together, Elizabeth has the feeling that she's composing a fictional creation, the heroine of an un-authorized biography. "Was she a tomboy?" says Elizabeth. "Did she do well in school?"

Mrs. Bright puts her head to one side. "A tomboy? No, I don't think I'd call Maribel a tomboy," she says. "Too sly, and much too fussy about her clothes. Maribel's favorite game was dressing up, and I suppose I was popular because my great-grandmother had beautiful clothes and never threw anything away. My mother kept everything packed up in camphor in our attic; if I had to be perfectly honest about it, I'd have to say I think that was probably my main attraction for Maribel—but only till she got old enough to buy her own clothes and do her own dressing up; after that she left me in absolute dust. My father served in the navy under her grandfather but the families were never close; my mother disapproved of Maribel—I sup-pose all the mothers did. Maribel was precocious, to say the least, but her father doted on her; as long as the money held out she could always get exactly what she wanted from him. The mother was a bit of a social butterfly, I think: a great gar-dener, completely mad about flowers. In fact, she didn't just grow them, she painted them, morning, noon, and night. With the result that Maribel was mostly raised by servants. Well, but of course lots of people were in those days, you know."

Elizabeth is due back at Calpurnia in an hour but Mrs. Bright lives in a world made timeless by too much free time, and, downing celery sticks with a kind of respectful attention to detail, Elizabeth has forgotten to look at her watch. From the corner of her eye she checks out the Sully ancestress over the fireplace, the Savery highboy and Capshaw chairs. Mrs. Bright reminds Elizabeth of her own Virginia grandmother and her determinedly winning ways, but it's hard to make sense of her picture of Maribel as a gamine in training for a bohemian femme fatale.

The martinis have turned warm in the bottom of the shaker as the canapés go back and forth across the table one last time untouched. Elizabeth closes her notepad and puts it back in her bag; this is not the time or place to talk dollars and cents, and she has too much on her hands at Calpurnia to work up any but the most preliminary figures till sometime after the sale. Time's probably not of the essence anyway: Mrs Bright may need the money but she doesn't need it immediately, and Elizabeth guesses that when the moment arrives to part with her father's memorabilia she'll almost certainly have second thoughts. She wants Elizabeth to give her a dollar figure on these items not because she's going to sell them but because they represent a kind of inventory in her head: what her estate is really worth in cold cash, what she's still got to hand over to her children and grandchildren after her final expenses are paid and the nursing home claims its share.

Mrs. Bright reaches for her cane; she gets up with great difficulty and, after several false starts, begins to show Elizabeth to the door. "Tell me," she says, sotto voce, as if what she's asking is morbidly indiscreet, "whatever became of Maribel's pretty niece, the one with the dress shop in Clover Hill? Nancy, was it, or Nanette? I always felt so sorry for her, caught between her mother and Maribel, those two terrible mischief-makers, struggling for her soul. Maribel gave her a painting as a wedding present, one of her more scandalous ones probably, knowing Maribel, and her mother refused to let them hang it on the walls."

"Nina," says Elizabeth. "Nina English. We've been working on the library together. She's fine. The shop is flourishing."

"Oh, I'm so *glad*," says Mrs. Bright. She shakes hands and stands aside for Elizabeth at the door; she seems genuinely sorry to see her go. "It was so nice of you to come visit an old lady in this awful place," she says; but the place isn't awful and she clearly doesn't think of herself as old.

Elizabeth holds her hand a second or two longer than the occasion calls for; how else can she make the point that she's really happy to have met her, to have seen the adolescent Maribel's pen-and-ink sketch of the adolescent Mrs. Bright, the ship prints and Japanese screens, to have had a look at her incredible highboy and eaten her touching canapés?

"I'll phone you in a few days, if that's all right," she says. "I'll have to do some research before I can get back to you with any kind of estimate."

Down at the other end of the almost endless hall the doors to the dining room have been bolted back, opening up a ribbon of waxed daylight like an extra lane on the polished terrazzo floor. It's dinnertime; doors up and down the corridor are opening on cue, and a column of gray figures has already begun to converge on the dining room. Mrs. Bright squares her shoulders for the long march; she would ask her to stay to dinner, she says, but she knows Elizabeth must have better things to do. "I hope I didn't bore you to tears talking about old times with Maribel," she says.

Elizabeth squeezes her hand. "No, just the opposite," she says. "I've become a real fan of Maribel's; I can't get enough of her." Pleased, Mrs. Bright shifts her cane from her right arm to her left. "One thing I'll never understand," she says. "The way people talk, the things people say. I mean even now that she's dead and in the ground."

Far away at the entrance to the dining room there's a traffic jam in the making, where someone's wheelchair has got meshed with a potted areca palm. "What sorts of things?" says Elizabeth.

Mrs. Bright shuts the apartment door behind her and locks it; The Hollies is famous for its tough security, but you never know. She sets off slowly in the direction of dinner with her left hand tucked into the crook of Elizabeth's arm for support. "About how she died, you know," she says. "About whether she died a natural death or not. Whether she knew she was dying, say, and then just decided to take things into her own hands."

She steps backward to let a very bald man in a wheelchair go by, and lowers her voice to a whisper. "Suicide," she says. She unhooks herself carefully from Elizabeth's arm and plants her cane on the ramp to the dining room like someone about to board a plane. "Not that I would have blamed her if she did," says Mrs. Bright. "Play God, I mean; but isn't that what artists are always accused of doing anyway?"

12

LLIOS says, "But my God, at last, how wonderful to see you again." She has opened the door on the second ring, and to Elizabeth it seems as if he has been standing there since sundown in the studied informality of his black silk shirt and starched linen pants, waiting for her to let him in. "Of course I'm not going to embarrass either of us by asking why it's taken you so long—ten months? A year? Or is it maybe even more? But never mind. Old friends have their privileges."

Ellios trades on the international ambiguity of his accent, musical but difficult to place. "Oh, it can't possibly have been that long, can it?" says Elizabeth. Still, she's shocked by the familiarity of his voice and its little signature smile—old friends indeed. Ellios's punctuality is famous, but his insistence on the rules and regulations has always surprised her; it shows a side of his personality—Teutonic, or bureaucratic anyway—that's at odds with those overhanging shoulders and meaty hands, the irreversibly agnostic eyes. She's gone to the door with her smile prepared: small and cordial, not too warm and not too cool.

Ellios is in his shirt sleeves, but the shirt is silk, the belt expensive, his black hair slicked back from his temples as if he's just gotten out of the shower. "Am I on time?" he says, then kisses the hand she's given him to shake.

Elizabeth feels like the hostess at a party as she shows him into the hall and shuts the door behind him. She can see him making his own critical appraisal of Calpurnia: a quick cost analysis of the Palladian fenestration, the towering rhododendrons, the square footage of the long streetside façade. "Absolutely," she says, "to the minute," and makes her face a blank as she leads him into the hall.

Outside it's still daylight but in here night has already begun to fall. It's eight o'clock, and Nina and Clemmie are both safely home, it being a rule of thumb that there's never anything to be gained by introducing prospective buyers to the family, let alone outside experts with well-known reputations for buying cheap and selling dear. Elizabeth remembers the summer night not unlike this one when he first made a pass at her like a crash victim remembering an almost fatal accident: including the smell of lemon cough drops on his breath, the touch of his hand inside her dress, exploratory and not quite friendly, and the flash of her own astonishment like a surge of high voltage arcing through a wire. Though she'd be the first to admit she might have brought it on herself. Because from the first he must have misread her reticence; and isn't silence always taken for consent? Was it that night or some other that Ellios had said, "I never understand men who say they don't know what women want. When it's so obvious, isn't it, that what women want is attention: am I right?"

Ellios may be right about women, and if so Elizabeth has spent the better part of the last two years doing whatever she could to prove that she doesn't want his. On the other hand, it was obviously in the nature of this business that they would run into each other from time to time, and this time at least she's prepared. This time she knows what she's up against: his casual greed, the opportunism that he's so famous for; and, now and then, and always when you least expect it, some surprisingly deeply shared judgment about what's beautiful and what isn't. It's the consensus in the business that Ellios has a remarkable eye, though maybe, like Rodin, an eye that doesn't draw as fine a line as it should between the created and the real; but forewarned is forearmed. Elizabeth leads him across the hall, keeping him at bay with her invincible politeness—a trick learned from watching her mother deal with tradespeople she despised, hung-over gardeners, and cleaning ladies she was about to fire.

IT's BEEN another day of record heat; if this keeps up, she says, chattering over her shoulder, she'll have to go out and buy at least half a dozen fans to cool down the studio and the second floor. Maribel seems not to have minded the heat; in the whole house there's only a single air conditioner and that one's in the maid's room at the back of the second-floor hall. Another item to add to the list on the clipboard in the hall.

It's amazing how stuck people get on their own frugalities; Maribel's refrigerator barely makes one tray of ice cubes at a time, her kitchen stove works by guesswork and good luck; there's no VCR in the house, no dishwasher, no microwave, and her old Smith Corona portable may or may not turn out to have much value as an antique (another item to research, if and when Elizabeth gets a moment to leave the house). But how does all this square with the prevailing notion of Maribel as a liberated woman, a member of some formerly official avant-garde, someone with pictures of fornicating gods and goddesses on her powder-room wall?

Elizabeth tries to put the day's work behind her as she leads Ellios through the dining room into the little brown library. There's a point in every project where the deeper you dig the more dirt you raise, and you can feel things crossing the line from the finite to the infinite; the more you do, the more there is to do, and the less hope there's going to be of ever getting the whole thing done. Watching Ellios as he zooms in on some unobvious first edition, she wishes for a fleeting moment that she could put him to work in here beside her. Of course there's no one like Clemmie; she's fast, she's all-seeing, she's as single-minded as a termite chewing through a beam, but you pay the price: at one of Elizabeth's sales she discovered twenty love letters stuffed into the hems of the bedroom curtains, and at another she found a nineteenth-century will documenting an ancient family quarrel; but her discoveries all make extra work for Elizabeth and end up adding hours to the day and days to the job. And Ellios would bring his cool art-lover's eye to the assembled cast of characters like a theater critic at a play. Whereas Clemmie's antipathies are instant and irreversible.

It was probably predictable, for instance, that Clemmie would take a dislike to Nina, all that artfuless and frou-frou, those floaty dresses, the airy Pre-Raphaelite hair. ("She's bird-dogging me," says Clemmie. "Every time I turn around she's there, counting the spoons. What does she think, I'm going to run off with the family jewels?") And Coby's fair game too: there have been mysterious disappearances from the moment he took to dropping in. A pair of old World War I binoculars went missing on Saturday, and two days later the third-floor bathroom light was unaccountably left on. "I don't like houses where things don't stay put," says Clemmie, "and the lights go on and off. I saw his truck in the drive Monday night when I cut through on my way to the store; and I don't exactly believe in ghosts, if you know what I mean." Clemmie's on to Coby; his report cards, unearthed from the back of a drawer in the butler's pantry, tell the story of a more than usually abrupt downhill slide from the sixth grade to the tenth ("We need more flashes of the Clarence Coburn Davies wit," writes his English teacher in the first quarter, but by the fourth she's thrown in the towel; the science teacher is reduced to listing the number of assignments he has not turned in, and by tenth grade everyone seems to have given up on him except the tennis coach). "Your basic suburban adolescent pain in the ass," Clemmie says, and she has her own equally unflattering idea of Maribel: "A woman who wouldn't even blow her own nose if she could get someone else to do it for her, what do you want to bet?" Because painting isn't work to Clemmie; art is something children do in school to break up the boredom of the day; and child rearing? Clemmie's met Coby, coming and going, overhead and underfoot, and the proof of the pudding is in the eating: if Maribel had been a better mother she'd have produced a better son.

Elizabeth loves to hear Clemmie's take on things, but she can't help wondering how different Ellios's would be. She looks for a lamp to light but he's already deeply at home in the library, pulling books from the shelves at random, checking for dates and quality, delighted with the prints. "Interesting grisailles," says Ellios, reaching for his glasses in the brownish semidark, and Elizabeth is as childishly pleased as if the prints were her own, not Maribel's or Calpurnia's. "Not really my cup of tea, but the decorators like them, and they always do much better at auction than you ever think they will."

She follows him to the window, relenting, easing off. In the year or year and a half since she's seen him last she's forgotten the pleasure she used to take in agreeing with him—or for that matter anyone—about pictures and objets d'art. "You can't help wishing you'd been here before they cleared the good things out," she says, trying not to think of the missing pieces, things that Maribel must have looked at every day. Not that it matters, because art should be independent of the culture it's embedded in, or of the business that people like Elizabeth and Ellios make their livings from. It comes to her with some surprise as she leads him out of the library and into the living room that she's worried about how well he'll like Maribel's paintings when he sees them, and what kind of price tag he'll be inclined to put on them.

Ellios crosses the hall as if he owns it; his passing interest in the wall art and the furniture, the architectural details, is proprietary. But inside the living room his whole manner changes, and Elizabeth can almost feel his temperature rising as she follows him into the room. Night has already fallen on Maribel's nicked brown coffee table and her dark red sofa but Ellios can see as much as he needs to in the dark; he comes to a stop in front of the coffee table at an unembarrassed distance from Lipscomb's portrait of Maribel in her fake Grecian gown, as Elizabeth makes her mock introduction. (Maribel, may I present Ellios? Ellios, Maribel.) In the sinking light the portrait has come weirdly alive: the shadows that have drained the flesh tones from the skin and swallowed the hair on her head have left the painting's eyes in eerie focus, like those of an animal caught in a car's headlights at dusk. The eyes, as some neurologist at a dinner party once told Elizabeth at an awkward moment between the salad course and the enormous planked fish, are actually bits of living gray matter extruded outward into the face, connecting one viewer's gaze to another's, cortex to cortex and soul to soul.

"What a great face," says Ellios. "So self-forgiving. So alive."

He leans closer and squints narrowly at the signature. "Ah Lipscomb; the great Lipscomb, yes, of course; the poor man's postwar Sargent. Not that anybody's still buying his stuff these days."

Lipscomb again. Elizabeth has mixed emotions: pleasure that Ellios likes Maribel's face, uneasiness at his possible interest. "The portrait stays in the family," she says. "It isn't up for sale."

"Well, of course; and who else would want it anyway?" says Ellios. "Poor Lipscomb. Gone but not forgotten: or is it the other way around? He had a wonderful run for his money, back in the thirties and forties, but portrait painters are out of style. Their natural clientele dies off; the children and grandchildren can't be bothered to sit still that long anymore. And who would commission a thing like this nowadays? Too expensive, and too immodest, if you want to know the truth. Husbands don't love their wives like that anymore, I'm afraid. Lipscomb was the end of an era. Nowadays the whole market is children and dogs."

Time is getting short and the room itself is getting too dark for comfort; Elizabeth leads him away from the portrait, out of the living room and up the stairs. "Well, we've got all the children and dogs you could possibly want right here," she says, pointing to the little drummer-boy in the hall, the bewigged eighteenth-century spaniels and hatted cats. She switches lights on recklessly on her way up, allowing Calpurnia's treasures to speak for themselves. In the studio, winded, sweating, he looks for a place to sit down and settles at the end of the divan with the paintings facing outward in orderly rows, like spectators. "I wasn't sure these would be up your alley," says Elizabeth, "but I thought you ought to have a look." She's conscious of holding her breath like someone making a wish.

Ellios mops his face and shakes his head, then gets up and looks again. A certain gallantry is one of Ellios's charms, she thinks; he would no more hurt the dead painter's feelings now, face-to-face with her orphaned work, than if the artist were actually present and alive.

"Interesting," he says. "I like her colors, that beautiful smoky blue; but maybe not the nudes. You can tell she's a woman from the way she paints the nude body. It's all surface; your eye stops dead at the skin."

Annoyed, Elizabeth turns the nudes to the wall; there are only four of them, faceless, their backs to the painter, hiding in their hair; though really, what does it matter whether Ellios likes them or not? "What about the interiors, though?" she says. But Ellios shrugs, as if paintings without figures don't count. He picks up one of the blue-gray interiors at random and brings it closer to the fading light. It's the largest of Maribel's small bore tabletops: a kind of still life, the spill of its objects unrelated to each other except by domestic accident. There's a jar of pencils, a white carnation with a broken stem, a cup without a saucer, and a silver spoon with a repoussé handle. Ellios looks puzzled; he picks up another and holds it out at arm's length from the first. "Spooky—isn't that the word?" he says. "There's always something missing, isn't there? What is it? What is she always leaving out?"

Elizabeth is suddenly and secretly pleased: he's put his finger on whatever it is in the paintings that she likes best: the empty mirrors, the absent lovers, the ghosts that Maribel felt too deeply about, perhaps, to paint. Ellios gets straight to the heart of things: it's the absences in Maribel's canvases that are her real subject matter—what she leaves out implied only negatively by what she chooses finally to put in. The little revelation strikes Elizabeth with such clarity that she can't quite trust herself to look Ellios in the eye. "Yes," she says, squinting at Maribel's saucerless cup and orphaned spoon. "Spooky is exactly the word. Do you think there might be some kind of market for them somewhere, then?"

He puts the second painting down beside the first. "My dear Elizabeth," he says, "both you know and I know there's a market for everything. Everything!" He's pleased with himself for seeing through her: she's as venal as the rest of them: she might as well have unbuttoned her shirt and bared her chest to him; welcome to the world. "Of course there's a market for them," he says. "The question is: what's the market, and where? Did she ever show locally, for example? If so, how well did she sell? These are the questions I'd ask myself if I were in your place."

"She did show from time to time, yes," says Elizabeth and turns away; for just a bare moment there she'd been so sure he was thinking of buying at least one of Maribel's paintings for himself. "I've got the name of the gallery here somewhere," she says. "Some German name. Friedrichson."

"Ah, Friedrichson," says Ellios. "Of course; the infamous Friedrichson. A sort of vanity operation: if you wanted a vernissage with full newspaper coverage and all the trimmings you paid for it yourself and Friedrichson lent you his assistant by the hour to help with the hanging, then got someone he knew at the *Bulletin* or the *Inquirer* to give it some sort of moronic review. Though I haven't heard of him in ages. God only knows if he's even still in business anymore."

Elizabeth feels herself stiffen but makes a mental note to look up Friedrichson. Because you can't prejudge these things; you have to go out and see for yourself. And masks her disappointment with one of her carefully off-putting smiles: Ellios isn't the only collector in town. Though he may be right: Maribel's gray paintings with their empty doorways and vacant mirrors must have been a hard sell in the era of huge museum abstracts and geometrical color fields, and may still be a hard sell now.

"And these erotic prints you mentioned," says Ellios, in a suddenly, mercifully businesslike voice.

Elizabeth turns Maribel's little gray tabletop back to the wall. Time to get down to business. She leads the way out of the studio and points him back down the stairs, following at a more than respectful distance, turning off lights in reverse order as she goes. Outside the last of a bloodred sunset is centered stagily on the western terrace, and the house goes dark behind it; in the stairwell glass-faced pictures catch each other's reflections blankly and bounce them from wall to wall. She's left the powder-room door open; it's hardly the place to make a grand entrance or set a scene. She can feel the pulse in her neck as she leads him across the hall, and tells herself it's only natural. One way or another, this is bound to be embarrassing all around.

The prints are where she's left them, in a Macy's shopping bag inside the powder-room door. Elizabeth unwraps Hercules and Deianira first, her favorites, and hands them to Ellios to study under the single lamp left burning on the telephone table in the hall.

With his glasses on and his hair slicked back behind his ears, Ellios looks serious and safe. He's a pro, he's beyond embarrassment; the prints are merely inventory to be bought or sold. He tilts the lampshade to bring more light to bear on them and reads off their titles in a pleased, approving voice. "Not bad, not bad at all, although these ridiculous ribbons may be a problem," he says. "Carracci, I'd say, but don't hold me to it. Dutch copies, possibly English; nineteenth-century, of course. Which shouldn't be held against them, by the way; but I'd have to take a closer look at them in broad daylight, at home, before I can be absolutely sure."

Elizabeth moves forward, to put herself between him and the shopping bag. "But I'm afraid that's not possible," she says. "The sale's only three weeks away. I don't have any kind of authority to let them leave the house."

"My dear Elizabeth, if you want top dollar I'm afraid you have no choice," says Ellios. He looks at her over the top of his small glasses; he's all business, affable, worldly wise. "I'm going to New York next Friday; there are one or two people I think might be interested, and you're more than welcome to come along. I have business at Swann's, and we could stop somewhere for lunch. These fellows don't make house calls, I'm afraid; you have to bring your little finds to them."

He hands the picture he's holding back to her, and Elizabeth eases the naked Vulcan back into its square of plastic bubble wrap and puts it in the bag. She hates having to make major decisions on such short notice, but it's now or never, probably; and, when you get right down to it, how many people would even notice that the prints are gone? As far as she's aware no one uses the powder room with its tricky toilet and tricky latch; both Clemmie and Nina use Maribel's bathroom when nature calls. She takes a deep breath, and then another. The light is fading. Yes or no? But it's probably worth the risk. And there may be a finder's fee in it for her if and when Ellios actually makes the connection or the sale.

Outside the open doorway the setting sun is nothing but a red line at the top of the hilly lawn. Elizabeth rewraps the pictures and ties the bag with string, then hands it to Ellios like a spy delivering secrets to the enemy. He says, "I'll see what I can do from here and get back to you by the first of the week. In the meantime there are one or two things in the library that interest me. But I have some calculations to make, a few phone calls to New York before I could even begin to put a price on your Carraccis. Assuming that's what they are."

Elizabeth pulls the door shut behind her and gives him her hand to shake, then locks the door. They've come in separate cars and that's the way they'll leave. "They're hardly *my* Carraccis, assuming that's what they are," she says.

Ellios fishes for his car keys.

"You must know that I've thought constantly of you," he says. The shift in his tone is like a change in the weather: portentous, heavy, barometrically incommutable.

"That's so kind of you," says Elizabeth.

He stands between two urns, blocking her way to the steps.

"How I wish I were a painter," says Ellios. "How I wish I could paint," he says.

13

F ACE-TO-FACE with him finally, Coby has nothing to
say to Littlefield at all. Having come to say good-bye,
that is, he's tongue-tied and stupid; but surely it's too
late now for true confessions or any other kind of heart-to-
heart? And anyway, his luck has changed, is changing as they
speak: on this last day of what will surely be their next-to-
last session, why dredge up old disasters and plumb old depths
of despair? Instead, he talks about the wall art in Littlefield's
waiting room, a sore subject for them both. Littlefield's taste in
paintings runs to the pastel, the unmenacing, and the highly
designed: dark geometrics in thick impasto like dried cement:
where does he find these things?

But Littlefield's impassive. "What are your associations to
these paintings of mine?" he asks. "Is it the colors that make
you uneasy? Is it their shapes? Their imagery?"

Coby takes a deep breath and counts to ten; they've had this
dialogue before. Coby doesn't know much about painting, but
he does know good from bad, and he talks painting to Littlefield the way stockbrokers quote stock prices to their cardiolo-

gists: it's a way of asserting normalcy, agreeing to agree or disagree on common ground.

Littlefield says, "Clarence, this is your time, your hour. Are you sure you want to spend all of it talking about the meaning of art?"

Coby says, "Yes, I do. What else is there to talk about?" At school he used to sell his classmates rough pencil copies of Petty girls and *September Morn,* first for pocket money, later for pot and acid (those were the days), though he has only Maribel's word for it that he could have been a contender. (Coby sees things like a painter, Maribel said; he has the eye.) Maribel didn't believe in psychoanalysis, he tells Littlefield in the voice he reserves for talking about his mother, a bass monotone barely audible in that room with its myriad electronic buzzes and hushes: the blinking intercom, the voice-activated tape recorder that Coby suspects Littlefield of using without ever having actually caught him in the act. If you were a painter you wouldn't need psychology, Maribel used to say. Maribel's own idea of psychotherapy was to go up to her studio and paint.

"And yet it was your mother, wasn't it, who strongly urged you to get help?" says Littlefield.

Coby can't deny it, though it went against her grain and she must have seen it as a last resort: but not before she had tried everything else at least once, including putting him to work (and that was just for starters!) on a copy of the little Whistler seascape she admired so desperately at the museum. The deal was a painting a week in exchange for half his rent, copies of mostly impressionist local masterpieces, with Maribel calling the shots on what got painted when. It lasted just over three months, which was about par for the course for Maribel's stabs at active motherhood. And in all probability a mother can no more teach her own son to paint than she can teach him how to conduct a love affair or drive a car.

Littlefield says, "I think you might want to ask yourself what this period of collaboration with your mother brings to mind."

Collaboration? Coby draws a blank. It wasn't a collaboration so much as a rescue operation, the blind leading the blind; and besides, what use is a copy, as opposed to the real McCoy? Degas said that you have to learn to copy before you can begin to paint even a radish or a frog, but Maribel herself always painted from memory: hotel rooms she had stayed in maybe all of one night before the war, or people's guest rooms; or the second-class cabin of an ocean liner going God knows where. Once, years after Lipscomb was gone, she saw a drawing of him in someone's book; it was such a poor likeness that she took up her pen and drew him from memory on the back of an envelope down to the last frown line and dented ear, then dredged up a photograph to prove her point; and Coby has never forgotten it. The point being that the eye is not a camera: to paint the simplest object, Maribel said, you have to have memorized it first.

"Who is this person you say she painted from memory?" says Littlefield. "Someone you remember? Someone you ever knew?"

"If we're talking about Lipscomb here, let's not," Coby says, because he makes it a point not to discuss Lipscomb with Littlefield, except in very general terms. Maribel's honor is not defensible, but he defends it anyway. Littlefield believes that Coby's never gotten over his adolescent anger at his mother's affair with Lipscomb, and that his more or less permanent flirtation with various drugs is his half-blinkered way of protecting his own rage and keeping it under wraps: to the point of committing suicide in protest, if need be. Well, if his theory holds any water at all, then Maribel's death should have freed Coby permanently from the world of mind-altering drugs: an instant cure, some kind of posthumous miracle. Which, he supposes, in the absence of any kind of dependable cash flow to keep himself supplied since her death, is something that remains to be seen.

Coby doesn't want to talk about Lipscomb, at least not to Littlefield, but it was Lipscomb who said that you get to know people by painting them in a way that you can never otherwise get to know them in real life. Which is what turned him to portrait painting, he said; and not, as is commonly believed (ha ha) because there was so much money in it. Coby hated Lipscomb and hates him still, but he believes to this day that, having painted her, Lipscomb knew Maribel in some way that Gerald never did and nobody else ever will.

"My mother thought people were their faces," he says. "She thought their faces were the only part of them that really counts."

Littlefield has that look in his eye that means he thinks he's on to something; Coby sees him reach for his notebook with his right hand, then scratch out his little message to himself, and withdraw. He doesn't want to be suckered into talking about Lipscomb, whom he suspects Littlefield of knowing socially or at the very least by hearsay and reputation around town. And Coby despairs of Littlefield's understanding, of his ability to see beyond the obvious, the quick and dirty psychoanalytical *aha!* Coby's no shrink, but even he can see that there's no subtlety to Littlefield. He paints by the numbers, not by the eye or the ear.

In the end, therefore, as if he had no choice, he simply

blurts it out. "I didn't come here to talk about Lipscomb," he says. "I didn't come to talk about Maribel. My money runs out next week. I came to say good-bye."

Coby's not as stupid as they think he is and he's under no illusions about what he means professionally to Littlefield (interesting case, sporadic or late payer, substance abuser, and lazy layabout), but in the here and now the man's reaction takes him completely by surprise. To Coby's astonishment Littlefield looks dumbfounded; he's profoundly and not merely professionally at a loss for words. And his amazement humanizes him; it carries him over the top of his therapeutic cordiality into the realm of the personal, man to man. For the first time in their many months together in this room Coby sees Littlefield for what he is: a poor fuck just like all the rest of them, as vulnerable to astonishment as anyone. Openmouthed and foundering; another equally lost soul.

Coby would like to try to explain this sudden insight of his to Littlefield and make one final effort at merely human connection, but what would be the point? To make his case he'd have to undo months of brittle sparring, misspent hours, and half-assed insights, clinical one-upmanship, sneers, and double entendres. But isn't it too late? Too late for Freudian open-heart surgery, that is, or classic head-shrinking of the old-fashioned kind, and way too late for any kind of negotiable absolution; or even plain and simple common garden-variety understanding, probably, if it comes to that.

Coby takes out his next-to-last cigarette and puts it in his mouth without lighting it, a habit that drives the nonsmoking Littlefield mad. After all these months Littlefield doesn't know Coby any better than he knows Maribel, whom he knows only through Coby's eyes, and will never know any more accurately than that now that her money is no longer coming in. Because

Littlefield has no eye or ear for the small stuff, and without an eye for the small stuff how can you ever hope to see the larger picture at all? And what, when you get right down to it, can you therefore say to someone like Littlefield about the dread that wakes you up in the morning and puts you to bed again at night? How can you talk to a man like this about real pain and real painkillers—your own or anyone else's, including Maribel's?

Coby gets to his feet. Time's up; they've come to the parting of the ways. Is it against the rules and regs to shake the man's hand at this juncture, clap him on the back, profess good wishes for a long and happy life? Littlefield's merely a pro, a paid confessor: your secrets might be safe with him but your soul will always be high and dry. Coby nevertheless extends his hand across the desk, and Littlefield surprises him by shaking it. Though you might be better off converting to Catholicism, Coby thinks, and sticking it to some poor Fishtown parish priest. Give him an earful in the dark of the confessional some drunken Saturday night; then go home and let the poor fuck take it up, however he sees fit, with God.

14

ROBERTO has walked all the way from the station, red-faced and out of breath, but he doesn't care to drive: as a New Yorker, what would be the point? He's given himself the day off, Dotson having broken their appointment for the second time in two weeks, while the board members are all out of town; and just as well. Roberto's not in the mood to talk convincingly about neo-Expressionism to a committee of would-be CEOs and vice presidents of This or That, to make light of their ignorance and pretend to respect their enthusiasm for the bottom line. You think that people with cash in their pockets and an express corporate assignment to spend it in very visible ways will be easy to deal with, but they're not. The more money these men have, the more they have to show you how hard-nosed they mean to be about disbursing it. Roberto takes refuge in his academic status, his unpressed jackets and unfaked absentmindedness; it's not as if he's selling them any-thing from his own collection, is it? Although God knows he's been tempted, now and then, to slip in something of Maribel's among the macho Franz Klines and the high-colored Frankenthalers they love so much. If only to see whether he could get away with it or not.

Elizabeth urges him into the path of the single working fan. Stooped and slow, he wears what's left of his unnaturally black hair in a ruff over the back and sides of his large square head; from a distance he looks like one of those cheap bronze busts of the aging Beethoven, though without the scowl. She's been up to her elbows in soapy dishwater for the last half hour, giving the Limoges a bath before Clemmie gets here to dry it and set it out. Clemmie's eyes are a problem these days; you can't always trust her to see the grime.

"I hope I'm not disturbing you," Roberto says. The card he hands her reads Roberto Vega Leal, Ph.D., and nothing more, and Elizabeth wonders if she ought to have heard of him. Based on this card he's either a nobody or someone whose name should be on the tip of every tongue.

Roberto stands midway between the door and the stairs; Maribel had kindly promised him one of her paintings, he says, and Nina English was good enough to tell him to come by and pick one out. He doesn't mention the fact that he has the key and could easily have let himself in if he'd been so inclined, but it's understood. Elizabeth leads the way; she's got into the habit of coming up here to the studio whenever the chaos downstairs becomes overwhelming or she simply needs a little break. Communing with the old lady's ghost, says Clemmie; and in a way it's true: the paintings have become a kind of company. She's already picked out her favorites; one of these days she'll know them all by heart.

Roberto's step on the carpet behind her is so soft it's all but inaudible, and she has to remind herself to slow down; in broad daylight now it's obvious that he's much older than she thought and probably a lot frailer than he looks. But his eye and his memory must be as sharp as ever; he comes to a full stop on the second-floor landing, at a patch of bare wallpaper almost halfway to the third. "The Alinari prints?" he says. "They're gone?"

Elizabeth feels a twinge of curatorial guilt. "I understand that they went to a member of the family," she says.

In fact they went to Coby, the day before yesterday, with her own implied permission and no questions asked: three pages of drawings from Leonardo's sketchbooks—noses, hands, a face in three-quarter view in sepia ink on a tea-colored page. Nineteenth-century prints of not very good quality and, she was sure, very little intrinsic value, after all. Roberto doesn't ask which member of the family took the prints, and he must know as well as she does how little they're really worth. "I didn't think they added all that much to the value of the collection, really. Did you?" she says.

"Ah, the collection," says Roberto, and traces the outline of one of the missing prints on the wall where it had hung. He folds his *New York Times* in quarters and fans himself with it metronomically. "Yes, maybe not. The admiral was a great art lover, but the kind of art lover who loved everything; he bought whatever came his way. And Maribel's grandmother could never resist a dog or a cat or a pretty flower. Of course they all painted; it was in the blood. The women in that family could hold a paintbrush before they learned to walk or talk."

Elizabeth backtracks to move the standing lamp in a corner of the landing out of Roberto's way as he resumes his climb. "I'm sorry I never knew her," she says.

Roberto looks at her through a curve in the intervening banisters. "Don't be sorry," he says. "None of us did. No one did." Including me, as he supposes he doesn't need to add. But this posthumous faultfinding has got to stop; if he thought once upon a time that by knowing her, by sleeping with her, he would know what made a painter paint, he's long since come to his senses on that score. They climb the rest of the way in silence with Elizabeth in the lead again, but more and more slowly, in deference to Roberto's age. She fumbles briefly with the little padlock on the studio door, giving him time to catch his breath. There's probably even less need to keep Maribel's paintings under lock and key than her grandfather's Alinari prints or oriental rugs, but locking the studio is a gesture of respect she feels she owes to Maribel, marking off this refuge from what she thinks of as the rout and disorder downstairs. Elizabeth stands aside for Roberto at the door. This is his moment; she doesn't want to seem to be intruding on his grief.

Roberto pauses on the threshold for a second, with light from the oval window in the south wall splintering around him on all sides so that he seems almost to disappear in it until, reappearing at the far end of the room in dazzling black and white, he lowers himself to his knees among Maribel's canvases joint by joint like an archaeologist lowering himself into a dig. Elizabeth backs away. Sometime this morning she has to rearrange the living-room rugs and furniture to make space for Clemmie's card tables, while downstairs there's a sinkful of soapy china waiting to be cleaned, and she doesn't want to be caught up here alone with Roberto if he should start to cry.

Down on his hands and knees in front of Maribel's paintings like a man at prayer, Roberto inches his way from one canvas to the next, handling each one as slowly and carefully as if it were made of glass. He's looking for the painting she was working on the week before she died: a still life of the little Cairene table he'd bought for her in Alexandria with its starched white sickroom kerchief and teardrop vase, one of three pill bottles overturned at its base as if someone had reached out for it in the night, overshot their mark, and knocked it permanently out of reach. It's a kind of memorial pastiche, a blending of past and present: the final conversation they'd never quite managed to have. She had fallen in love with that table, the smell of its wood as Egyptian and everlasting as the Nile. Now that it's too late he wishes he'd kept some kind of written record of the transaction, a signed gift card or a bill of sale with his name on it: proof that he'd known how to make her happy while that was still even remotely possible.

Elizabeth can't bear the sight of him down there on his hands and knees; inching snail-like along the studio floor like that, he reminds her of penitents climbing Gethsemane on their knees at Eastertime. Unlike Ellios, who had taken his pick of the paintings at random from those within easy reach, Roberto is leaving no stone unturned; he's like a man looking for a needle in a haystack, dogged, methodical, and grim. And it isn't until he's kneed himself painfully almost three quarters of the way around the room, inspecting each canvas, then turning it carefully back to the wall, that he finds whatever it is he's been looking for midway between the divan in the corner and the easel under the north-facing window, and comes to a stop with one of the paintings in his hands. From the look in his eyes you can tell he's hit pay dirt: any minute now he's going to start to cry. Elizabeth offers to hold it for him as he struggles to his feet.

She sneaks a look. The painting is one of Maribel's typically smoky rooms caught at the defining moment between dusk and night: *l'heure bleue,* the color of the color-drained sky before all the lights come on. At first glance it doesn't look much different to her than any of the others, and it's certainly not one of the ones she's come to know; she has only the vaguest recollection of the paisley pattern on its half-drawn curtains, or its corner of patterned rug and clutch of miniature glass bottles on the tiny tabletop. Though on second thought the table itself rings a kind of bell: a hexagonal top on a plinth of X-shaped wood—something she knows she's seen somewhere before; but couldn't you say that about any of Maribel's empty rooms? The canvas is medium-sized, and there's nothing startling in its perspective or its colors, so typically Maribel, but from the look on his face and the certainty with which he lights on it, Elizabeth can see that to Roberto, at least, it must be one of a kind.

He pulls himself to his feet and steadies himself on Maribel's easel; he'd begun to think he'd never find it, and now here it is, but just in time: the heat up here is terrible (how did she stand it?) and his knees are on the verge of giving out. After all, the painting wasn't marked, it wasn't in the will; if he hadn't seen her working on it he'd never even have known it existed and would have had no reason to believe she'd ever even finished it. Now, thanks to Nina's kindness and Elizabeth, it's his. Like that little Cavafy poem she'd read to him in Alexandria instead of the guidebook he insisted on buying for her that day ("One afternoon at four o'clock we separated, just for a week; and then that week became forever . . ."). The usual story, he supposes, but thank God not theirs; though the threat was always there: something about the way she held herself apart made him wonder, always, whether every day would be the last, whether she might not turn a corner in some godforsaken city on some godforsaken street and simply disappear into thin air someday: until, as the poem says, that day, that week, or the next one, or the one after that, indeed became forever. As it has now.

Roberto braces himself against the gabled wall and holds the painting out ahead of him, wrong side to, so that only the stretcher is showing: not for Elizabeth's eyes. She might recognize the table; he might be called on to explain, and although he likes talking about Maribel to anyone who'll listen, he doesn't exactly care to be seen conversing like this with tears in his eyes. (Roberto's ashamed of himself; since when has he become one of those old men who cry at the drop of a hat?)

"Philosophers make these claims for the uniqueness of the human race," he says, talking fast to mask his disarray. "Only man has speech, for example; or only man is conscious; or only man can count; but to me the only real difference is art. Man is still the only species that can draw and paint." It could easily be a line from the little speech he gives to the corporate committee members who consult him about what paintings to hang in their boardrooms, and he has the social science data to back it up; but Elizabeth doesn't challenge him. When she hands the painting back to him, he takes out his handkerchief and touches it lightly to his forehead, his cheeks, and, last of all, his eyes. "Not that you could ever mention the word 'art' to Maribel," he says. "To Maribel painting was just a skill, something that ran in the family like perfect pitch. Her grandmother taught her how to draw a rose when she was five. It must have come so naturally that she thought she had no choice."

Elizabeth assumes he's crying for joy, not grief, and pretends not to notice the tear working its way down the left side of his face; she feels warm with the generosity of someone conferring happiness at no emotional or financial cost to themselves. "You get the feeling that she's still up here somewhere, don't you?" she says. She remembers Oscar's comment about artists and their immortality, and wonders where Roberto stands on such things. "That she's left so much of herself behind, I mean," she says.

Roberto feels his age—all that crawling around on his hands and knees: he'll have to put ice on them tonight when he gets home. "Yes, much too much," he says, "considering that she sold so little of her work." And doesn't add: but that was Lipscomb's fault. Roberto has never met Lipscomb and just as well: if he had they'd have come to blows. It was Lipscomb who had kept her from showing in a decent gallery, or even a not so decent one: Lipscomb who convinced her early on that she had no future as a painter, that if you couldn't do portraits you couldn't do anything. Roberto kept these ideas to himself. He wasn't a painter, he wasn't a member of the tribe. He had never stretched a canvas, mixed a color, or held a brush: so what was his judgment on any of these subjects worth? Case closed.

Roberto tests the painting of the table with his forefinger, superstitiously, to see if the paint is really dry. "She refused to do what she had to do to get her name in the catalogs," he says. "As long as she had enough money to live on, she never cared whether she sold anything or not. As long as she had enough money to buy the next tube of paint. Or so she said."

Elizabeth edges toward the door: she should never have let him stay up here so long; you can see that the heat is beginning to get to him. "You don't happen to know Friedrichson, do you?" she asks.

He falls in behind her, happy not to have to look her in the eyes. "The dealer?" he says. "No, only by reputation. They say that Friedrichson did very well with her, but as long as she showed with him no serious critic would go near her. You're known by the company you keep, in art as in everything else. I would have helped her if I could, but my field is seventeenth- and eighteenth-century French paintings." Though she would no more have let him help her than she would have let anyone else. Because Lipscomb's verdict on her had become final by then. Sentenced to life imprisonment in her own studio, she had stopped painting people and become a painter of empty rooms instead. But he's never spoken ill of Lipscomb and he won't start now; Elizabeth would mistake it, as Maribel had, for jealousy.

"I think Friedrichson was not the problem," Roberto says. "The problem was the buyers, especially the ones who wanted to meet the artist face-to-face. Maribel couldn't take the social side of it: the old ladies with dachsunds, and the rhapsodic newlyweds."

What do they want from me, Maribel used to ask him; they have my paintings; isn't that enough?—and Roberto never pushed the point. Because painting, like any other art, is a kind of public nudity, and Roberto understood that you pay a steep price for undressing your soul in public. Maybe that's the difference between the artists and the simple spectators. The rest of us would never take chances like that.

He follows Elizabeth into the hall, nervous about the possibility that he might start to cry again and that she might catch him in the act. She closes the studio door and locks it behind them, shutting out the smell of turpentine and dust and linseed oil. "This must be so hard for you," she says.

Roberto starts down the stairs, keeping the painting at a safe distance from the side of his sleeve, though he knows how ridiculous this must look: it's not as if she had just stopped working on it yesterday; it's had at least two months to dry. "Well, yes and no," he says. He's glad for this opportunity to tell someone what these last months have been like, a subject otherwise undiscussable at Calpurnia: some Protestant prohibition against any outward acknowledgment of grief. "People think cancer is an awful death, and of course it is," he says, "but at least you can always see it coming. This is not exactly a disease that creeps up on you and takes you by surprise."

It's the same argument he had used with Maribel, though it

seems to him in retrospect that the longer she lived the more firmly she believed she was never going to die. Amazing, when you think of it, what hard work it is to take your own life: what a daunting project to organize, both for the body and the soul. Not the kind of thing Maribel would ever have been good at, obviously: at least not without confederates, people to do the legwork and the follow-through. His heart goes out to Coby. If she'd asked Coby to help and he had turned her down, Roberto has no illusions about whom she would have turned to next.

Roberto remembers the last time he made love to her—at her insistence, not his—sharing the desert between her legs like two nomads trying to scare up an oasis from the Sahara, until the weight of her own body became too much for her to support and she let him off the hook, a command performance of unbearable awkwardness. Their last act as lovers, and his last, he supposes, ever, as a man. "Of course if you want to know what immortality is really all about," he says, "all you have to do is look at cancer cells in a petri dish."

Elizabeth nods; she's never seen cancer cells in a petri dish but she can imagine them—infinity in action, perpetual motion—and she's more than willing to concede that when it comes to immortality a single cancer cell probably has it all over a Picasso or a Goya: art doesn't stand a chance. Roberto shifts the painting from his right arm to his left. "This little painting," he says. "She must have been working on it just days before she died. A miracle, if she was as sick as they say she was, because it must be the last thing she did." He thinks of it as his gift to her, returned to him transformed. They say that only God can make a tree, but Roberto knows better. Don't painters make trees and flowers every day?

Her last painting, Elizabeth thinks: is that why he wants it so much, is that why it means so much to him? She stands two steps above him under the skylight; at this level they're almost eye to eye, and for a moment she wishes that she could run back upstairs, collect Maribel's canvases, and pile his arms high with them: a parting gift she's in no position, obviously, to make. Tomorrow she'll do the right and obvious thing, call Friedrichson and set up an appointment to see what kind of agreement she can come to with him, flatter him, and egg him on; because what other choices does she really have?

Downstairs in the kitchen she scares up some odds and ends of wrapping for Roberto's painting and a plastic supermarket bag to carry it in, then offers to drive him to the station, but he turns her down and Elizabeth doesn't push the point: she can see he needs to be alone. She stands in the open doorway between the two urns with their untrimmed beards of dusty ivy stirring in the invisible breeze and watches him turn the corner into Weavers Way, carrying his plastic bag out ahead of him like something combustible. It's a ten-minute walk to the station and he's all alone, the sole pedestrian, probably, for miles around: a foot soldier from a forgotten war. From the back, lurching downhill at his rocky snail's pace, Roberto looks more elderly and much less surefooted than he does face-to-face, but even so she envies him. Like Tosca he's lived either for art or love, or maybe even both; but unlike Tosca he has Maribel's painting, at least, to show for it.

15

ELLIOS says, "I brought you here because I know you're a connoisseur of all things Italian."

Elizabeth can't think what she's ever said or done to deserve this label. Her fondness for Puccini is not something she talks about in public, the only Gucci bag she owns was once her mother's and she's never even been to Italy, but she nods pleasantly to hide the fact that she already regrets letting him out the door with Maribel's prints, which now stand upended in their big brown shopping bag on the floor at his feet. He moves them out of her way as proprietarily as he waves her into the booth, but the prints still make her nervous, even down there under the table, out of sight and under wraps. The restaurant's soaring ceiling and triple-height windows make it seem much more public than it really is; people walking past on the street could easily look in on her dealings with Ellios if they wanted to, and the tables are close enough for eavesdropping; the waiters are never very far away.

"I have bad news about your prints, I'm afraid," says Ellios.

"A question of quality. So let me be the first to offer my condolences and get that out of the way."

Condolences? She fights the little spike of disappointment rising in her throat and tries not to let it show in her face; but she wasn't born yesterday, and this isn't the first time she's been let down over what might just as easily have been an important find. All the more reason to regret having brought him into this. Though if he's right it's a minor setback, not the end of the world. "These things happen," she says, and tries to mean it. Look, this is business. Life goes on.

Ellios smiles at her across the tabletop. He's pleased with his little bombshell, and maybe a bit surprised at his own power to evoke cracks in that otherwise admirable façade. She's got her old uniform on, the dark blue blazer and the girlish pearls: how do these blue-blooded blondes stay so cool in this slimy tropical heat? Ellios can see she's disappointed; he's become a connoisseur of the stiff upper lip in all its local variations, male and female, professional and amateur, but he raises his glass and clinks on hers. "Let's look on the bright side, though," he says. "Your Carraccis may be worthless on the face of it, but their backsides, so to speak, may be worth their weight in gold."

She refuses to laugh at his obnoxious little joke and looks at the menu while he reaches into the bag at his feet and unwraps one of the prints, shedding newspapers and bubble wrap as he goes. "Allow me," he says, and removes the menu from her hands. "Have a look at this. It's what I found behind your little Carraccis when I took them out of the frames."

The drawing he hands across the table to her is slightly off-center, its left edge bent and pebbled where it's been cut to fit the frame. The luminosity of the background has a tarnished quality, gray on gray, with the figure emerging only reluctantly from its background like an afterthought: you have to look twice even to see it's there. It's the picture of a girl with masses of Medusa-curly hair, lying naked on a baroque divan. The subject holds a small silver-backed mirror in her left hand, and with the mirror she's moodily inspecting the dark and otherwise invisible space between her legs.

Elizabeth cringes; she has a sense that everyone in the enormous dining room is suddenly looking at them, like children at a birthday party roused by the rustle of wrapping paper and the rat-a-tat of party poppers. For a moment the figure in the center of the page fades in and out of focus like an image emerging from a photographic developer's bath, and once she gets a clear fix on it she sees that there's something dangerously familiar about both the objects in the background and the figure in the foreground. The couch, the egg-shaped face with its bull's-eye of a round and deeply dimpled chin, the crazy hair, the dormered wall: but on closer glance the resemblance is unmistakable. The face is Nina's, held like a flower on a stalk above the all too naked body of someone undressed for a life class or a pelvic exam. Elizabeth reaches for her water and drinks it down. She's seen enough. She turns the drawing facedown and slides it back to him across the tabletop as if were his, not hers, to deal with.

Ellios puts the picture back in the shopping bag unwrapped. "Lovely little thing, isn't it?" he says. "Unsigned, of course, which is too bad, but you can't have everything. And who knows, a little detective work might even turn the artist up. I'd be glad to take it on, if you think I could be of help. Though of course it's a very special market; not quite the thing for your average Main Line estate sale, probably."

He lifts his glass to her again before he drinks, admiring what he thinks of as her unnatural composure in the face of obvious provocation; but who's provoking whom? If he were a painter he would paint her as a Sargent or even an early Eakins, one of those summery outdoors girls of the American elect—luminous, pitiless, ageless; unbeatable at croquet or badminton. "Would you like to see the others?" he asks, and watches her carefully to see if she's as surprised as she pretends to be.

Their waiter is already setting out bread, olives, and *cornichons* in little pottery bowls, and she waits till he's called away before she retrieves the menu and takes refuge in it. "Could we possibly do this later?" she says.

She waves the olives away; then the bread; then the wine. The chin is the giveaway, she thinks: Nina, aged fourteen or fifteen; the hair and the face are just corroborating evidence. In Maribel that gaze would be challenging, but on Nina it's merely insolent—an adolescent's defiance of a grown-up dare. Elizabeth orders the plainest salad on the list and closes the menu like a book; unfolding her napkin, it dawns on her that she doesn't just know who the subject is, she knows who the artist is too. Venus with mirror and pearls: the play on Velázquez, not to mention Balthus, is inescapable. Elizabeth feels the slow burn of embarrassment in her throat and on her face. Who could have persuaded the teenage Nina to get up on that couch and spread her legs like that?

Ellios closes his menu as noisily as he does everything else, a man unreservedly comfortable in his little local limelight, admiring her perfect teeth as she eats a carrot stick: all those years of good dentistry and timely vaccinations in every bite. Sitting across a table from Elizabeth is an almost aesthetic pleasure to him; it's not just her beauty, it's that she's so true to type: patrician, well mannered, and well kept, someone with no possible axes to grind in his world—which he thinks of as the real world, and therefore the only one. He knows the gossip about her (the husband who decamped to California with some other and no doubt equally handsome blonde; curatorship of the doubtful Americana and some disputed nineteenth-century documents in a bankrupt Rosemont millionaire's collection), but it only confirms him in his first impression of her. She's struggling for a foothold in a business whose ramifications she doesn't really understand, both over-educated in the generalities and undereducated in the particulars, and, either way, severely undercapitalized. An art lover out of her depth among money lovers and people with sharper elbows than her own. He could be helpful to her there. No, more than helpful: he could save her life.

He could be helpful to her but only if she lets him. Because Ellios is not as thick-skinned as he looks; he loves women; he's supported his ex-wife Dorothy in the style she was accustomed to long after the divorce agreement itself ran out, and would have adored his children if he had had any, and spoiled them as mercilessly as he could afford to if that had ever been in the cards. And he still loves women, notwithstanding the miseries of his last years with Dorothy and an unfortunate tendency to pick his lovers by their faces, then spend the rest of their days together trying to remember what he first saw in them, and work his way back to common ground from there.

Elizabeth keeps her eyes on her plate. Buttering her bread, spearing radicchio, cutting her spinach into smaller and smaller bites, she asks herself whether Ellios can possibly know Nina. Have the two of them ever met? Has he seen her here and there around town? Or, if not, has he picked up on the likeness to Maribel's face in the portrait, jumped to whatever conclusions people like Ellios obviously jump to, and started planning his next move from there? Elizabeth wishes again she'd never brought him into this, let alone shown him the stupid prints: if those drawings fall into the wrong hands it could cost her her job or even, if worse comes to worst, her career. She has no need to see the other drawings he's unearthed; they'll only be more of the same, and from the look on his face she can all too easily imagine what they're like. Ellios presses her to take dessert and reads off the menu in minute detail (tiramisu, zuppa inglese, zabaglione) but Elizabeth shakes her head. Does she look like a woman that easily bought off, someone with a sweet tooth: a woman who lets herself eat dessert?

Outside on the hot pavement he takes her arm above the elbow with that showy old-world gallantry that makes him so popular with local women of a certain age. It's high noon in the parking lot; opening the door and handing her into the car he assumes personal responsibility for the heat, and Elizabeth struggles to keep the blood out of her face as he hands her the remaining drawings, one for each of the xeroxed Carraccis: all the same size, and all by now recognizably Nina. All variations on a single theme.

Her heart sinks. Like the first one they're takeoffs on various well-known nudes. In addition to the Velázquez there's a silvery riff on Boucher's *Mademoiselle O'Murphy,* and a deadpan counterfeit of Manet's *Olympia.* All three show Nina English's signature dimple, and all have her signature head of hair. Elizabeth turns them facedown beside her on the front seat, one by one, and moves as close to the door as she can get, pointing her knees toward Ellios like guns.

"Priceless, aren't they?" he says. "At least once you get the hang of them." And laughs. "Well, I hope so, anyway, literally for both our sakes."

There's a thread of cold air on her forehead as the car's cooling system finally kicks in, and Elizabeth resists the urge to look in the mirror to check her makeup, but she refuses to ask him the obvious questions: how he found the drawings, and what he thinks they're worth. (But wouldn't anyone be red-faced in this ungodly heat?) Now that it's too late it's clear to her that Maribel would have hated Ellios and everything he stands for; and would have hated Elizabeth, in all probability, for letting him in on these family secrets of hers.

Stacked on the seat between them as he drives her back to Calpurnia, the drawings have already begun to take on a life of their own. Elizabeth disowns them; she refuses to give Ellios the satisfaction of taking a second look; and it's only hours later, counting spoons in Calpurnia's silver drawer, setting old table linens out for Clemmie to bleach, that it occurs to her to wonder why she didn't simply reach into the back of the car then and there, while she still had them in her sights, and put them back in their frames and hang them back up where they belong while she still had the chance.

16

ROBIN says: "No, I was *not* sleeping, I was just waking up, but don't give it a second thought."

Elizabeth hears the edge of irritation in her voice, a filial reflex (the sleeper awakened): grudging, barely polite. "I know you're busy," she says, "but I just wanted to check this out with you. The sale is scheduled for the thirtieth, there's this little Biedermeier bureau, four drawers and ebonized mounts, and you're always saying that you need more drawer space. Or I could take a Polaroid and put it in the mail."

At the other end of the line she can hear Robin shift the phone from one ear to the other. There's the creak of bedsprings, something heavy rolling to the floor. "Mom, I'm not going to have a minute to myself this weekend," Robin says. "And anyway, I'm trying to simplify my life. I want to travel light. The last thing in the world I need is a Biedermeier chest of drawers."

Elizabeth makes allowances for Robin's surliness—she was probably just as awful to her own mother in her own day—but she still isn't used to this new version of herself as someone always in the wrong. She relinquished her son Pen to Douglas without a fight at an early age, a conscript to baseball and the stiff upper lip, but by common agreement Robin has always been hers: a kindred spirit, bird of a feather and good friend. "And just where is it you're planning to travel lightly to?" she says.

"God, no place," says Robin. "Wherever. What difference does it make? When the time comes I just want to be able to pick up and go."

There's silence at both ends of the line, and Elizabeth wishes she'd kept her mouth shut; more and more these days their conversations have taken the same path: assertion of dissonance on Robin's side; assertions of harmony on hers. "Mother, this call must be costing you a fortune," Robin says.

It isn't; it's Sunday morning and the rates are low, but agreeing is the only easy way out, and Elizabeth resigns herself to giving up without a fight. "I know," she says. "I'll keep you posted," and hangs up. It doesn't matter; for the moment at least Robin's not traveling anywhere. She's at college, safe and sound; and, thanks to Calpurnia, her next two semesters' worth of tuition, room, and board are safely in the bag.

IT'S SUNDAY, the sun's already high in the eastern sky, and Elizabeth has the day to herself to catch up on paperwork and square personal things away. It's the time she would spend in church if she believed in God, or felt any residual loyalty to her mother's fussy Episcopalianism and obsession with keeping up appearances. But there are, thank God, no appearances in Elizabeth's quiet Sunday to keep up. Instead the day ahead is a windfall of empty hours to get her life in order, draft letters, pay the bills.

Elizabeth makes herself a tall glass of iced coffee, takes off her sandals, turns off the phone. Writing ads is as much of an art as writing love letters: you don't want to promise more than you can actually make good on, but there's a certain leeway for poetic license and hedging your riskiest bets. What if the Peter the Great–era gilt bronze and blue enamel mantel clock turns out on closer inspection to be Russian art nouveau? What if the grimy Mahal in the living room is not quite as antique as it seems? There's no place in this business for curatorial exactitude, but if you say something is eighteenth-century it had better not be a nineteenth-century copy; if you call something French it had better not be Belgian or Dutch. Elizabeth knows her customers: rich widows with time on their hands, collectors posing as dealers, dealers posing as pickers, people who will buy anything if it's cheap enough; and others who will buy anything at any price if the house has a certain atmosphere and a strange or storied past.

Elizabeth uncaps her pen and closes her eyes, trying to see Calpurnia from the outside in: a bargain hunter's treasure trove, ripe with surprises and one-of-a-kinds. The secret of selling anything is to remember yourself as a buyer—that sense of love at first sight, the little death of ownership postponed. *Silhouettes, shadow boxes,* she writes; and: *glazed tile chinoiserie plaque; red and black Bokhara rug; (pair) nineteenth-century fauteuils; (suite) Hepplewhite-style chairs.* The real ones having gone to Sotheby's along with the Pissarro, the Dewings, and the Milton Avery, no doubt. *Empire mirror, Empire console,* she writes. She stars the Empire console and the Hepplewhite chairs for further research; it might be wise to get Oscar's opin-

ion on these before she prints the ad. And leaves the Biedermeier chest out of it altogether for now, until Robin has had
some time for reflection and second thoughts.

Writing an ad is like painting a picture: the magic of the
place has to come through in the list of its furnishings, with
each description carrying the full weight of the object, sight
unseen, but you have to earn your adjectives and ungild the
lilies as you go along: no superlatives, no wishful thinking, and
whatever's listed in the ad had better actually be out there on
the floor. She's given the Alinari prints to Coby, as if they were
hers to confer, and two days ago she'd been ready to hand over
as many of Maribel's paintings to Roberto as he'd have been
willing to carry away. *Nineteenth-century serigraphs,* she writes;
grape leaf chandelier. Things that Maribel must have inherited
from her mother or her grandmother, the good taste (or otherwise) of a bygone day. Or is taste the enemy of art, as Duchamp
is supposed to have said?

Elizabeth considers those smoky hotel rooms of Maribel's,
which seem to her to be beyond taste, either good or bad; but
they make her seize up with pleasure, and isn't that the point?
Elizabeth can't paint, and if she could she'd never be able to
live with the mess and the smell of turpentine, but she knows
the real thing when she sees it, and she sees it in Maribel. She's
going to meet with Friedrichson next week; she'll size him
up, sound him out on the possibility of a retrospective, and,
if he turns her down, just keep on going till she finds someone else who will. Someone who sees things her way; someone
who responds as she does to Maribel's gray twilights, her half-
masted windows and unmade beds. Someone like David, she
thinks, or for that matter like Ellios: a true believer in the past-
ness of the past and the power of art to change your life for

good. *Inlaid Moroccan table,* she writes; *converted nineteenth-century gasolier. And other items too numerous to describe.*

SO MUCH for the ad; it's a decent start; tomorrow she'll go over it again for the errors and omissions, but for now it will have to do. She needs the rest of the morning for her letter to David, already two weeks overdue: a measure of the toll Calpurnia's already taken on her private life. She pulls the heavy white curtains shut and chooses a record for the stereo: Spanish guitar, to set the mood. *Dear David,* she writes, and draws a paralyzing blank.

Over the years she's addressed him much more passionately and much more wantonly than this, but it can't be helped, because even at this great distance in time and space is there any love in the world that can stand up to the passage of the years at anything like the same heat and pitch and depth as when it was new? She understands that lovers can't afford to be boring, or to be any less desirable on paper than in the flesh, but it's a challenge; she's known him since she was nineteen. She was already engaged to Douglas when they met, but they stood next to each other in chorus and when he sang she could feel the vibrations in her bones. Till she met David she has never known a boy who read poetry and went to museums of his own free will, or who would rather listen to music than a game of baseball on the radio.

He took her to New York for a performance of *La Bohème* in March of her junior year, and more than twenty-five years later she still flashes back to his kiss in the leather-curtained darkness at the rear of the homebound train. In April they went to Atlantic City to see the sun go down, and in the standing-room-only bus going home he sat with his arms around her and begged her to take off Douglas's ring and throw it away. It was the only kind of blackmail she wasn't open to: in public places she froze up, speechless with decorum. Everyone was listening, or seemed to be, and she shook her head; she would not and could not make a scene. They became lovers only after her divorce, like people coming into an inheritance they never had any reason to expect.

BECAUSE lovers can't afford to be boring, the letters Elizabeth writes to David now take the form of an old-fashioned romantic serial, complete with unsolved mysteries, eccentric secondary characters, smoking guns. Calpurnia's fair game, a gold mine of unanswered questions and unfinished arguments. (Did Maribel die of blood poisoning, as Nina said she did, or of cancer, as Dr. Giles made such a point of spelling out, or was it suicide, as Mrs. Bright seems to think? And what about Peg's weekly hints of things too dark to tell, and Clemmie's missing binoculars, and lights going on or off; and the ghost or ghosts who shattered the glass in Coby's hand in the living room that day, way back at the beginning, before she'd even signed on for the job?)

Elizabeth adds more milk to her glass and returns to the blank page. She'll tell him what little she knows about Maribel's lives and loves and invent the rest—describe those watery nudes and tone-on-tone interiors in their half-lit and permanent afternoons, and the doctored Carracci goddesses with their hovering putti, trying to keep things short and sweet, suggestive but underplayed. Elizabeth thinks of her love affair with David as a work of art, carefully edited, plotted, and compressed to fit the number of hours available to them. And wonders, not for the first time, what David does with the letters she writes him once she sends them off. Eight years' worth of them by now: if she were to look at them on her deathbed would they read like the story of her life? Once, years earlier, she'd rebelled against the limits his marriage imposed on their relationship and tried to break it off; in the resulting silence she had half expected him to send back her letters tied up with red ribbon, an Edwardian convention as sturdy as common law. But he never did, and she still has only his half of the correspondence to show for all their years together till now.

Elizabeth caps her pen and reaches for a fresh sheet of paper. David is the story of her life, the narrative thread that connects her present to her past, her youth to what's shaping up to be, from all indications, an uninflected and unmoneyed middle age; after she dies Robin will read his letters to her and understand once and for all why Elizabeth never even thought of remarrying after the divorce. True love is like lightning: it only strikes once, and once it does nothing is ever quite the same. *David darling,* she writes, and it's the recklessness of the word *darling* that unlocks the dam. The words come fast and furious; she might as well be writing pure fiction, ghost stories, travelers' tales.

Elizabeth covers the paper in her neat and ropy backhand; a page for Maribel; a paragraph for Coby and three for the Carraccis; a quick line or two for Nina and even less for Hugh and Giles. Peg's easy; and she sees no need to mention Ellios at all. Ellios isn't a member of the cast of characters; he's offstage, not even a walk-on part; and what place could her upcoming trip to New York with him possibly have in the overall story of Calpurnia's decline and fall? Describing Hyacinth's hand on Apollo's leaping member she tries for the tone of a certain kind of shameless Victorian pornography, all innocent adverbs and sneaky double entendres. There's no need for David to know how easily this language comes to her, or how acutely she misses him in the flesh as she comes to the end of the page.

17

FRIEDRICHSON, a small gray-faced man with aquatic eyes and a fishy mouth, escorts Elizabeth fussily through the gallery, down several halls, around corners, under an arch. He has a hand-wringing habit that he tries to mask by stuffing his fists in his pockets or clasping them behind his back; it gives him a desperate air like someone in permanent crisis but much too polite to mention it. Following in his wake Elizabeth is always on the verge of bumping up against him or losing him at some critical turning point. It's like driving behind someone who speeds up and slows down at random on a narrow road.

"It was so nice of you to see me on such short notice," she says. She's gone over various scripts for this conversation in her mind on her way into town and she's still not sure what she really wants to say to him or where either of their real interests will turn out to lie. As she follows Friedrichson into his bare skylit office at the garden end of the gallery, Elizabeth reminds herself not to set her hopes too high; not to set her heart on a retrospective, for example—the best of all possible worlds.

Although, everything else being equal, it's the only way she can think of of getting the paintings out of the house all at once, with or without a decent commission if and when they finally sell. Not to mention the goodwill it would presumably earn her with the family, and Roberto, who must know better than anyone else how valuable the paintings really are. And, last but not least, for that matter, a way of honoring Maribel's name.

"Not at all, not at all," says Friedrichson. "If you hadn't called when you did, you would have missed me. I'm going to London on Saturday, worse luck. Maribel Archibald Davies is (was?) a very great favorite of mine, I can't tell you how sorry we all were to hear that she was ill." He points to the chair beside his large black desk; it's leather, Adams, in a burgundy so dark it's almost brown, and from the smell of it quite new. "Let alone dead," he says. "My God."

"I'm sorry to say I never actually knew her," says Elizabeth. "Although I feel as if I did: you get such a sense of people from the things they leave behind."

Elizabeth wonders what sense she would have of Friedrichson if all she knew of him were the paintings in this gallery of his and the furniture in his office, where everything is a reproduction of the very best quality, minutely and brilliantly maintained. The pictures that line the gallery walls behind them are all figurative—updated versions of seventeenth- and eighteenth-century genre paintings, competent still lifes on blackish backgrounds, fantastic landscapes, smiling and confidential nudes. The paintings seem unconnected to one another except in scale; they're all the same size, roughly three feet by four, a good shape for hanging over the living-room couch, except for the page-sized ones, which seem to come in pairs.

"Especially their paintings, don't you think?" says Friedrich-

son. "But then I'm a special case; I couldn't live without paintings on the walls; if my friends would let me I'd hang them all
the way to the rafters and down to the chair rails too. Are you
an art lover, Miss Oliver?"

Elizabeth hates this question; it always seems far too personal for the circumstances. "Well, yes and no," she says. "I'm
afraid at the moment all my walls are bare."

"Ah, a minimalist," says Friedrichson. "We'll have to do
something about that, won't we?" He gestures toward the front
of the house, but there's a calculated twinkle in his eye; he's
fishing, wondering why she's come but careful not to ask. Elizabeth wouldn't be caught dead with any of his fake Dutch genre
studies and nineteenth-century storms at sea, and wonders
what Maribel's pictures would look like hanging on Friedrichson's overfriendly walls.

"I understand you've handled Maribel's paintings in the
past," she says.

Friedrichson looks at her knowingly. "Oh yes, yes indeed,"
he says. He hooks his small gray hands into the opened desk
drawer. "We had that great pleasure in 1969."

"Such a long time ago!"

"I suppose this dates me terribly, but I don't think of it as all
that long ago at all," says Friedrichson, laughing. "*Ars longa*,
you know. Though as far as I know she never showed anywhere
else. Maribel was, how shall I say this? well, of course Maribel
had her own money, she was never hard up for cash, and unlike
most painters she had an absolute horror of fame. Well, fame in
the wrong quarters, let's say. Because I could have done very
well with Maribel, just between the two of us, if she'd given me
a free hand, very well indeed. But I'm afraid we had to agree to
disagree about it, in the end. Because, just between the two of

us, who she sold to was much more important to Maribel than what or how much she sold." He leans back in his impressive chair, clubby, confiding, and episcopal. "You know, the world is full of snobs," he says, "and I'm sorry to say I'm probably one of them in my own small way; but aren't we all? Though Maribel's snobbery was quite unique. If she didn't like you, she simply wouldn't sell a painting to you, and that was that."

"And what were her reasons for liking a buyer or not?" asks Elizabeth.

"My dear young lady, if I knew that I'd have been a very much richer man than I am now," says Friedrichson. "Those interiors of hers would have sold like hotcakes if she'd given me the green light with them. I don't mind telling you, there was a gold mine there; she'd have died a millionaire. We both would have died millionaires, to be exact, ha ha."

Elizabeth tries not to look surprised. There's something contagious about the simplicity of Friedrichson's greed, and it's tempting to think of Maribel as a successful painter, feted at fashionable openings, reviewed in the *New York Times.* "There's been talk of setting up the house as a kind of museum," she says. "A showcase for the family collections and, obviously, for Maribel Davies' work. I thought it might be a good idea to speak to you first, see if you wanted to have a look at her most recent paintings, before the committee comes around to take their pick."

Friedrichson shuts his desk drawer and lays his hands squarely on the table, side by side, as if inviting Elizabeth to inspect his fingernails, his shirt cuffs, and his wrists. "On what basis, exactly, would I be looking, if you don't mind my asking?" he says. "As a buyer? As a seller, for that matter, ha ha? As an old friend?"

The edge in his voice is cautionary, and Elizabeth reminds herself that men like Friedrichson don't get where they are by vulgarity and doggedness alone. She reminds herself to look at his hands, not at his eyes. "Well of course that would be up to you," she says. "Though of course I can't help thinking in terms of a retrospective of some sort. Now that Calpurnia's in the news again, for example, because of the museum."

It's true; the museum controversy is free advertising whichever way you look at it and however the zoning decision goes; but if Friedrichson doesn't bite Elizabeth will have her work cut out for her: unless she caves in and sells every last one of them for a song, knocked down to the highest bidder at the end of the sale. Or buys them herself, and hangs them on her own four walls.

"A museum—really?" Friedrichson swivels toward the light and makes a little steeple of his restless hands. Interest, self-interest, enthusiasm, and cunning come and go in his half-hooded eyes. He stares past her at the tiny stone garden outside his office window with its miniature Japanese footbridge and grainy gravel paths, and Elizabeth holds her breath. Friedrichson must know this business backward and forward; he's been in it for over thirty years, and in a way his opinion of Maribel's work is therefore worth more than Roberto's: if he says her paintings are salable, they are.

Outside there's the wail of an ambulance dopplering past a curve; somewhere behind them in another room the phone rings twice, musically, then stops. Friedrichson pulls a big leather appointment book toward him from one corner of the desk. He sighs and flips two pages ahead, then several pages back; it's ridiculously short notice but he thinks he's found an hour for her, give or take a few minutes either way, he says, and

Elizabeth feels a surge of dangerous self-congratulation as he reaches for his pen. They're in this together: buyer and seller, bride and groom, neither of them willing to admit how indispensable the other has suddenly become. He'll come and have a look on Thursday at four o'clock if that's all right with Elizabeth, he finally says.

Shaking her right hand he covers it with his left, and Elizabeth tries not to look as happy as she feels. "Terrible timing, I'm afraid," says Friedrichson, "but that goes with the territory, doesn't it? And when is the timing ever good, ha ha? Still, speaking as one art lover to another, it's a wonderful profession, isn't it? Full of adventures and surprises, even when you can't always quite make ends meet, ha ha."

He follows her to the door, but this time she walks two steps ahead of him, guided at critical intersections by his hand on her arm as if she's a member of his inner circle, expected to know the way. They pass a quartet of red-and-yellow clowns; two seascapes; a pair of flower studies in elaborate gesso frames. The immaculate carpet is new, and the red walls are probably supposed to remind you of the Louvre. Handing her a business card from an outsize and unnaturally shiny silver bowl near the door, Friedrichson turns to her for one last handshake and says, "Tell me. Is it true what they say?"

"About making ends meet?" asks Elizabeth, confused.

"About Maribel Davies' death," he says, looking over his shoulder, lowering his voice. "Did she really die of cancer, or did she commit suicide, the way the grapevine says she did?"

Elizabeth takes his card and drops it into her purse. He's the third person who's asked her this, if you don't count Clemmie and Oscar, and it must be a measure of how far she's come as Maribel's curator that the question has become so irritating. For a moment, standing by the door, she sees Friedrichson through Maribel's eyes: a hand-wringing philistine masquerading as a patron of the arts, a predator pretending to be prey. If she had the guts she'd cut him loose, find some reason to undo their appointment, and go out in search of some other and better gallery for Maribel's work.

"No, not that I know of," she says.

18

COBY'S awake, but barely. He hardly ever manages to catch the start of the day at Wimbledon, but England's six hours ahead (or is it five?), and since Maribel's death either the days have gotten longer or the nights have gotten shorter; as a result he's never too clear anymore where night leaves off and day begins.

Coby watches tennis the way Peg watches the soaps and figure-skater champions of the world. It's a fix on an orderly universe, the beauty of opposing extremes. Peterson's the designated underdog today, and Coby always roots for the underdog, no matter what his skin color happens to be. He draws the line at women, but otherwise he's a democrat through and through, and he'll even watch women, if the truth be known, when there's nothing else up there on the screen.

Up on the screen the clock reads 3:50 with Peterson leading 7–5. Coby braces for the first serve of the next set's starting volley. He's hungry; to the best of his recollection he hasn't eaten since yesterday at noon. There are six dollars and eighty cents in his pants pockets and Nick lets him eat at least one meal a day on the tab, but Nick is Coby's lifeline, his last resort, the only person still left in the world who will extend him any kind of credit at all, and he tries to keep that in mind. Especially now, because Nina is executing the estate as if it's the goddamn United States Treasury, and Hugh has let him know in a not so roundabout way that the will may not be probated for months. His only hope of keeping body and soul together in the short term, as he sees it, is Peg. Peg, and, if he's lucky, Elizabeth.

Elizabeth has taken a liking to him, fortunately; she let him have the Alinari prints without a backward glance and if he plays his cards very carefully he thinks he can get her to cut him a break on a few other small items here and there as well, things that no one will ever miss. In truth Coby only wanted the prints because he likes them, and because the face in one of them reminds him of his father. It wasn't until the day before yesterday, strapped for pocket change at the state store buying cheap wine, that he actually had the bright idea of trying to turn them over somehow, somewhere, for hard cash.

Coby's given up any idea of finding his father's stamp collection, appraised at six thousand dollars twenty years ago, or the Civil War coins he buried in the rose arbor when it was still standing, and those aren't the only things that have never come to light. What about her jewelry? That big yellow stone she always wore around her neck, and her grandmother's diamond earrings; what about those famous pearls?

Pete Peterson is twenty-three, short-legged but ready to go to the farthest corners of the court to make up for it at the drop of a ball; if he wins today he'll be a modest millionaire. As Coby could have been, possibly, if he'd stayed the course. Peterson has curiously long and inflated forearms, like Popeye's: they're all muscle and bone, maybe nature's way of compensating for the shortness of his legs; and because he isn't really built for the game, and knows it, the guy is all over the court. He's hard-working, a true overachiever; it's a pleasure to watch him churning the court for his points.

Tennis as art form: this is an argument Coby often tried to make to Maribel, but she wasn't a game-player and he could never get her to see it from his point of view. When he was a kid it was all you could do to get her to sit still for a game of checkers or a hand of Go Fish. She wanted him to be a painter, not a Philadelphia lawyer or a clubman like his father, and it didn't help that Coby had a natural talent for drawing. Although in the final analysis all he ever drew were nudes, half-dressed Petty girls, tennis players, and racquets that Maribel could not possibly afford to buy for him; and wouldn't have, probably, even if she could.

Coby loved his mother, he loves her still; he dreams that she's still alive, that she walks all the way from Calpurnia in her sun hat in the broiling heat to bring him fresh-baked bread—although to his knowledge Maribel never baked a loaf of bread in her life for him or anyone, and the sun hat has not been seen in years. Coby loves Maribel in the dogged and unapologetic way that a vine loves the sun but he never had any time for her friends, the arty types who hung out at her studio, talking about who's making out with whom and the drying times of paints. Tennis was Coby's way out, his path through the jungle toward a wider world, swinging his racquet ahead of him like a machete through the bush. It's true his father wasn't much of a tennis player, but so what? Maribel used to complain that Coby's tennis lessons were the only thing that Gerald ever willingly paid for after the divorce, and even now, after all the water that's flowed over and under that bridge, it's money from his father's will that still pays Coby's dues at the Cricket Club: a special bequest, completely separate from the trust. Not that it matters much at this late date, because the Cricket Club is still harassing him for back bar bills, and he doesn't have what it takes physically anymore anyway. He'd need hours of mixed doubles to get himself up to speed, and a whole new lifestyle to boot. Unless he suddenly gets lucky at cards or falls in love with a rich woman, Coby will probably never play serious tennis again. Or any other kind either, if it comes to that.

Lying in bed, waiting for the right moment to get up and shave—a commercial break, a surge of forgotten energy from what's left of the caffeine in his system or some other unknown bolt from the blue—Coby considers the odds on his lasting out the disbursement of Maribel's will. Because as you get older (is this some law of nature?) it gets harder and harder to put one foot in front of the other and hoist yourself out of bed. Depression, Littlefield says, but refuses to give him a prescription for anything, and Coby's not blaming him; in his shoes he wouldn't write himself a prescription either. Besides, isn't money the best energizer there is? Good old lucre, filthy or otherwise, much better than any pill. Coby was thirty-seven years old on Friday, and except for a fifty-dollar check from his great-aunt Ibby, a *GQ* subscription from Peg, and a tie from Nina (little yellow tennis racquets on a dark blue ground), the occasion went unremarked. On bad nights (Coby can't help it, these thoughts keep popping up) he seriously wonders whether he'll ever see thirty-eight.

Up on the screen Peterson's beginning to flag; he's sacrificing strategy and stamina to speed, and Coby's heart goes out to him. The guy is fresh from two back-to-back doubles matches, and although he made it to the semifinals in both against all imaginable odds, the effort has clearly taken its toll; you can see it in the way he moves, and the curtain of sweat on his forehead in that otherwise impassive face tells it all.

Because talent isn't everything, let's face it—not by a long shot, it's not. You've got to have the right character for the game, not to mention the energy and the knees. And last but not least the eye for it: above all the eye. Because in tennis as in art, as he used to try to tell Maribel, the eye is half the battle; or maybe even more. To which Maribel replied: It's not as if you'd need a strong backhand or steady knees to paint. And Little-field agreed. This isn't two women you're being asked to choose between, he said. We're living in the twentieth century, in the land of opportunity. It's not as if anyone's asking you to make a choice between tennis and art.

Well, Coby concedes the point. He's a graduate of a decent prep school and an Ivy League college (though both, to be fair, by the skin of his teeth), and he knows lots of people, some of them rich: if you get right down to it his career options are probably as good as anyone's. It's true that things never worked out for him in the incentive and fulfillment business that Conrad tried to hook him up with or the brokerage house where Ibby once pulled strings for him; but those aren't the only games in town. Maybe he should become an antiques dealer, or an estate liquidator, like Elizabeth. Elizabeth can quote the price and provenance of everything, and you can see she knows her way around. Over the last two weeks he's let himself get into the habit of hanging out at Calpurnia with Elizabeth and her sidekick, Clemmie, a trip down memory lane, now that it's too late: but isn't that the story of his life? Clemmie's a tough nut to crack but Elizabeth turns to mush when he puts on the charm; if he handles her right there's no reason why she couldn't take him in hand someday, educate him, show him the fucking ropes.

And Coby could show her a thing or two too, if you get right down to it. His contacts in the old money crowd around here could keep someone in her line of work in clover for years. Not to mention that when it comes to Calpurnia he has to be the world's leading expert on where the bodies are buried, what goes where, and who owes what to whom. There's sunken treasure in the rose arbor, if he can resurrect it, and what about those dirty pictures of Maribel's in the powder room? She'd made one of her artist friends ink in big black cartoon-style ribbons over their private parts, then hung them down there as a joke for all to see. Though the powder-room toilet's been iffy for at least ten years—a long time ago Maribel made him jam the door shut with shims in the strikeplate, and as far as he knows no else has ever been in there since.

Coby hasn't thought of those pictures in a hundred years. They were a big embarrassment to him in days gone by, so that whatever thrills and chills they may have raised were instantly canceled out by the shame. What other kids' mothers would have even stood still for something like that inside the house? Coby's such a little Puritan, Maribel said, his father's son, putting her arm around his shoulders in front of all her friends: that fat-lipped Frenchman of hers, the one before Roberto, and the commemorative medal heiress, and the bug-eyed mushroom millionaire. It was the cocktail hour; the lot of them were always drunk by five o'clock. You've got to toughen up, she said. Life isn't a game of tennis. Not by a long shot, no pun intended, honestly; ha ha ha.

Well, maybe life isn't a game of tennis, maybe she was right, and yet with all that and to his own seemingly permanent confusion he misses her—misses her the way you miss drugs or drink when life forces you onto the wagon against your will. Which seems strange, after all these years, and especially the last six months when, quite honestly (and he won't admit this, not even to Littlefield), she was often a burden to him, a great albatross around his neck. Knowing she was dying, that is, and wanting everything squared away before she died, including Coby and his sad, unsettled life. Though as Littlefield sometimes said, at least you can't say you didn't communicate, and just think how rare that is between mothers and sons, don't sell yourself short. (And things must be really bad, Coby thinks, when your own shrink has to tell you not to sell yourself short.)

Coby remembers the line from Auden she said she wanted on her gravestone: *And so, for all eternity, I forgive you, you forgive me.* Or something to that effect, though he sat up all night for two weeks after she died trying to locate it in the *Selected Poems,* and came up dry; as if it even mattered, now that Maribel is dead. As if Maribel of all people ever forgave anyone for anything in the long run, anyway.

Coby turns off the TV. The set is going into its final game; he can tell from the way Peterson returns Rowley's serves that he knows he's never going to score. Why lie here and watch it happen, look at it unfolding in all its ugly inevitability up there on the jittering screen? Not every unhappy ending has to be experienced face-to-face. You can't turn off life but you can always turn off the television screen, and Coby's still feeling some residual luckiness left over from the other day in front of Littlefield's office, some promise of better things to come: why squander this last gasp of anticipated happiness on the sight of yet another pointless televised defeat? The night's no longer young but it's still dark enough for breaking and entering, and since Maribel's death Coby's become an expert at both.

COBY MAY not be a kid anymore, he's not as light on his feet as he used to be and he can't play tennis the way he used to; but as a kid he used to break into Calpurnia half-stoned, and doing it cold sober is child's play, especially now that there's no one living there anymore; and some things still come perfectly naturally to him anyway.

Maribel never threw anything away; there's still that old wooden sawhorse in the toolshed, too heavy for one man to move alone and therefore considered immovable; but Coby doesn't have to move it far, so that standing on it he can easily hoist himself onto the kitchen roof, and from there it's nothing to climb into the guest-room window. He remembers every toehold from nights of predawn debauchery with his Davies cousins and kids home on vacation from Lower Merion, one of them the favorite younger brother of the guy who collected door receipts at the Electric Factory and let them in on slow nights for half price. It's a climb Coby could have made in his sleep, and he'd purposely left the guest-room screen an inch up from the bottom on the inside the last time he was in the house. The alarm's unarmed; it's a safe bet that in all the confusion no one has ever got around to fixing it yet.

In the guest room Coby lowers himself onto the draped table under the window. This time he doesn't intend to make the mistake of turning on the lights. But the guest room faces away from Peg's bedroom, and Coby's got a soft spot in his heart for Peg. Many's the time in days gone by that she's taken him in, fed him, given him somewhere to sleep off a drunk (or worse): not to mention the big black Citroen she signed over to him his senior year, her dead son Mikey's first car, until Maribel made him give it back. But, let's face it, that's all water under the bridge; and Peg's a light sleeper, she has eyes in the back of her head. All he needs to do is rig up something black at the window; he's got his own flashlight, the batteries are almost new, and anyway he intends to use it sparingly.

Coby walks flat-footed into the hall and down the stairs,

testing the darkness for displaced boxes and furniture. He tries not to think about his aborted look around two weeks before because it makes him see red when he does: how could they go and change the locks on him, then hand out new keys to Elizabeth and all her helpers and hangers-on? Just another one of Nina's little ways of showing you who's the boss. Or possibly Hugh's, but never mind: Coby knows at least three ways into this house that the rest of them don't and that don't require a key. It's the house he was born in, isn't it? Coby knows Calpurnia the way a rat knows its maze or a conch knows its shell, and he'll come and go as long as he has to, keys or no keys, until he finds whatever he's looking for.

Downstairs the circle of moonlight on the bare hall floor looks stagey and engineered. There are two rugs rolled up on opposite sides of the hall, a standing lamp without its shade, framed pictures stacked six deep beside the stairs. Even though he's alone in the house Coby crosses the floor on tiptoe, careful to avoid the warped floorboards at the end of the hall, but the powder-room door opens more easily than he has any right to expect, and down here under the stairs he's at the opposite side of the house from Peg's property: if he turned on the light he doubts there's anyone on Weavers Way who would either notice or care.

It's years since he's been in here, but the smell of dried lavender and chamomile from the basket under the sink is as instantly familiar to him as the smell of his own sweat. He plays his flashlight over the striped wallpaper on the stairwell, green to match the tiles, up and down and side to side; it takes him only a second or two to remind himself what he's here for and not much longer to realize that the wall he's looking at is bare. Someone's been here before him. The famous prints with their famous gods and goddesses are gone. There's nothing hanging, no pictures, no mirrors, no anything on either side of the stairs.

Coby sits down on the old pot-bellied commode; the stored heat from the week's heavy weather has sucked up most of the oxygen in the little room, leaving him without much air to breathe. He's sweating and his hands are shaking; if he didn't know better he'd say he needed a drink. It's Elizabeth's doing, it has to be. This is her handiwork; she's been at it in here, doing her job, dotting her goddamn i's and crossing her goddamn t's. She'd given him those Leonardo prints just to get rid of them, probably, and get them off her hands; God only knows who she's given the randy gods and goddesses to. She's handing out his mother's things like penny candy, first come first served. They could be fuck-all anywhere by now.

They could be anywhere, and if so it's the end of the road: those prints were his last hurrah. His mother had called him a Puritan and (scornfully) his father's child, and maybe it's true, but there's always a market for erotica, and Coby knows people who know the people who buy that kind of thing. At the very least the prints would have paid the arrears on his electric bill and wiped out his debts at the club. Not to mention his tab at Nick's; or, if worse comes to worst and his unpaid landlord takes it into his head to start eviction proceedings against him, some small token advance on next month's rent.

Coby's anger is slow to rise, and when it does it takes him by surprise. He doesn't ask for much from life, he never has, but those prints were his birthright, and where's his good luck now that he really needs it, now that his bottom dollar is really running out? Where is it written that everything he sets his heart on immediately turns to ashes, rage, and catastrophe before he even lifts a finger to cash in?

Coby gets up, runs the cold water, and throws some on his face, but it's no use; his head's too hot to cool down. With no one to hear him he curses himself out loud and fights his way out of the powder room like someone running from a fire. Because how much longer can he go on this way, sneaking into the house like a cat burglar in the middle of the night for the quick salvage operation, the raid, the instant getaway? He's thirty-seven years old, he could have broken his neck: can this be the way she meant it all to end? *(And so, for all eternity, I forgive you; you forgive me.)* Blind, light-headed, invisible to himself in the dark hallway, Coby bumps into a shadeless lamp and swings at it like something alive; then, as if he were drunk or high on speed, goes on swinging at whatever else gets in his way—the wall, the lamp, the dangling crystals of the ceiling gasolier—cutting a path for himself into the living room toward Maribel's face in the middle of Lipscomb's portrait on the wall above the couch.

It's weird; for a minute or two he doesn't even feel the pain. The powder-room gods and goddesses are gone but Maribel's still here, and she will have to do: face-to-face with that sardonic goddess in her halo of barbed-wire hair, he pulls the sofa out as far as he can and slams it into the coffee table, and it's at that very moment that the blood decides to start to flow. And when it does it's everywhere—on his hands, on the floor, all over the back of the sofa, red on red: and even on the frame of the portrait as he lifts it off the wall.

The painting is much heavier than it looks, but it's too late to turn back, and the sound of glass from the ruined gasolier smashing overhead and underfoot doesn't even begin to match the sound of the thoughts inside his head. It's just lucky for Maribel she's dead, and lucky for the rest of them that he's alone in the house and they're all safe at home in their own beds. Because Coby doesn't trust himself. Reaching for the farthest limits of his own unaccustomed rage, all he knows for sure is that he's beyond reason, seeing red, redder, reddest, and feeling no pain at all. He hoists the enormous picture onto his shoulders like Christ shouldering the cross; he's had nothing to eat since Tuesday and there's blood on his hands but the picture weighs nothing, nothing at all, and the cuts on his hands are so painless he might as well be dead. He shifts the portrait and resettles it, making a shelf for it midway between his shoulders and his neck. He'll walk out of the house by the front door carrying the one thing in the house that everyone agrees is his, whatever it's worth, whatever it weighs, and he doesn't care who sees him; let them call the cops, let them put him in jail or take him to court. The portrait is his, and he's walking out of the house he was born in with blood on his hands and his head held high and his mother's face on his back, his own inalienable albatross, for all the world to see.

19

PEG LEADS Coby into the kitchen, quick, trying not to think about her new dining-room carpet, the blood on his hands, bloodstains on the rug in the hall; she has to wrestle the painting out of his hands and lean it against the wall. Is he drunk? She can't smell liquor on his breath but drugs are something else; the stuff you see at night on the television, that's another world. Peg's getting old and it's a long time since Coby last actually set foot in her house: how is she supposed to know what a drug maniac looks like, or smells like, or even acts like, if it comes to that?

In the kitchen she sits him down at the zinc-topped table and wraps his hands in clean dish towels, blue and white. She keeps a can of Band-Aids down here somewhere but you can see at a glance you're dealing with way too much blood for that: what's needed are surgical bandages, the real thing—big wads of gauze and adhesive tape and other things she hasn't had on hand, probably, since Mikey was a child, if then. Peg puts on water to boil, then peels back the cuffs of Coby's jacket and inspects the damage to his hands.

"What happened to you, for God's sake?" she says. "Did you get in a fight with ten angry cats?"

It's the note of panic under the motherliness that does him in. Coby fights tears; his hands come alive with pain. In Peg's kitchen, safe and sound, the rage drains out of him as the pain flows in.

"The gasolier in the hall," he says. "They must have lowered it to clean it. I couldn't see where I was going; damn thing just caught me right in my goddamn face."

She doesn't ask him what he was doing there in the hall in the first place after midnight, all alone at Calpurnia, feeling his way, crashing into things in the dark. "I'm driving you to the hospital," she says. "You're bleeding like a pig. There could be glass in those cuts."

Coby doesn't argue; it's her house and they're her dish towels he's soaking with his blood: let her call the shots. Because Coby understands something that Maribel never did: that you need people like Peg around to keep things going, water boiling, traffic moving, time passing, life going on. And Peg's not, thank God, someone who goes faint at the sight of blood. Coby tops off his tea with milk and gulps it down. In this house with its ancient bathtubs and four-legged stove, the washer and dryer are always the latest models, the best that money can buy. In Peg's laundry room there's always at least a month's supply of detergent and two different kinds of bleach, and nobody is ever going to starve or go thirsty or wear a bloodstained shirt.

Peg waits till he's finished his tea to rinse out the first round of dish towels, then folds fresh ones around his palms and anchors them with twine. A messy job and not one for an amateur, but she's an old woman and she's got arthritis in both hands; they'll know what to do with him at Lankenau, if she can get him there before he bleeds to death. Coby's already that ghastly shade of grayish green that people turn before they pass out, the color of death, if you want to know the truth; though it isn't until she offers to make him a piece of toast and jam before they go that it dawns on her he may be dying of hunger as well as loss of blood. "When was the last time you ate?" she says.

She watches him crushing the toast into his mouth, two pieces at a time. Where are the famous Coburn Davies table manners that used to charm everyone so much when he was still a little boy? But Peg knows a starving man when she sees one. It's none of her business how people treat their relatives, she's barely passed the time of day with Nina since she got married and opened that shop of hers, and she hadn't seen Conrad for years until they met again at the funeral, but Peg has no use for people who let their own people starve.

Peg remembers the days when Calpurnia was all orchards and woodland as far as the eye could see: including the row of pear trees on the south side of the house and the Belleflower apples that were Maribel's mother's pride and joy. The octagonal goldfish pond had already been converted to a swimming pool and the chicken run to a rose arbor by the time Peg and Justin moved in, but Peg's beloved cat Salome killed one of the fine-feathered Dorkeys (or was it one and a half?) one summer night and had to be put out to pasture with a favorite aunt in Maryland. "My cat for two chickens!" said Peg, for years, whenever anyone asked her about her famous neighbors; but she's lived to have the last laugh. By the swinging sixties the whole spread was down to the villa with its old stable converted to a three-car garage, and that little mustache of a garden on the south-facing hill. The tennis courts where Bill Clothier once played Bill Tilden are Peg's property now; she bought them from Maribel to tide her over the years between her separation and her divorce, and for the last four years Peg's instructed her yardman to clip the hedge on Maribel's side of the line as well as hers. If she thought she could have gotten away with it she'd have sent him over there to weed the pachysandra too, all in the name of preserving property values, her own as well as Maribel's. Though even Maribel had her pride. Trimming the hedges was one thing, but turning over that car to Coby—Peg must have crossed the line. There were limits to Maribel's ability to look the other way. In some ways she was still her mother's child: she had no use for the largesse of the lower born.

Peg takes the dishes to the sink and leaves them for the girl to wash when she comes in. There's gas in the car and she can air out the guest room later this morning when she gets back. She can't remember the last time she had the windows washed and the walls haven't been painted since the year Mikey died, but that blue never did show the dirt. She sends the girl in to dust three or four times a year and she uses the closet for storing her winter coats, so a good cleaning is probably long overdue. She'll have her wash down the woodwork and baseboards, change the bedspreads and vacuum the rugs, see if the drapes need cleaning.

Peg runs hot water on Coby's dishes, once over lightly, then wraps sandwiches and packs a thermos for the road. It's a long time since she's had to drive a wounded person to a hospital, but she remembers the drill, the paperwork, and the long waits with nothing to eat or drink except whatever you can scare up from those stupid vending machines. It wouldn't be the first time anyway. As a kid Coby was always running away from home and the home he ran away to was always Peg's. It took her a long time to realize that Maribel was not as amused by his takeoffs and landings as she always pretended to be. Surely, even so, she must have known Peg would look out for Coby in the long run; and for all Peg knows, in her heart of hearts she may have even counted on it. Maribel may have kept him on a short rein but one way or another, to her dying day, she always kept him afloat.

Peg waits till he's finished the last of his tea, then packs a shopping bag with clean dish towels, just in case. Mikey's been dead for seventeen years now, and as grown men the two of them, inseparable as boys, might not have had the time of day to spare for each other, but Peg chooses not to dwell on this; what would be the point? Mikey's dead and so is Maribel: she owes it to both of them to get Coby to the hospital and see him safely home. And she has no intention of mentioning the fact that she saw him drive his truck out of the porte cochere and up the street the night his mother died. Why should she? It wouldn't be fair. To him or anyone.

20

LLIOS says: "They say that when the pope objected to certain indecent frescoes Michelangelo had painted at the Vatican the artist replied: But the pope has merely to change the world, and I will paint the new one."

She smiles, but barely. The train pulls into the open, crosses the web of long-distance lines, and heads back underground. "Well, the world hasn't changed all that much in the meantime, has it?" says Ellios. "And they say those frescoes are still there, although I for one have never seen them. Have you? Has anyone?"

Elizabeth shrugs and Ellios sags. Her politeness is a sinkhole so deep he can't begin to see the bottom of it, but still he takes his soundings, reluctant to go down alone. Ellios isn't new to this game; she'd called him out of the blue after all these years with these amazing pictures of hers: she can't be as cool as she looks.

Elizabeth turns her head to get away from the sound of his voice because God only knows who might be sitting behind them on the moving train. Coming out of the tunnel the late-afternoon sun explodes in her face like shell fire. She has spent the day as Ellios's guest, first on the Metroliner, then at lunch with his dealer friend Verry, and is torn between thankfulness at not having to pay her own way and anxiety over the expected quid pro quo.

"Of course one of the reasons erotic art is so rare is because in the old days most dirty pictures were burned either before or after the artist died," says Ellios, as unselfconsciously alone with her on the crowded train as he was that summer night at the empty intersection, nursing the growing suspicion that she was other than what she had always gone to such great lengths to seem. He wants that version of her, naked under her dress, restored to him; he thinks she owes him that. Like the naked Fornarina on Raphael's easel in that wonderful Ingres double portrait; because, having revealed herself so unexpectedly that night (however briefly, however regretfully), what right did she have to go and close back up again? If he had it all to do over again, he might have acted differently, but it's too late to turn back the clock, and Ellios is nothing if he's not patient. "Painters' widows, especially, have a lot to answer for on this score," he says.

She doesn't answer and her nod is so fleeting he can't really be sure it was really what it seemed to be at all. "Although hopefully the sexual revolution will eventually change all that," he says. He smiles at her sideways, an honorary feminist, though he suspects she may not be that much of one herself, judging by the way she let him pay for the train without a murmur and made no fuss about letting him pick up the tab for lunch. Well, and so much the better. Ellios likes to feed women and give them little gifts, offer good advice, hand them in and out of cabs.

The train picks its way through a landscape of burned-out

factories and brave industrial slums, a gridwork graveyard, a little treeless park. "Fortunately there's always something that makes it through intact to the next century, something left for the rest of us to buy and sell," says Ellios. "And do whatever else it is we choose to do with it, of course."

Elizabeth's exhausted. It was a mistake to come today; she's left Clemmie in charge at Calpurnia but the kitchen is still in an uproar, the studio will have to be rearranged for Friedrichson's visit, and it's a given that anything that can go wrong will go wrong. Instead here she is with Ellios, headed through the state of New Jersey on her way back from the big city, asserting her right to have been present at his negotiations with the dealer he was so sure could tell them the provenance of Maribel's drawings and give them a fair idea of a price. Or, better yet, at least from Ellios's point of view, make an offer on the spot. Though from the moment she saw him waving to her at the head of the ticket line at Thirtieth Street that morning, she'd had a strong presentiment that she would live to regret the trip.

Unruffled by the heat and their long day on the town, Ellios still looks wealthy and well groomed in his silky Italian suit; there's still a faint breath of bay rum as he shoots his shirt cuffs and unfolds his *New York Times*. Standing aside for her in the aisle, then taking his place on the seat to her left, he's his usual courtly self—safe, settled, and at least superficially unthreatening: just another Philadelphia businessman on his way home from New York after a day in the marketplace. And all for nothing, because Verry, the dealer he's conjured up, is no longer buying: or if he's still in the market at all it's only, like Elizabeth and Ellios, to sell.

"Or so he says," says Ellios.

He's waved her to the window seat but with the sun in her

eyes she's forced to turn her head toward him more often than she wants to, giving him her undivided attention by default; when he offers to buy her a drink it hardly seems worth the energy it would take to refuse. She settles herself as far over in her corner of the seat as she can. There's no point in being rude. It's either speak or resign yourself to being spoken to.

The day's disappointments play back in her head as Ellios heads for the bar: including the narrow streets south of Murray Hill; the cryptic lettering on the Korean restaurant signs; the seedy office of Ellios's dealer friend Verry with its sooty windowsills and rain-scarred glass. "People find it hard to believe, but there isn't a living in it," said Verry, gesturing to the cluttered shelves and the grimy windows behind his head. Verry's little warren of interconnected offices is in a narrow building with five other businesses on the lobby directory: an underwear manufacturer's showroom, an oriental rug merchant, and two more that can't really be identified from the names on their nameplates or the logos on their doors. "Not anymore," said Verry, tipping back in his chair and clasping his hands behind his head. "Believe it or not, the whole market for this sort of thing is dead. *Playboy* changed the name of the game in the sixties and after that it's been all downhill. It'll never be the same again."

To Elizabeth, Verry had seemed surprisingly cheerful for someone whose business is down the tubes; a sandy-haired man with an Australian accent and a loud tie, he'd kept pushing unframed drawings and mezzotints of suggestively posed nudes in plastic passe-partouts across the desk like fabric samples, while Elizabeth made herself look the other way. It wasn't just the artwork that bothered her, or the suspect delicacy with which he steered it past her toward Ellios, but the assumption that they'd come as buyers, not sellers: that there was money in this for Verry if he played them right.

"I've been in this field for a long time," Verry said, "and I've seen it change in front of my very eyes. The market for serious pornographic art has collapsed into the general art market itself: all the people who were in it for the thrills can simply walk as far as the nearest newsstand now to get their fix. Or men with special tastes, as they used to call it, can go to Forty-second Street and find whatever they want in four-color Technicolor for three dollars a pop." Verry laughed, flashing a mouthful of bad teeth and a tongue stained red by the strong-smelling cherry cough drops that he kept offering all around. "Or shall we say: in the flesh?" Looking at the cluttered office with its unwashed windows and undusted windowsills, Elizabeth senses the end of an era: old inventories left unsold for years and leases that will never be renewed.

Verry had laughed his matey Australian laugh and offered his cough drops to Elizabeth, furtively, like drugs. "In the fifties all my buyers were men, but not anymore," he said. "Nowadays, the big buyers are women. Middle-class women, actually." He turned to Elizabeth. "Women—please don't be offended—like yourself. They want it for the artistic aspects of the thing, or so they say. Art for art's sake, you know!" He giggled, and waved his hands at the mess on his desk. Elizabeth crossed her legs at the knee and tightened her grip on her purse. "Your prints now; quite interesting," said Verry, "but probably not in that class. They're poor-quality nineteenth-century reproductions of some rather well-known and widely collected seventeenth-century works, in my very humble opinion, no offense. And on top of that they're bowdlerized—these rather comical ribbons and draperies that someone has inked in to preserve the niceties. Charming in their own way, but only as cartoons or someone's little joke, when you get right down to it."

"But what about the drawings?" said Ellios.

"The drawings, yes," said Verry, "of course." His voice sank half an octave to what must have been its true, everyday pitch, and his eyes shifted to the window and its view of urban brick. "There might be some interest in the drawings, actually, yes. Not without a signature, though, or at least some evidence of provenance: not for the kind of money that would make it worth your while to sell. Well, let's be blunt: you'd need a pedigree." He smiled and spread his hands like a man with nothing to hide: the word *provenance* hung in the air between them like a note held too long. Elizabeth had felt Ellios's eyes on her face and made a point of looking at the view.

THE TRAIN breaks out of gray industrial wasteland into suburban coziness: boxy houses each with their single flowering dogwood; a graveyard as immense and shipshape as a golf course, climbing its rolling hill. Maribel's little jokes are in Ellios's briefcase now, homeward bound, and Elizabeth is left with the problem of getting the pictures back up on Calpurnia's powder-room walls without being noticed or called to account for them.

Ellios hands her the little cardboard box-top tray with their drinks, then makes a point of pouring out her wine for her, and Elizabeth braces herself for his tasteless small talk, almost another hour and a quarter of it; she prays that there's no one who knows her on the train. She drinks the strong red wine he's handed her; she's his hostage, won in battle, for the duration of the ride. Men love to believe that women are secret hedonists, ready for whatever comes along, and Lipscomb's drawings of

Nina are a case in point; but what could have possessed Maribel to let Nina pose for them? To Elizabeth's mind there's no way to reconstruct the scene of that sitting that doesn't make a monster of Maribel and a debauched schoolgirl of the adolescent Nina. In two days she has an appointment with Lipscomb, to which Ellios is not invited and about which she sees no reason to tell him in advance. Because if provenance is as key as Verry says it is, then surely Elizabeth holds the high cards here. She knows who drew the damn things, after all; and if she can't sell them for a decent price on the open market, she can at least find out what they're worth to the artist himself—the perpetrator, as she has come to think of him, of the pictures' crime. She wonders how much Lipscomb's name on the pictures would be worth to someone like Verry—either with or without an actual signature.

You learn these lessons the hard way; never mix business with pleasure, never give anything away, and never show your hand, regardless of whether you've got high cards or low. She's tried to put that night in Ellios's car behind her but he won't let her off the hook, and what good does it do her to make an enemy of him? Elizabeth is a realist, first and last; if she has to, she can get along with anyone. She turns her back to the sun and toasts him in stale airline bordeaux.

"Thanks for an interesting day," she says.

It's her first concession to what he thinks of as the reality of the situation, and Ellios lifts his little plastic glass to hers, barely touching it, turning it to the quadrant where her lipstick has painted half of her mouthprint on the rim, his square, well-kept hand on the edge of the tray table flashing onyx and gold. The sun behind her disappears into a black-edged cloud as the train approaches a ribbon of river and clatters into New Brunswick, a toy colonial scene, all neat brick Federal façades, sudden spires, and golden domes. From this angle she's the line-for-line likeness of Miss Elizabeth Linley in the Elkins collection's Gainsboroughs: soft, distant, and so unconscious of the painter's eyes on her that she might be all alone in the studio, or for that matter the whole wide world, give or take the jewelry and the tall eighteenth-century hair. He'd like to ask her if she knows the painting but thinks better of it.

"Yes, a wonderful day," says Ellios, with a sense of pushing his luck. "Though maybe not such a profitable one. But Verry isn't the only game in town, and it shouldn't be all that hard to find out who drew these things. Shall we play detective, you and I? Would you like to pursue it? Are you game?"

ELIZABETH lets herself into the lobby without checking her mail. It's a day wasted, the longest so far of an unnumbered series of long days, but she's brought it off without crying or losing her temper, and without any obvious public shame. Ellios can think what he wants about that night in his car at the intersection, but she's never made or broken any outright sexual promises to him, or anyone else for that matter either, in all the years since she's been divorced. It's not as if she had ever come right out and asked her randy accountant to do her taxes for next to nothing, for example, or her fanny-patting divorce lawyer to accept payments of a hundred dollars here and fifty dollars there. And it may be true that along the difficult road her life has taken since she left Douglas, or vice versa, she's learned the art of postponing the unthinkable in a way that makes it seem as if she's only postponing the inevitable; but the accountant and the lawyer both still cash her checks, the bronze collector who took a shine to her at one of Oscar's parties still takes her out to dinner on some hopeful and unchanging timetable of his own, and David still takes her fidelity for granted. As he can. As he has every right to do.

Peachy thinks she's crazy to keep herself pure for a man she only sees three or four times a year. "How do you know who he's sleeping with himself?" she says.

But Peachy doesn't know David.

"I know who David's sleeping with," says Elizabeth. "He's sleeping with his wife."

ELIZABETH looks at herself in the mottled elevator mirror, all shadows softened and all lines erased, and wonders exactly what it is that Ellios sees in her. She's a woman of only average looks without any influential friends or steady source of income and already well on the way to showing her age; or are single women just fair game? And, to turn the question on its head: what exactly is it that she sees in him?

The easy answer is that what she sees in Ellios is some sort of strategic reserve: a deep well of desire and know-how and connections to be called on in cases of professional emergency. She keeps men like Ellios on the line because it's prudent, because it simply makes good business sense. He knows everything, he knows everyone, he's respected in his field, and, let's not beat around the bush, wherever they go he always pays her way. In their own way men like Ellios are therefore, let's be honest, irreplaceable; you need them the way you need tax experts and lawyers and dependable gynecologists. It's nothing to be ashamed of. You don't have to admire them, or love them, or sleep with them; you don't have to marry them.

But with or without men like Ellios in her life Elizabeth has trained herself to expect the worst; and with good reason, unfortunately: because the first thing she sees when she closes the door behind her after her day in New York is the light on her answering machine, blinking steadily and scarily in the semidarkness. There are five new messages since she reset the tape this morning, and even from this distance the silent tattoo has a kind of sickening urgency. Days later, when she knows all its messages by heart and there's no turning back from them, she'll tell herself that she could see just from looking at it across the empty room that the tape was full, and that what it was full of was bad news.

Elizabeth takes off her shoes and throws her limp shirt into the hamper, then pushes the playback button full of yesterday's calls, and listens to the day-old voices unscrolling on the day-old tape. Robin, exasperated and short-tempered as usual, returning Elizabeth's Tuesday evening call; Oscar reminding her to bring the punch bowl for his July Fourth lawn party; and Clemmie, of course, both third and fourth in line, distraught and out of breath ("Liz, this is Clemmie. Is this Liz? I'm at the house. *This is an emergency.* Please call me at your earliest convenience, ASAP: six-six-seven-one-five-seven-eight.").

CLEMMIE'S voice at the other end of the line when she finally picks up the phone is exhausted and spiky with disbelief. "Honestly, Liz, your guess is as good as mine. I was out there at seven-thirty in the kitchen cleaning the Meissen, like you said. I had the back door open for the cross ventilation but the screen was locked, and you know me: I never leave it open, I never would, so help me God; not in a million years. I was minding my own business, I got all the plates done, those two big platters and the soup tureen, plus about half the cups and saucers. Then I started in on the demitasse cups, just like you told me to, right? By now it's nine-thirty, ten o'clock, and I go down to the powder room to get rid of those dried flowers, when all of a sudden I'm halfway through the dining-room door and I see all this blood. Yes, I said *blood*. Blood all over the doorjamb, and this god-awful mess in the hall, that big lighting fixture in a million pieces all over everything, the bobeches all cockeyed, what's left of them, anyway; and trash, broken glass, you name it, the whole place looked like a cyclone hit it. Well, I know trouble when I see it, you know me, I just went back to the kitchen and called Mrs. English on the kitchen phone. I got her at her shop. What are you doing up there all alone? she says. I go, What do you mean what am I doing, I'm Liz Oliver's assistant out here for the estate sale, that's what I'm doing, sorting the silver and cleaning the damn chinaware: as if I wasn't just doing my goddamn job? Well, she gave me an earful, you know how she is; and I don't have to tell you, Liz, you know me, I don't take that stuff from anyone. So I left the dishes right in the sink, put the keys on the windowsill, and left. I mean, what was I supposed to do? I locked the back door behind me, and good-bye. And I'll tell you something else, Liz, although I didn't say anything to her, or anyone else either, but I'll say it to you, right here and now: wild horses couldn't get me to go back there, not today, not tomorrow, and not yesterday, so help me God."

Elizabeth puts the phone on the floor, unzips her skirt, and hangs it over the back of a chair. It's years since anyone has called her Liz, and the sound of her schoolgirl nickname in Clemmie's mouth still rings like a voice from the distant past. Clemmie's a born storyteller and Elizabeth sees the scene unedited in her mind's eye: the blood, the broken glass, the ruined gasolier. She unwinds the phone cord as far as it will go and inches her way toward her own all-white and bloodless kitchen floor. "Poor Clemmie, it must have been awful," she says.

"What on earth do you think could have happened? Was it a burglary, or some kind of accident? Did somebody break in overnight?"

Clemmie quiets down, slowly, like a tea kettle taken off a stove. "Liz, I didn't stick around long enough to find out," she says. "I saw all that blood and that was enough for me. I mean, what about AIDS, what about all the evidence for the cops? And after the way that woman talked to me, dead horses couldn't drag me back. I put in a good two hours there yesterday: two and a quarter if you want to get chintzy about it: not counting the fourteen hours last week, and seven the week before. That's twenty-three total, not counting travel time, or meals. Or the aggravation; because, you gotta know this, Liz, my blood pressure was through the roof."

Elizabeth says, "I know, I can imagine, poor Clemmie, my God." Her voice is shaky but her head's a blank. She needs a drink, she needs time to sit quietly and let the bad news sink in, but getting Clemmie off the phone is always dodgy and at the moment she isn't even sure she wants to, because who knows what else she might have to cope with once she hangs up? "Look, Clemmie," she says, checking her liquor cabinet for something (anything) to drink in place of the soured wine in the fridge, "let's just be thankful you weren't there when it happened; that it wasn't your blood. That you didn't catch the burglar in the act."

"No, you're right; I wasn't hurt; not a scratch," says Clemmie. "I took one look and that was enough for me; I never went anywhere near that glass. I may be crazy but I'm not dumb."

Elizabeth stands in the kitchen door with the phone cord stretched out behind her like a lifeline, unwilling to let go until she's found another to replace it with. "Clemmie, I can't tell you how sorry I am," she says. "I'll call Nina English tomorrow.

Just give me a bill for your hours and I'll see to it that you get paid. Try not to worry about a single thing." And realizes only after she's said good-bye and started to hang up that it's her own fears she's trying to deal with now, not Clemmie's.

ELIZABETH has no taste for whiskey, it's something she only keeps on hand for male visitors, but it's either that or the Swiss beer left over from David's last visit. In the dark bathroom she reaches blindly along the first shelf in the medicine cabinet for the bottle of aspirin she remembers from another life. At times like this, it's human nature, you can't help asking yourself: why me? Elizabeth isn't a troublemaker; she's never bent the rules. She didn't sleep with a man till she was twenty and having slept with him she married him: all her life she's kept her car washed, sent in her taxes on or before April first; she's pretended to be kind to people she hated; pretended to be patient with her kids when they were violently unreasonable; tried to do the right thing without fanfare whenever it was at least halfway obvious what the right thing was to do. In the course of her life she's taken in two stray cats, saved a neighbor's child from drowning, helped numerous blind people cross innumerable streets. But who's keeping score, and what do all your good deeds add up to anyway in the face of a single day's one random moment of bad luck?

Belatedly Elizabeth steels herself to replay the last message on the tape. She listens for the little buzz that heralds the call (is there no end to the people who have waited to phone her till yesterday, the one and only day in months that she's actually been out of town?). The voice is Nina's, and so much the better. Time to get it over with. Elizabeth can save herself a call.

She tucks the receiver under her cheek and reaches for her

notepad. Till now she's spoken to Nina on the phone so rarely that even though she's half expected it, there's still a moment before she actually manages to recognize her voice. In contrast to Clemmie's outraged call to arms, Nina's tone is as expressly unexasperated as that of a queen giving up a throne or a diplomat announcing his departure from a war zone. She's sorry she hasn't been able to reach Elizabeth all day, Nina says; she's tried her repeatedly, she says; she's left two messages on the machine at Calpurnia, and she deeply regrets any trouble she may be causing her, but there's been some trouble at Calpurnia. She prefers not to go into details on the phone, she says, and hopes Elizabeth will understand, but for the moment she has bad news. She'll explain things later, face-to-face. In the meantime, though, she's afraid the family has no choice, unfortunately, and to her personally very deep regret, except to call off the sale.

TO ELIZABETH the click at the end of the tape sounds like a door being shut and locked. So that's that, she thinks. Amazing how little it takes, isn't it? It's the end of a summer's worth of plans, a daybook full of urgent things to do, a bank balance pleasantly (momentarily) in the black. Elizabeth shuts her eyes and replays Nina's message twice, listening carefully, testing for insincerity, indignation, or deceit, but she can't hear anything in the words beyond a kind of regimental courtesy, noblesse oblige. And, underneath it all, the all too obvious desire to finish speaking and get off the phone.

Well, these things happen, Elizabeth tells herself. Promises get broken; sales get called off: it isn't just her, they happen to other people too. In her mind she constructs a list of all the professional disappointments and near misses she's ever had, going back to the Hepplewhite fauteuil she mistook for Directoire, the Venetian dressing table she passed up at the Ormsby auction, the Milton Avery drawing ruined by Windex under the glass. Taken all in all, a list that anybody else in this business could just as easily come up with too, if pressed; and why not count your blessings at a time like this, instead of your defeats? There's still money in the bank from the settlement of her mother's estate; if she has to she'll tap it for next month's rent, and after that, who knows?

Elizabeth makes herself a scotch and water and drinks it down like medicine, then takes her best blue-linen dress off the hanger, inspects it for creases, and hangs it on the back of the closet door. She'll steam it when she takes her shower in the morning: tomorrow is another day. She'll have to cash in some chips immediately to cover her costs at Calpurnia to date; she had counted on paying at least some of Clemmie's hours off in Meissen from Maribel's pantry and miscellaneous kitchen things. Clemmie's brother-in-law has already put in billable time running trash to the junkyard, and Henry will have to be paid for weeding the hedges and daffodil beds. There's still time to cancel her meeting with the rug dealer, and the ad will have to be pulled immediatcly. Then, last but not least, there's the small matter of getting the pictures back from Ellios and hanging them up on the powder-room wall before she turns over her key to Nina or Jaxheimer and locks herself out of Calpurnia for good.

But not, perhaps, on second thoughts, before she has a chance to meet with Lipscomb and get his slant on them?

Because nothing ventured, nothing gained, and whatever they do with the house in the long run, they'll have to come up with some plan for Maribel's paintings, at which time it can't hurt to have spoken to Lipscomb about them in the meantime, obviously? Including (why not?) the erotic drawings of Nina on Maribel's divan. It's much too late to get out of the meeting anyway; the appointment's been scheduled for over a week. If she canceled now she'd look like an ingrate or a fool. Anyway, Lipscomb doesn't have to know the sale's been called off until later; if at all.

Elizabeth resets the tape on her answering machine and opens her Filofax to the last page of the week, then starts crossing things out one by one and penciling in alternatives: a kind of photographic negative of the original master plan. Because even disaster has its protocols, its countdowns and quid pro quos. Number one, pull the ad; number two, contact Ellios about getting the drawings back; number three, work out some intelligent scenario for their meeting before she goes to see Lipscomb Thursday afternoon.

Time to get going, Elizabeth tells herself; and sits dead still with her legs crossed at the knee and her hand on the silent phone. She isn't a fighter, she's always gone with the flow, but cornered she'll do what she has to do. David will or will not come in August as planned; she will or will not make it through this summer on what she still has in the bank; life will or will not go on. Unfinished business has a way of backing up like a plugged drain unless it's dealt with unflinchingly at the source. She has her work cut out for her, but for the moment it's all she can do and even a little bit more just to go on sitting here in her underwear with her eyes closed as she waits for the scotch to do its work. And anyway, hasn't she come too far and too fast over the last three weeks to rein herself in, burn all her bridges, and pretend she's no longer interested in what could have happened at Villa Calpurnia yesterday while her back was turned?

21

ONRAD doesn't want to say I told you so, it's not his
style, he doesn't like to rub things in, but let's put it
this way: he isn't exactly surprised. If Nina had put in
the new security system right after the funeral as he told her to,
none of this would have happened. Not that Conrad thinks
Coby's breaking and entering is exactly the end of the world,
not at all. Coby was born and raised at Calpurnia; it's only
natural that he'd keep coming back to the scene of the crime.
Assuming there was a crime, of course, and assuming that whatever crime there was was initiated by Coby. Assuming he'd
finally got it through his head that Maribel had left Nina in
charge as executor, instead of him. Assuming he'd finally fig-
ured out that Maribel had had it in her power to disinherit him
if she saw fit.

Well, Conrad knows how that feels. He remembers sitting
in Jaxheimer Senior's office after his grandmother died (aged
twenty-seven, dry-eyed, and beardless in those days) and the
reading of the will: primed to receive news of his rightful inheritance and listening instead, bug-eyed, to the collapse of his

great expectations and his sense of himself as a doting grand-son, loving and therefore loved. The women in this family always look out for themselves—low-slung *grandes dames* with their tiny talents and their elegant little axes to grind: when it's time to divvy up the spoils they leave everything in one another's hands, while the men are supposed to fend for them-selves. It's a family tradition, passed on down through the gen-erations like holy writ, old Samuel Archibald's idea of how to stiffen a young man's spine. And Conrad doesn't disagree in principle. Take Conrad's own only son, Hal, for example: his own worst enemy, a hard-drinking, guitar-thwacking couch potato with a year's worth of parking tickets to show for his dreams of musical grandeur, and an orange-sized bald spot on the top of his head at the age of twenty-two. Well, Conrad's fended, he can't complain, he's fended quite decently on the whole, if he does say so himself, but whether Coby's up to the job is an entirely different kettle of fish. Coby's how old (thirty-four? thirty-six?) and hasn't held a real job for more than six months at a time in his whole adult life. A deadbeat, yes; a lost soul for sure: but a "break-in"? If you ask Conrad, Nina's lucky he didn't break in and establish a whole opium den in the ser-vants' goddamn sitting room. All the more reason to go for-ward with the museum idea; otherwise there'll be embarrassing visitations and revisitations till the day old Coby dies.

Conrad's made that pitch already, of course—to Ibby, for what it's worth; to Nina of course; and, more than once, to Hugh. Because, let's be realistic, they're all in the same boat together taxwise on this issue, and what's good for one is obvi-ously good for all. All except Coby, of course, who hasn't got any income to tax in the first place; or won't until the paintings get auctioned anyway. And his share of the proceeds won't last long enough to get taxed, judging by past experience: Coby's got expensive tastes in drugs and women and clothes; but what he doesn't have is an income, a lawyer, an accountant, or for that matter even a savvy Dutch uncle, since Conrad gave up on that role a long time ago himself. Coby has never been able to see beyond the end of his own nose; all he wants is cash in hand. Which is probably just as well: because in Conrad's experience people who just want cash can always be bought off.

Ibby's friend Julia Romaine has been on the phone to Conrad twice since Thursday; the museum is her idea, supposedly, and she appears to have smelled a breakthrough, a meltdown in the united family façade; all the more so now, presumably, after Coby's recent escapade. Conrad's not sure what Julia thinks he can do to swing the vote; God knows he doesn't have much leverage with his niece, but perhaps Julia isn't aware of that. Her only source of information is Ibby, after all, and Ibby sees things through the rose-colored glasses of family harmony. Where he does have leverage, possibly, is with Hugh. Old Hugh's a pragmatist, and Hugh's got fiscal issues of his own. That shop of Nina's has to be a money loser, and Hugh may welcome the additional write-off that Calpurnia would be sure to bring as a museum. Or then again he may not, depending on how long it takes him to amortize either or both losses in the long run.

Conrad's been pro-museum from the beginning. Number one because it makes such good sense taxwise for all of them (well, almost all of them) and, number two, because he thinks of it as doing honor to the family name—ridiculous as that may sound, coming from him, the ex-Philadelphian, the outlander: but still. Conrad pulled up stakes as a young man, and he's never regretted it: why should he? Conrad's not a snob, he's always the first to acknowledge that the family fortune was founded on dentures and dental instruments: never mind

Calpurnia and its famous gardens, his grandmother's equally famous flower paintings, or his grandfather the admiral at the Battle of Tampico. Conrad's never cared where a man's forefathers came from, his own or anyone's; he doesn't believe in ancestor worship and royal blood. Hell, he wouldn't even mind if they put some of those original ads for the old Archibald false teeth up there on display right alongside the little Sargent and the famous Dewings; why not rescue Calpurnia from its bohemian limbo or even restore it to its days as a working farm, the way Conrad remembers it from when he was a kid: the hayrides and humming honeybee hives; the legendary tennis games; his grandfather's horses and dogs: why shouldn't there be some respect paid to that side of things too? Turn back the clock to the days before Maribel got her hands on things and converted Calpurnia into her Petit Trianon, and poor old Gerald had to go out to the pagoda or drive to his club to read the Sunday paper and smoke a good cigar. Coby used to play a decent game of tennis as a kid but he never did learn to ride a horse, and wouldn't know a honeybee from a bluebottle if it stung him on the ass. They have all kinds of museums these days. Art isn't the only game in town.

Poor old Coby, poor kid: things might have been different if he'd gone with Gerald when the marriage broke up, but that was never in the cards. Conrad suspects Gerald didn't want Coby—that ghastly custody battle was just a bluff, a way to get Maribel to back down on the settlement terms; and if so the strategy paid off. Old Gerald can't have been as stupid as he looked, because Maribel didn't get beans from the divorce. Even if everything they said was true, dirty books and all, hell, even if she was screwing that painter in Gerald's own bed five nights a week, including the pictures he was supposed to have painted of her in the nude—still, she was his wife, wasn't she? I mean, after all, wasn't she the mother of his goddamn child?

Conrad isn't surprised that Coby keeps showing up at Calpurnia. He's looking for buried treasure: a good thing they got the good stuff out of there on the first go-round or those pictures would be sitting in some shady backroom by now, sold for half of what they were worth, and/or collecting dust till the coast was clear. Coby lives from hand to mouth, he always has, and getting him to sign off on the museum is not going to be an easy task, but credit where credit's due: the kid may be a layabout and a liar, Conrad's not disputing that, God knows; he may be a procurer, a small-time drug purveyor and an unreconstructed mama's boy. But whatever else he is, Conrad's sure, Coby is certainly not a, quote, murderer, unquote.

All the more reason, then, to reconsider the idea of a museum. Something to remind Coby of his heritage, and maybe even set him up with a kind of lifework into the bargain. They could appoint the kid as curator, let's say, and put him on some kind of salary; it would be a way of killing two birds with one stone, wouldn't it? Then bring someone in to do the actual work, and let Coby sleep till noon. Give him the run of the house, since he's going to take it anyway: why not?

Conrad's not sentimental, he has no nostalgia for old Philadelphia or the girls and parties of yesteryear; he remembers all too well the way certain doors closed to him when his father died and the money disappeared in a town where blood is supposed to be so much thicker than water and what you have in your wallet is supposed to be beside the point. The sale's off, and good riddance; a bad idea from the start, inviting the whole township in to ogle Calpurnia's tattered upholstery and dirty linens, poke through the old coats in the musty closets,

pinch the old ashtrays, and look down their noses at the over-
grown hedges and the unkempt lawns. Who needs it—aside
from the gossip columnists and the blond estate sale lady, who
probably stood to make a tidy fortune from the take? Nina's
idea: she said it was the only way to clear out the house without
calling in the demolition derby, plus make some money for
Coby to tide him over till the paintings went up for auction
in the fall. But Conrad never bought that line of reasoning.
Because if she was so concerned about keeping Coby's head
above water, why didn't she just slip him a few thousand dollars
on the side till the Sotheby's sale went through?

Conrad knows Coby at his worst, no one more so, he doesn't
fool himself, but you can't help feeling sorry for the guy. A
mother who went broke fighting for his custody, then couldn't
or wouldn't be bothered driving him to tennis practice after
school; a cousin who cut him out of what little was left of
his childhood at Calpurnia, then married a man who wouldn't
even let him into the house; a father who might as well have
been dead for at least twenty years before he actually lay down
and died: not an easy row to hoe. If Conrad had been there
he'd have tried to right the balance any way he could, but by
then he was married and living in Cleveland, making his own
way, and the best he could do for Coby was to take him out
for dinner and hoist the odd glass with him, or put him in
touch with people he knew in the crass world of commerce,
profit, and loss, whenever he was back in town. Though Maribel had not approved. She didn't want her one and only son to
be a businessman: she kept trying to make a painter of Coby
till her dying day.

A painter! Conrad has to laugh. Just because a kid's good at
drawing cartoons for his school yearbook, or anatomically cor-
rect cocks-and-balls on the walls of the boy's bathroom at

school, doesn't make him an artist, does it? A tennis player, maybe, or the pro at a local country club (assuming he'd ever learned to stay off the sauce); even a salesman for some gimmicky line of sports equipment, for that matter, or a recruiter for college athletic scholarships—who knows? Things Coby could probably have done half-asleep with his eyes closed and his arms behind his head. There are lots of things a kid like Coby could have done with his life when you start to think of it—but painting? Painting isn't one of them. Maribel should have had her head examined, knowing how little money there is in that line of work, knowing the kind of miserable life she'd led as a painter herself. Why would she want to wish that on Coby, for God's sake?

Because anyone with half a brain can see that it takes more than talent to make a painter of someone; and just because you end up starving in a garret doesn't mean you're an artist, does it? Just because you can draw a wicked likeness of the lower-school headmaster, or a line-for-line medical-textbook rendering of the adult female sex organs, doesn't make you a goddamn Rembrandt or Vermeer. Conrad's always been Coby's favorite uncle; hell, he's his only one, if you want to get technical about it, and if anyone knows the kid it's him. But what he knows is this: Coby hasn't got a single artistic bone in his whole goddamn body. Not one, never did, never will; so: *artist?*— please; don't make Conrad laugh.

22

ELIZABETH gives herself an extra half hour to find a parking space. The house on Franklin Square is on all the tourist itineraries; it was built as the rectory to the famous nineteenth-century church from which most of the city's first families were once either married or buried, before people moved to the country and the country became the suburbs and the old farmhouses became hot properties in the multiple-listings books. Elizabeth's own mother, good Episcopalian though she was, had never gone to the same church for five years in a row, and even then only if the flowers were beautiful; when the altar arrangements and the soloists no longer met their standards her mother and her mother's friends all moved by preagreement to another church like theatergoers to another show.

Elizabeth hasn't been to church since her mother died. She's impatient with the American stained glass and the secondhand Tudor of the local architectural canon. The flower arrangements at St. Mary's seem businesslike to her, and at St. Asaph's the preacher puts her off. She misses the hymns, the smell of damp stone, and the sense she once had of being a credit to her mother, a good girl and a happy one. Her mother took to her bed when told that Elizabeth was leaving Douglas and never really got up again, the divorce overlapping with the final stage of her own fatal illness; Elizabeth would have tried to outwait her if she had known.

Along the river the dogwoods have finally finished flowering; the sculls are locked up in the boathouses again after the June heats, and there's a golden drift of pollen on the off-ramps; under the yellow-green trees Elizabeth has the road mostly to herself. It's that secret, semisweet moment of the year when spring shades disappearingly into early summer, the nameless season between the end of the flowers and the first signs of any kind of fruit. Elizabeth fumbles in her open bag on the seat beside her for her Filofax to check Lipscomb's address, but it's wasted effort; the church is visible from ten blocks away. Next to it Lipscomb's house has a worldly look that seems unsporting in this leafy setting. Its limestone façade is late Renaissance revival, the bell ring a brass oval knob shined to a fare-thee-well and set squarely in the middle of the door; even from here Elizabeth can hear the baritone chime as it echoes musically inside. A rich man's house, well kept and carefully appointed, mindful of the face it turns to an increasingly watchful and dangerous world.

Elizabeth introduces herself to the small scurrying woman who comes to open the door: the nurse, to judge by her white dress and stockings, her sensible rubber-soled shoes. Inside another door there is another woman: elderly, white-haired, with small classic features in a shapeless face, her mouthful of perfect teeth bared in an official-looking smile.

"Madeleine Cavanagh, Charles's sister; oh, Charles will be so pleased," this woman says, initiating a flow of almost seamless small talk (the noise, the traffic, the weather) like a deejay or master of ceremonies. "It's so kind of you to drop in; we get so tired of each other's faces here, don't we, Charles?"

"Don't we what?"

The voice is an old man's, but unmistakably a man's; it comes from a leather wing chair at the other end of the room and reminds Elizabeth, jarringly, of someone she knows. David, she thinks suddenly. Something about the inflection, the self-certitude, and the pitch.

"It was so nice of you to see me, Mr. Lipscomb," she says. Elizabeth never calls people by their first names unless and until she's invited to, and sometimes not even then. She follows Madeleine Cavanagh the length of the impressive Aubusson carpet and comes to a standstill in front of Lipscomb's leather chair. "This is Elizabeth Oliver, Charles: a friend of Freddy Friedrichson's," the old lady says. And, trilling girlishly, to Elizabeth: "A friend of a friend is a friend."

"Friedrichson's girlfriend, did you say?" Lipscomb asks.

Elizabeth laughs. "No, no; just a colleague," she says. "Hardly even that."

Lipscomb raises his head and gets a fix on her, squinting to bring her into focus like a statue on a plinth. "No, of course not," he says in that rich, young, uncanny voice of his. "Too bad for Friedrichson. A girlfriend's about the last thing poor Friedrichson would ever need."

Elizabeth looks for a way to get this dialogue back on track: Friedrichson's sexual proclivities are no concern of hers. "I've been talking to Mr. Friedrichson about arranging a retrospective of Maribel Archibald Davies' work," she says.

There's a moment of raw silence. In the background the brown-haired nurse makes herself useful adjusting the angle of the window blinds, and daylight advances a foot or two into the room, then recedes again, leaving the sepia shadows intact. The browns, Roberto had called the school of Academy portraitists of which Lipscomb had once been de facto dean. "Mrs. Davies was a painter," says Elizabeth. "I think you knew her once; she sat for her portrait with you in the forties or thereabouts, if I'm not mistaken. A wonderful painting. The lady of the house as Aphrodite, looking at her reflection in Ares' shield."

"Oh, my dear, *Maribel* of course," trills Madeleine Cavanagh, picking up the thread. "Charles, you remember Maribel Davies; of course you do." She turns to Elizabeth: "And how is Maribel? But didn't someone tell me she was ill? It's been so long; we see the same faces here day after day. Can I get you something to drink, Miss Oliver? Iced tea? Or something with a little kick to it—just say the word; we have everything under the sun except sherry and beer. Charles never goes out anymore, and neither do the rest of us. We try to keep him company, so we do all our drinking at home."

"Mr. Lipscomb doesn't want hard liquor," says the birdlike nurse. "I'm sure."

"Something cool would be wonderful," says Elizabeth. She hasn't come here to get drunk with Lipscomb and his sister; her mind is fuzzy enough these days as it is.

"Does Friedrichson know Maribel?" says Lipscomb. "Clever son of a bitch. On to a good thing, Friedrichson. Every little Sunday painter and painter's wife up and down the Main Line has had her little show with Friedrichson. I wish I had one tenth of the money that fellow's managed to salt away."

"Oh, be a good sport, Charles," says the old lady. "You've salted some of your own away in your time too."

"Yes, I have; and I'm sitting on every last bit of it right here in my own living room," says Lipscomb. "House rich; that's why Bettina left me: money in the bank. That's why Vivian left me. That's why Miss Oxtoby is going to up and leave me one day too, aren't you, Miss Oxtoby? Women always know what's good for them. Money in the bank, and the hell with pictures on the wall."

The nurse laughs unmusically. "Oh, no, Mr. Lipscomb," she says. "You know I wouldn't leave you. Doctor's orders. You'd have to fire me first."

Elizabeth smiles politely with the rest of them; they're performing for her, showing off their accustomed comic riffs. "I know," she says. "I was surprised to hear that Maribel had shown at Friedrichson's. Did you know that she died last month? I hope I'm not bringing you bad news."

There's another of those moments of sudden and intractable silence. Conversation stops; motion ceases; even the clock on the mantelpiece seems to go up a notch in pitch, and the ice in Elizabeth's tea sinks toward the bottom of the glass with a small explosive sound as the air conditioner gasps, then soldiers loudly on. "Oh my dear," says Madeleine. "You see what happens when you stay home all day and never open your mail? No one in this town ever tells anyone anything anymore. I heard she was sick, of course."

"It had to be in the paper, Madeleine," says Lipscomb. "How could you miss it? You've got eyes in your head. You can still read a line of print."

Madeline Cavanagh defends herself from his easy sarcasm, the invalid's revenge. "Maybe so, but not the obituaries," she says. "They're much too depressing. That goes for all the wars and murders too; too frightening. And politics, why bother? I never keep up with politics. Because *plus ça change, plus c'est la même chose,* don't you agree? (Is it Miss Oliver or Mrs?) In fact I'm not even sure I'd know who the British prime minister was today if it didn't happen to be a woman this time around."

Lipscomb clears his throat and says: "Maribel was a decent painter, she studied with the best. Including, if I may take a small bow, yours truly. Until she went off on her own tack— expressionist, Kierkegaardian, Teutonic, not my cup of tea. But of course that's all very ancient history by now."

Elizabeth sips her drink and settles back in her brown chair, smiling in a small way, hypnotized by the sound of Lipscomb's bizarrely familiar voice. Lipscomb's an old man now, he must be well up in his eighties, but his masculine presence is still intact. He doesn't paint anymore, he says; he gave it up a long time ago; first his sight went and then his hands: he could throw paint at the canvas like Pollock but that's about it, and since he has never had a good word to say about abstract expressionism in his heyday, he's not about to start pretending to promote it now. The skittery little nurse clicks her tongue at him, afraid that he may be speaking ill of the dead. In his youth, Lipscomb says, he knew John Sloan, he knew Glackens, for that matter he still knows de Kooning—he's known them all, and he knows one or two things about them that you won't find in *Art Forum* or Bettinger's archives, no indeed.

Elizabeth nods in her high-backed chair, more than happy to be impressed by the impressive names. Lipscomb's handsome profile is still matinee-idol in its exactitude; it's easy to imagine him as Maribel's lover, dispensing a ruthless and unbending charm, and the voice is still as rich and resonant as a much younger man's. When she sees David in August it will be seven and a half months since their last visit, the longest they've ever been apart since her divorce. Long enough for him to fall out of love, meet someone else, or decide to recement his wavering attachment to his long-suffering wife, for all she knows.

People are always after him to write a book, says Lipscomb, but he's not tempted, his lips are sealed: discretion's his middle name. He remembers Maribel, yes, of course he does; but his memories are polite and sanitized; he's sorry to hear she's dead but then, if we live long enough, isn't that what happens to all of us in the end? A wonderful woman, though, he says, marvelously talented, but she never had the courage of her artistic convictions. He'd tried to get her to open up, paint the human body, paint her way into or out of those claustrophobic interiors she was always so obsessed with, or, if not, at least bring some light and color and reality to bear on them—but it was a hopeless task. "It's all in the eye, of course," says Lipscomb, "but people forget that the eye can look either in or out. And how can you paint something you can't even see? Maribel didn't paint from life; she painted from memory."

Miss Oxtoby plunges in. "Now, now," she says, "time out. You promised we weren't going to think anything but happy thoughts today."

Lipscomb opens his mouth as if to laugh but starts to cough instead, and Elizabeth looks pointedly away, at linen-fold paneling on both sides of the fireplace, paintings on the walls. Portraits, as expected, and studies of human heads, ink and wash, pastels, red chalk: mostly of women, and most of the women just this side of beautiful. You could date them by their hairdos and cut of their collars if you had to, they're that accurate, that reportorially acute. Who are these women, Elizabeth wonders, and are they still among the living? Did Lipscomb seduce their daughters, did their husbands pay the bills? She has the feeling that if she saw any of them in the flesh she would know them instantly, anywhere; and, waiting for him to finish coughing, waiting for his blood to fill back up with oxygen and life to regain the upper hand on death, it dawns on her that she doesn't need Lipscomb's signature to know who drew the studies of Nina in Maribel's powder room. The signature's unimportant, a mere detail. There's corroborating evidence right here in this room on every wall.

Lipscomb goes on hacking. His cough has a sad, organized sound to it, as if it were something he does every hour on the hour, on doctor's orders, but without enough muscle behind it to make any real difference to respiration or longevity. When he's finally finished, the hand that he uses to raise the water glass to his mouth is trembling and there's a film of sweat on his forehead that wasn't there when he began.

Nurse Oxtoby has gone to get something for Lipscomb's cough, and with Madeleine Cavanagh mixing drinks by the door Elizabeth is suddenly alone with him in this otherwise uninhabited corner of the room. She pulls her chair closer to his and leans forward into his line of sight. It's now or never: for a split second she feels the sick bravado of a reporter at a crime scene, thrusting a microphone or a camera into the face of the next of kin.

"I came across some drawings of yours at Calpurnia," she says, keeping her voice low, her eyes on his. Once the words are out she's amazed at her own fearlessness; it's as if she's reading lines from someone else's script. "The house is on the market, Villa Calpurnia, up for sale; we're in the process of appraising the effects, and I wanted to ask if you could authenticate the drawings for me. Assuming that you agree they're yours."

Lipscomb looks at his hands and shakes them slightly as if he's touched something hot. "Mine?" he says, and adds, "Are they signed?"

It's not clear whether he's asking her or telling her. "They're unsigned, actually, yes," says Elizabeth, "as far as I can tell."

Lipscomb turns his impressive profile to the light. "If they're unsigned it means they're probably unfinished; and vice versa; which means they could be anyone's. We're not talking about old masters here, I assume? Nowadays you don't sign things until you're sure you're finished with them. Unfinished means unsigned."

Elizabeth tries to read the expression on his face. Is he pleased by her attention, or leery of possible reprisals come back to haunt him in his golden years? Or, for that matter, does he even have any idea what she's talking about? Is it possible, that is, that artists don't always necessarily remember everything they paint? Elizabeth watches his inscrutable profile with its single unreadable eye. At the other end of the room Madeleine Cavanagh is arguing with Nurse Oxtoby about the ice, an old lady in nonstop communication with a narrowing world. "Or inauthentic, even," says Elizabeth. "I mean, who knows?"

"Or inauthentic?" Lipscomb asks. "A forgery? I like that; imitation being the sincerest form of flattery." Once, in the old days, back before Elizabeth was born, he says flatteringly, there was a young woman who tried to paint a series of Lipscombs and pass them off as the real thing. "It caused a lot of trouble, more than you might think." Lipscomb breaks a small and wavery laugh. "But that was in another country; and besides the wench is dead."

"I've admired your portrait of Maribel so much," says Elizabeth. "I never knew her, but your painting has made her very real to me."

And in a way it's true; apart from the odd snapshot and posed family portrait from the fifties, the only idea she has of Maribel's face is Lipscomb's, true or false, its layers of allusion

and irony inseparable from Peg's tall stories and Coby's childhood memories of his mother, variations on an undocumented
theme. Lipscomb is known for his uncanny likenesses, but how
far can that take you in the throes of first love or, better yet,
its terrible aftermath? "I wondered if I could bring the drawings around for you to look at sometime soon," she says. "And
possibly ask you to help me put a price on them, before the
sale."

She's skating on thin ice here; but what does she really have
to lose? The old man takes his glasses off and puts them on the
table beside his chair. There's a remote tattoo of footsteps on
uncarpeted stairs, a telephone ringing in a distant room. "I
suppose they could be mine," he says. He crosses his long thin
legs, and then his hands; she has the strong impression that he's
enjoying her uneasiness. "Or then again they might not."

Elizabeth nods and holds her breath; then lets it out. "But
wouldn't it be best to know?" she says.

"Would it?" he says. "Why?"

Elizabeth works at keeping her voice steady and reasonable.
"Well, for the record: I mean what about the biographies? The
catalogs, the retrospectives, and so forth."

Lipscomb bares his teeth in what she supposes is meant to
be a smile; but he's beyond flattery. "Yes, indeed, the biographies," he says, and laughs. "All fifty of them, authorized and
otherwise." He puts a wadded handkerchief to his temples,
gingerly, as if there's no place on his skin that doesn't give him
some degree of pain when touched. "Although it might surprise you to know that there's a fellow at the University of Virginia who's actually sounded me out on the subject once or
twice."

"But it doesn't surprise me at all," says Elizabeth.

Lipscomb gropes for his glasses on the tabletop. "These

drawings of yours," he says carefully, in David's ghostly voice. "What makes you think they're mine?"

She's stumped. It's a ridiculous question: what makes people think a Rembrandt is a Rembrandt, or a Degas a Degas? What makes anyone think her face is hers, for that matter, or his is his? Elizabeth says, "I'm not a painter, and I'm afraid I'm no good at nailing down provenances." And then, before she can stop herself: "Does the name Nina Archibald English mean anything to you?"

As soon as she's said it Elizabeth feels the space between them go dead and she knows she's gone too far. At the other end of the room the women's voices rise and fall like traffic on a quiet street, but Lipscomb's eyes on Elizabeth are unblinking, and, when he finally speaks, something in his voice makes it clear to her that he knows exactly what she's talking about and remembers the drawings perfectly.

Lipscomb leans forward in his chair. "Look, my dear young woman, I don't know what your game is and I'm not sure I even care," he says. "But for the so-called record—or what did you say: for the biographers?—here's all I have to say, and I'll say it under oath if I have to, to you or anyone else, in any court of law. These drawings of yours could be mine, they could be yours, they could be anyone's; but if they don't have my name on them there's nothing I can do for you. Or you for me."

Elizabeth pulls back into the shelter of her chair, out of the line of fire. She's gone too far too fast; she should have waited, made herself indispensable, baited her trap with flattery and goodwill. Lipscomb unfolds his hands from his belly and leans back, a lion retreating to its lair. His tone softens. "The old eyes, my dear," he says. He points two fingers to his scored and deeply knotted temple. "The old eyes aren't what they used to be. Miss Oxtoby has forbidden anyone to mention it, but the fact is I'm legally blind. If those things aren't already signed my word on them one way or other wouldn't stand up in any kind of court at all. The plain fact is I can't see them; I can't see the wallpaper on the wall; I can't see the newspaper to read it or the lamp to read it by. That painting above the fireplace is just a blur to me; your face could be beautiful or you could be a fright: I can't see anything. The only paintings I've still got it in me to authenticate are the ones up here inside my head. The unpainted ones, to be exact; and nobody's beating down my door to ask for them; not anymore."

Elizabeth drains her glass of iced tea and puts it down, ready to go, glad that he can't see the rush of color in her face if what he's said is true. "These drawings of yours," Lipscomb says. His voice is confidential, almost boyish in its intensity, and so uncannily like David's that she has a hard time focusing on the words. "All I can do is imagine them. Did you think you'd brought me some pearl of rare price?" He smiles: a brief baring of his old man's ridged, chewed-down, and grayish teeth. "I've drawn a lot of things in my day, finished and unfinished, sketches, scribbles, you name it, signed or not. Works on paper, including paper napkins and the backs of envelopes, forgettable and otherwise, scattered far and wide." He puts out a hand in search of hers, misses it, and takes it back, one finger at a time. "I'd ask you to describe these particular specimens to me," he says, "but I have a feeling you'd prefer I didn't; or am I misjudging you? Were you a such good friend of Maribel's? Do we understand each other? Am I wrong?"

He flails the tabletop beside him for his handkerchief, then flails the front of his shirt for a pocket to put it in. "Please be sure and give my regards to Miss Archibald," he says, "assuming she's still alive. Or Mrs. So and So; or whatever name it is she may be calling herself these days."

23

ELLIOS, in love, combs his hair forward to hide the bald spot and plants his feet on either side of the wet bath mat to shave. He can honestly say that he had no idea, the other night, stepping off that train, driving her to her car, that he'd made such good progress with her. Had not expected it or planned for it, had not dressed up or down for it, had not even really allowed himself the luxury of imagining it in anything but the most general way, and can't believe in retrospect how easily he'd talked her into coming to New York with him in the first place, to shop those prints of hers around: let alone meeting with Verry and letting him take her out to lunch. He's given himself a day and a night to think it through, but he could probably have come to the same decision on the spot: in just a minute, as soon as he's shaved and dressed, he'll call her up and make her an offer on the drawings, then phone Albrecht's and put in an order for roses and baby's breath. A new page in a new book; and a long one, he hopes. Because Ellios knows the signs of a lonely woman when he sees one. If there's a man in her life there can't be much of one.

Her telephone call was a long time in coming, but Ellios has the patience of his kind; in this business you learn to bide your time or you're through before you've even begun. And the moment she came to him with those drawings he'd known the game was up. Pen and ink overdrawn on Conte crayon or pastels, or whatever they are, but beautiful either way: that dimple-chinned coquette with her amazing head of hair, and those delightfully tongue-in-cheek references to Velasquez and Bouchard; unsigned, artist unknown. Because it's true that a picture is worth a thousand words, and those pictures said it all; she didn't have to spell it out for him. Twice now, as far as he's concerned, she's given herself, both literally and figuratively, away. Even assuming she hadn't known they were there behind the Carraccis in the first place, which he seriously doubts.

She isn't young anymore but she's still beautiful, and Ellios likes his women, like his paintings, with a little age on them: virgins and young mothers have never been his cup of tea. Ellios loved his mother and his mother's friends, survivors of a hundred wars, living Boldonis with their feathered hats and little dogs, their parasols like lecture pointers, and their half-smiles behind tiny veils, refugees and war widows of empires that no longer even exist.

Ellios rinses the last bit of lather from his face. He's leaving for Brussels in seven hours, just time enough to pack, order the flowers, call Elizabeth, and remove Dorothy's photograph from the top of the little white piano she never played and where it's stood all these years waiting for resolution or reconciliation or redecorating, whichever happened to come first. When he comes back he'll throw away the odds and ends of used emery boards, empty perfume bottles, and monogrammed notepaper that his ex-wife left behind her when she went away. He has no picture of Elizabeth except an old clipping from the *Main*

Line Times, holding up a Victorian glass painting at some for-gotten charity raffle and beginning to shred at the edges by now, which he's nevertheless kept between the *o*'s and *p*'s in his address book for years.

Ellios wishes he could paint. Knotting his tie in Selena's mirror he tries to see himself as Elizabeth must see him: a man no longer young, as the saying goes, but no better- or worse-looking than the next and with his own uniquely unambiguous credentials: his money, his patience, his desire. Not to mention his need to get to the bottom of her, to know her from the inside out the way he knows early Chinese graphics, say, and precolonial Orientalia: because isn't that what women want? To be known; and, once known, to be loved and spoiled a little anyway. He'll offer her a thousand dollars each for those draw-ings of hers, and, if she doesn't like it, two. No, better make it two from the start; he doesn't want to begin this thing by hag-gling over a few thousand dollars more or less. A serious error, like the gaffe he committed that night in the car. He can't risk it; he's waited long enough. And so, he assumes, has she.

Elizabeth fancies herself a businesswoman but Ellios knows better; in that department she still has a lot to learn, and he'd be more than glad to teach her what he knows. He'll take her to Malaysia with him and give her the run of the bazaars, get her feet wet, let her get the hang of things. He'll introduce her to some of the money men and see how she handles the social end of things, then give her her own little stake to spend. Ellios is a risk taker, because in this business you have to be, but he's never gone out on a limb. And he knows what he needs to know: she has a good eye, and in this line of work that's the only thing that really counts. The rest is all on-the-job training; the rest can all be learned.

Ellios knows better than to underestimate the intelligence

of women. His mother's friends were all cutthroat card players: they spent hours in the hotel reception rooms of faraway cities with unpronounceable names playing bezique and cribbage and gin—games that nobody plays anymore, but all of them for high stakes. One of her best friends won the cost of three steamer tickets from Shanghai to San Francisco for herself and her two half-grown daughters less than two weeks before the Japanese occupied Nanking. The husband had committed suicide in Milan and the girls had unpronounceable Polish nicknames. He wonders what became of them. He hasn't thought of them in years.

Ellios checks his pockets for the essentials: passport, tickets, the envelope with its small wad of Belgian francs. He uses Selena's open sofabed as a staging area for the trip, his suitcase opened to its full width at the foot of the bed with last-minute items on the pillow at its head. He saves the shoes and paperwork for the end, among all the other last-minute decisions about what to take and what to leave behind. Traveling is a way of life and you either like it or you don't, but in this business you have no choice: objets d'art are like migrating birds, you have to follow them wherever they go. But Ellios has been on the move since the day he was born; he would miss all the coming and going, probably, if he ever settled down. (Dorothy said: You're never here, I never see you for weeks at a time; how am I ever supposed to unpack all this stuff and turn this place into a proper home?)

On second thought, though, he thinks, maybe two thousand apiece is too low. What's six thousand dollars to anyone nowadays? It's best to make her an offer she can't refuse, or at least not easily, and six thousand's barely more than a peace offering; though if so, why even bother? He doesn't want to insult her; he doesn't want her to think it's a gift or a bribe and not a serious trade. Otherwise, why not just go out and buy her a bracelet or a watch, lay his cards on the table, and be done with it? His mother's friends had lived on their jewels for years and sold them off one by one, a ring per city or a necklace per continent, until they were down to the bare essentials—a wedding ring, a watch to keep the time—and had no choices left but the gaming tables anyway. Maybe those little bridge parties in the card rooms of the old hotels were more desperate than they had seemed to him at the time.

Ellios stuffs his socks in his shoes and puts the shoes in the pale blue shoe-bags he inherited from his father, Egyptian cotton so old it's falling apart. His mother, thank God, had never had to live entirely by her wits; his father's health had held out long enough to get all three of them to the promised land and sow the seeds of a very modest fortune in the antiquities business before he died. As for those friends of hers, they took whatever ships they could get to whatever cities would have them; one to San Francisco, two to Buenos Aires, and one to Panama, where Ellios would have run into her in the plaza outside some famous church one day on his honeymoon except that Dorothy had pulled him suddenly away, and by the time he turned back to look for her she was gone. A Hungarian, he thinks; her name was Marita and she was the most beautiful of the lot; she had been painted, once, by Otto Dix. He remembers the painting better than he remembers her. He saw it in a gallery in Rome not long after the war; a beautiful thing, Marita at her dressing table in something so diaphanous you could almost see her backside, just hidden by the rise of the chair; he would have bought it if he could.

Verry's right; erotica's a lost art, an endangered species, as lost as the lost Aretinos; the genre simply doesn't exist as such, and if it did it probably wouldn't even be salable anymore. Pornography can't flourish without repression, and what is there left to repress when every little suburban housewife knows how to perform all the best perversions exactly like the most accomplished whore, while every bored divorcée keeps a battery-operated dildo in her bedside table along with her cough drops and her remote control?

No, six thousand is still not enough; on sober rethinking he'd probably do best to offer her ten right from the start, a nice round figure, something anyone in their right mind would have a very hard time turning down. He'll hang the drawings in here on the wall above Selena's Scotties, his inner sanctum, where he can see them every night as he makes his Indonesian calls. It's outrageous, of course, the pictures are hardly worth a quarter of that if Verry's guess is right, and he supposes he ought to have his head examined; but nothing ventured, nothing gained; and art is art. Ellios looks at it this way: it's an investment in his own future, professional as well as sexual. After all, what's ten thousand dollars to him, after all these travels and all these years, especially once the Belgian thing goes through?

24

HUGH COLLECTS his file folders and puts them back in his briefcase in alphabetical order. Upstairs, traffic is light; there's the ping of the shop door as people go in and out; there's the rustle of someone flipping through the racks, pivoting for the mirror, zipping and unzipping, trying something on. Hugh should be back at the office going over depositions in the Shawcross case, but the trial date has been pushed back for the second time in as many months, and it's been a long time—much too long—since he's had a chance to go over Nina's books. With the Shawcross postponement today's the only opening he sees in his schedule for weeks; and he's always happier doing the books when she's not around. Nina knows in the abstract at least that he's doing her a favor, and she swears she's grateful for it, but when they're both downstairs together in the cramped little closet that she calls her sales office, it can't be helped; they have a hard time staying out of each other's hair.

Hugh snaps his briefcase shut, locks the file cabinet behind him, and climbs the short flight of steps to the sales floor, where

Gillian stands poised behind a customer, inserting shoulder pads into a yellow caftan. Customer and saleswoman stare into the pier-glass mirror on the shop's western wall as if they're posing for a family photograph, and Gillian's hands on the smaller woman's shoulders seem to imply a sense of possession or patronage: her height alone is persuasive, as if that's all she really needs to get the customer to buy the dress. A golden dress cut like a bathrobe, shapeless, intricately wrinkled as if it's come premangled in the wash, and with little grommets and nailheads in unexpected clusters along the seams.

But that's all right; it's not Hugh's job to understand the clothes Nina buys and sells. Far from it; in fact he'd be a little concerned about a man who actually did understand such things, and on the whole he's more than happy to leave that end of the business to her. Unless her sales figures are so low and her returns so high that the operation goes south and stays there for more than the space of one normal business cycle, end to end. So far that's never happened, though; and with his help, it won't.

Hugh may not understand what makes women buy the clothes Nina stocks, but what he does understand is cash flow, taxes, profit and loss. Which is why he makes it a point to go over the books himself at least once every quarter, or even more often if he has the time. It's not that he doesn't trust Nina's clerk-bookkeeper; or Gillian, the aging blonde whom Nina calls her head of sales; or the office services company that he himself originally hired to do the paperwork; or even Nossiter, his own personal accountant, whom he has had to bring in to make sense of the books from time to time, as an occasional last resort. No, in all fairness, they all do the best they can with what they've got, and Hugh's always there with encouragement and support—or even rescue if need be. Over the years he's set up various foolproof filing systems and trained everyone to handle the invoices and bills of lading and tax receipts with all due respect for the letter of the law, so that there are no nasty surprises at the end of the year and everyone gets what he or she has coming to him within at least sixty days. After all, Hugh's the administrative partner in his own firm, so who should understand better than he does how important it is to keep the paperwork on track?

Hugh doesn't understand women's dresses, it's true, but one thing he does understand is that women can't have enough of them; that the desire for something new to wear is a bankable commodity and therefore a good source of income for anyone who cares to stock the goods and second-guess the trends. Those form-fitting dresses that his sister wore to weddings and cocktail parties in the sixties, each with its mile-long zipper like a second spine down her back, are out of fashion now; she had at least twelve of them in her closet, in every color of the rainbow: Hugh knows because he counted them. Hugh doesn't understand women's dresses and he doesn't understand women either, as he'd be the first to admit—except for the raw essentials: the mysterious ups and downs of emotional heat that punctuate their otherwise uneventful lives, and their more enduringly passionate connections to their own clothes and jewelry and household furnishings. Nina thinks he bankrolled her shop out of indulgence, a kind of masculine largesse, and of course that's part of it, because they never got around to having children, and Nina obviously needed something else to do. But if you asked him, he'd have to say there's more to it than that. It was (a) one way of keeping her out of his hair; and (b) a calculated business decision as well. Either she'd make good money or the thing would run at a loss, in which case he'd have a tax write-off on their joint return. One way or another he'd come out ahead; and by and large that's exactly the way it's turned out.

Hugh briefly ducks his head at Gillian in the mirror on his way through the door, but he doesn't wait to see how the transaction turns out. Women are a mystery to him, and maybe if he understood this mystery better he could turn Nina's business around for her, put it permanently and irreversibly in the black: but is that what he really wants? Over the years he's wrestled with this problem, one way or another, off and on, but in the last analysis he always ends up deciding to leave well enough alone. If her shop were a runaway success there'd be no dinner on the table. The house would be left on permanent autopilot; she'd be too tired at night to make love.

Hugh slams the car door and locks it. Clover Hill is trendy and the main drag is heavily policed, but there's a dubious patch before you cross the river and he prefers to avoid unnecessary chances. He takes one last look at the window display before he pulls out of his space: three willowy wire forms decked out in black-and-white organza stirring in the faint breeze from the shop's air conditioner vents as it cycles off and on. Hugh was only eight when his sister Alicia started dating, and only fourteen when she got married, and he was a virgin till he was twenty; until he met Nina the most he'd ever done was to get a girl to unbutton her blouse in the front seat of his father's car, and by the time Nina showed him Lipscomb's drawings (that sweet little girl's face and those big breasts with nipples like bull's-eyes below it) he was already half in love with her. Though he hadn't planned to propose to her for months: if ever. If at all.

He's had a long time to think of the legal ramifications of that business since then, God knows, but he still isn't sure where he stands, or what kind of case could have been brought on her behalf if she had been ready to go to court. Was it libel to paint a picture of a nude woman you'd only seen fully clothed; or child abuse, or infringement of copyright, or defamation of character, or what? Art is a tough call. Drawings aren't widgets, or car parts, or bacon and eggs; and where do you draw the line between representation and misrepresentation, real and surreal, portrait and caricature? But of course (thank God) it never came to that. Because by that time they were practically engaged, and what would have been the point? Nina had put herself literally, as well as figuratively, in his hands; and in the back of his mind he always knew there was only one way to find out whose body the drawings actually portrayed. Nina was convent raised; in those days to see a girl naked you more or less had to marry her.

He spent the next three weeks researching the legal issues, and on Tuesday of the third week he took her out to dinner and gave her the benefit of his considered advice. Which was: forget it; burn the damn things, forget they ever existed, and go on from there. He had even offered to do the job himself; surely he didn't need to tell her how dangerous it would have been to keep them lying around any longer than she had to, did he? The wedding took place that June. Ibby was there in all her finery and so was half of the Merion Cricket Club, and Calpurnia blazed with candles and tapers; the dining-room floor had been sanded and revarnished for the occasion, and there were lilies and irises from Maribel's mother's cutting garden on every tabletop. Hugh has never regretted it, and it never occurred to him that she wouldn't have done what he told her to, taken his advice and burned the drawings or torn them up, with or without regrets. Why should it? Nina's the docile type; is there any time either before or since that she hasn't seen it his way, bowed to his best judgment, done more or less exactly what he's told

her to? Except when she forgets, or doesn't understand, or simply gets things wrong. Like the security system at Calpurnia.
Like some of the more imaginative entries in her books.

HUGH SHUTS the door behind him and crosses the street to
his carefully parked car; he's got the timing down pat, there are
still ten minutes on the meter: there always are. It's four
o'clock; Nina should be through at Calpurnia by now, and he'll
be glad when she's out of that cesspool once and for all. The
place is decrepit, unhealthy, full of Maribel's sordid secrets and
moldy ambitions for a bohemian life. Hugh guns the motor
and eases out of the tight space; he'll stop by Calpurnia on his
way home and see if she's ready to call it a day. Traffic is still
manageable at this time of day but he'll be driving straight into
the sun until he makes the first turn at Weavers Way and the
canopy of ancient street trees closes in overhead.

Hugh puts his hand signal on although there's still no one
behind him on the street, and there's never been any problem
with traffic on Weavers Way. At least not now; not yet; though
the museum could change things in that respect. Hugh has no
illusions on that score, and the neighbors are probably right to
be concerned; he makes it his business to be objective, but
when it comes to the museum he's tried to take a backseat. He
doesn't want people coming to him ten years from now and
accusing him of causing the end of the world. Personally, he
couldn't care less, one way or the other, as long as Nina's happy.
And as long as he and Conrad get their tax write-offs; as long as
Coby gets it through his head that Calpurnia isn't his to break
and enter and smash to smithereens whenever he pleases by
divine right.

Hugh makes it his business to be objective; to dig out and

master the known facts, then look at them dispassionately, ana-
lyze them down to the ground, and rebury them, if need be,
when all the evidence is in. There's no doubt in his mind that
Coby knows more than he says he does about the way Maribel
died, and, considering how hard up the kid's always been for
money, Hugh can't say it hasn't crossed his mind to think the
worst; but as long as there's no way to prove it, why bother to
press the point? Look, they've got to make their own decisions;
he's only a member of the family by marriage; and Hugh knew
what he was getting into when he married Nina. The grandmother was half French; the whole family was artistic; and the
gossip was that Coby was Lipscomb the portrait painter's child;
so what else did he expect? Hugh went into it with his eyes
wide open, and that's the way he intends to keep them, for
Nina's sake as well as his own, as long as they both shall live.

25

SLEEP doesn't come easily to Lipscomb, and less and less so as he gets older. His infirmities don't mesh: the pain in his left flank is at war with the ache in his right sinus; if he lies on one side it's at the expense of the other, and if he lies on his back he chokes. Worse yet, the available remedies all either cancel each other out or make each other worse. Drink puts him to sleep but the only kind of wine he likes gives him canker sores; whiskey stuffs up his nose; and the only pain-killers that really work tie your bowels in a knot for weeks. Miss Oxtoby's middle-aged cheer in the face of these complaints enrages him. She's fifty-seven and has probably never had a sick day in her life, but in the event she ever did he has no doubt that she would simply take two aspirins, brew a strong cup of tea, and soldier on. It's a long time since Lipscomb has been able to tolerate aspirin on an empty stomach, and tea has never done much for him at all. At bath time he takes his insidious revenge, pleading an old man's shaky footing while he stands with his hands on her shoulders a little too long as she dries the parts he can't reach, or says he can't reach, himself.

"Don't get old, Miss Oxtoby," he warns.

"Not on your life, I promise you. Don't you worry about it, Mr. Lipscomb," she replies.

Poor Oxtoby: an old man's body can't be much to look at, Lipscomb thinks. In his youth he had a passable physique, better than Dürer's, but even then he was not about to paint himself in the nude: it was women's bodies that interested him, not men's. But you have to pay your dues, financial as well as romantic, before you can make a lifework of painting nudes, even assuming you ever wanted to; and unlike Picasso and Bonnard, Lipscomb had an old mother and a flighty sister to support. He'd always had a knack for painting faces, though, and before he knew it, he supposes, he became like so many people of his generation the victim of his own success. Something in Lipscomb could never bring itself to turn down a commission; but he has no real regrets. He tells himself that he doesn't care that he's out of fashion, that the art world has passed him by. He owns this converted rectory and a modest securities portfolio, he still gets invited out to dinner in the best houses (though he rarely goes) while his portraits hang in some of the city's most handsome dining rooms and two of them have been bought by fairly respectable museums. And besides, if you look long and hard enough, there's at least as much true nakedness in a woman's face as in the most bare-all of full frontal views. Lipscomb's never been married but he knows a thing or two about women. A woman's body isn't necessarily the entrance to her soul.

Not that you could have told him that as a young man; he'd had to find it out the hard way—but what man doesn't? That young woman sitting opposite him in the other wing chair yesterday, for example—he couldn't see her properly but he guessed her to be about half his age: the voice, the manners, the way she moved has brought back a host of memories. And of course he remembers Maribel; don't they all?

Lipscomb has always been good at keeping his own counsel, but there's a statute of limitations on secrets, like everything else: sooner or later people get old, their tongues loosen, the other parties to the crime sicken and die, and someone or other simply forgets and spills the beans. Maribel herself never gave a damn what anyone said about her anyway, dead or alive. It was part of her pose to be above or maybe just beyond mere scandal. The Main Line bohemian, he called her, because there's scandal and scandal, isn't there? and even Maribel had her limits, drew her little lines. That was the game they'd played, over and over, in ever riskier ways and at ever riskier levels. Lipscomb couldn't bear to be called a social climber; Maribel couldn't bear to be called bourgeoise. Amazing when you look back at it that things had ended as quietly as they did.

The way to a woman's soul is demonstrably not through her body, and probably not even through the eyes: because Lipscomb has painted enough female faces in his day (male too, for that matter) to know how much privileged information is written into the set of the head, the tilt of the mouth at the corners, the connections or disconnections between the mouth and the eyes. Painting Maribel he'd felt like a scholar reading a text, Aphrodite in Ares' shield: that delicious conceit. Male bluster disparaged and turned to good use by feminine vanity: Mars's manhood subverted to the purposes of Venus's self-love. The old man had stipulated something classical, hadn't he? Lipscomb can't remember whose idea it had been to paint her *à la Grecque*.

Lipscomb was never sure exactly how he'd gotten the commission. The old man was retired, a bit senile, he'd run into him in the cloakroom at the Franklin Inn after a luncheon to honor some visiting man of letters, and he vaguely remembers some small talk on the subject of portrait painting as opposed to portrait photography as they put on their coats and scarves. Maribel's mother was recently in her grave; the old man had always regretted that he had never had a portrait painted of his wife, he said, and Lipscomb supposes he said something consolatory in turn, but if it went any further than that it's lost in the mists of time. Maribel was said to be the spitting image of her mother at an earlier age. Did he look at it as a way of turning back the clock, cheating death, treating himself to a posthumous portrait of his wife?

By something classical Lipscomb supposed he meant something timeless, or at least Edwardian, Sargentian. All things considered, though, and whatever he meant, it was probably a little cruel of them to take him at his word. What they gave him was Maribel in a diaphanous tunic, with classical allusions that the old man didn't get and certainly did not appreciate when they were finally spelled out for him in detail. Lipscomb was paid for the damn thing in full and on time, but he suspects that in the long run it may have cost him dearly. Isobel Aubrey hasn't spoken to him from that day to this, and her friends are legion and well to do. As Maddie never gets tired of reminding him.

Looking back on the Archibald Davies commission he sees it as the beginning of the end of his considerable success, the first downward dip in the curve of the arc, though at the time he didn't even really notice it happening and, if he had, would have put it down to any number of other causes. The general migration to the suburbs, for instance, and the small size of suburban dining rooms—much too small for the proverbial family portraits on the walls; as well as the growing prevalence of divorce. And, last but not least, something he can't quite put his finger on: the loss of a certain reverential quality in the way husbands used to feel, or at least used to pretend to feel, about their wives. All these must have played their role in taking the fizz out of the market in the fifties, after the war, and Lipscomb certainly wasn't the only portrait painter to feel the pinch. But he suspects in his heart of hearts that Maribel's jokey Aphrodite didn't help.

IT WASN'T his best painting: a painting that went for the mind, he always thought, and not for the eye or heart. Maribel's fault, he thinks: her insistence on posing the little boy, aged four, in his white sailor suit as a stand-in for the invisible Ares, holding up that stupid shield. And the shield itself was a compromise at best; he'd wanted to borrow something heraldic from a famous local collection, but that idea fell through; instead, at his own expense, he'd had one carved from composition board, and gessoed and gilded by a friend who made a living doing restoration work in churches and movie theaters.

The shield, though, had been a problem from the first. It was too heavy for little Coby to hold up without propping it from behind, whereas once it was adequately braced the child lost interest in it; he couldn't see why they needed him in the picture if the shield could stand up by itself. In addition, Coby had hated the sailor suit, which kept getting dirty and having to be washed and pressed, and it was clear from the outset that he would have had a hard time sitting still under the best of circumstances anyway. In the end Lipscomb had had to settle for what he could get. Maribel thought he was being fussy. In her opinion the look on Coby's face just underscored the prevailing irony (a child doing a man's work) and if Lipscomb disliked his expression so much, she said, why didn't he simply paint it out and paint in another one?

It was a question that cut to the quick of their ongoing argument with each other. Because what you paint is what you see; and how, he asked her, could he paint an expression that was not just absent from that four-year-old face but utterly unimaginable on it?

Maribel pretended to be amazed. She had originally consulted him (if that's the word) to help her overcome her problem with faces. She couldn't get a likeness, she said; it was a knack she'd had as a girl and lost as a grown woman; she didn't know whether she needed the ministrations of a teacher or a psychoanalyst. Lipscomb didn't know her well enough then to know whether she was absolutely serious, semiserious, not serious at all, or simply flirting with him. He had given up teaching at least five years earlier, but he made an exception in her favor because he was flattered by her request (who wouldn't be?) and because Maribel was one of those people—few and far between in his life till now, thank God—that you simply cannot refuse to take on when they ask you to.

Lipscomb had known Maribel all his life, but distantly, and as a party-goer, not a painter or a friend. He remembers the glamour surrounding her marriage to Gerald Davies after the war, and an opening of her work at Friedrichson's, which he pointedly did not attend; but he can't remember a time when he didn't want to paint her, or the challenge of that tensile, mercurial hair, and, after they met again one night at Isobel Aubrey's where he had gone to pick up his sister, her vivid face with its unsteady smile and brilliant, stabbing eyes.

He thought about ways and means of painting that hair and those eyes, off and on, for months, and when she called him six months later out of the blue, he read it as a kind of omen and went out to Calpurnia that week, still dreaming of that barbed-wire hair, to see what he could do.

The place was a circus. She held court in that enormous ballroom on the third floor, converted to a working studio by its immense skylight and mottled drop cloths, while downstairs the daily cocktail party started at lunchtime and went on till five o'clock. Her circle of friends included every unemployed divorcée and local flash-in-the-pan for miles around: widowed ex-flappers on dwindling insurance policies, trust fund paupers, would-be bohemians, and artists without an art. "How can you work in this madhouse?" Lipscomb asked her. But she had no idea what he meant, and anyway they all cleared out before dinner, didn't they?

Because Gerald's homecoming from the city was sacrosanct. Gerald was some sort of pool manager for an investment trust, a man of regular hours well thought of as far away as Wall Street, and he hated her hangers-on. Curiously, Lipscomb saw eye to eye with him on this; and he set out to get rid of them one by one, like Christ turning the moneylenders out of the temple. Not only could you not paint in that bedlam but you could hardly conduct a serious love affair. Lipscomb imposed order on that chaos, for Gerald's sake as well as his; but he never did quite get her to the point of painting an acceptable likeness, either by her standards or his own.

Lipscomb sighs and turns left to right in the bed Nurse Oxtoby has made for him: immobilized by her steely hospital corners, and without the strength in his legs to kick them loose. And she knows it. The women in his life all have their own unperturbable agendas; his wants and needs don't begin to come into it, no matter what they tell themselves about the great sacrifices they're always making on his behalf. Maddie has been effectively homeless since Roger died and left her without a roof over her head but his, while Miss Oxtoby is practicing for a kind of medical sainthood: it's the doctors she answers to, not him. As for that young woman who came to visit yesterday afternoon, who knows? He'd hate to second-guess her motives in peddling those drawings to him. From the sound of her voice and her laboriously good manners it's hard to impute anything as base as blackmail to her, but these are extraordinary times and people are no longer necessarily what they seem. You learn the hard way, but, God knows, you learn.

Lipscomb remembers the drawings, of course; remembers them line for line: how could he forget? The whole thing had started so laughably, so lightly, almost as a joke. He told her that he thought her problem with faces was overdrawn—or, more accurately, underdrawn: she was always in a hurry to put paint on canvas, she went straight for the brush and never stopped to draw. A few quick slashes, an eye with its thought as legible as newsprint, the head an unplumbed cartoon with its punch line left hanging, about to be delivered into the wide-open spaces of her empty rooms. Quite effective, those rooms, sometimes, in their own way; some of them quite brilliant, really, on their own terms, so that Lipscomb can't be sure, even after all these years, that what she really wanted was his help, and not merely (let's be blunt) his company.

She said she'd forgotten how to draw; he took out his sketchbook and sat at the end of that Freudian divan of hers and started to sketch her face. The husband was away somewhere on business, and the birdwatchers had all gone back to their trees; it was, possibly, the first time they'd ever actually been alone in the house. He drew her head, then her face (he already knew it by heart; it was like drawing from memory), but something happened when he started on her hair. Hard to explain, and certainly not the first time it had happened to him, though it was the first time he'd ever let himself give in to it. The hair came to life around her head as he drew, that wonderful tangle of human fireweed, as alive as her eyes or her mouth, and he was pleased with how easily it went, after all his trepidation—masses of it; it took him over an hour, but it wasn't enough; and when he got to her neck he simply kept on going, working from the top down, undressing her on paper, imagining the body underneath the clothes.

There was music on the record player—something for unaccompanied flute, and he remembers Maribel arguing with him about the pose, the angle of her head, the crick in her neck, the time it was taking him to work his little magic trick. But something had got into him. He had her pinned to the paper, at his mercy, bound and gagged; he felt that her life was, like her face, quite literally, in his hands. By the time he showed her the drawing itself the record had stopped playing and the room was as charged with his excitement as a giant battery. He let her change the pose, then made another drawing; and another. By the second drawing she'd unbuttoned her own blouse of her own free will; by the third she was naked. Neither of them, least of all Lipscomb, could believe how accurately he'd imagined her in the original sketch.

LIPSCOMB heaves himself over again and strains at the corners of the imprisoning bed. He's not going to give in to the temptation to reach inside his pajamas and test the strength of his sexual memories of Maribel. Nurse Oxtoby pretends to be all-tolerant and all-knowing and his blindness has its consolations; but it's one thing to joke about his loneliness or the time she takes to wash his balls, and quite another to present her with the ugly evidence of his residual needs. And whoever it is he dreams about on those rare nights that he wakes himself up out of a sound sleep by the force of his own desire, it's not Miss Oxtoby.

Lipscomb hasn't spoken to Maribel in over twenty-five years, and he's been spared the sight of her in her final illness, the stepwise slide from well to ill, from strong to weak, from bad to worse. The magnificent hair was already graying a bit in front and at the sides while she posed for her portrait as Venus lost in Mars's shield; he painted it out without so much as mentioning it, and she never took him up on it herself. Though Maribel, to her credit, was never vain. She must have been pushing forty in those days but she still had a decent body; the skin on her face was only just beginning to thin and her breasts had held up perfectly well. Besides, Lipscomb was never one of those men who could only make love to a woman if she was young and physically perfect or lightly used; and it wasn't just lust that he felt for the pretty niece, as Maribel supposed. Her jealousy on that score was totally undeserved. He never made a pass at the girl—what was her name?—Mignon, Ninon, it's on the tip of his tongue; just because he wanted to draw the damn girl didn't mean he wanted to make love to her, did it? Or could he have asked, in some moment of gross stupidity, or mere malice, or some other absolutely unmemorable whim, impossible to remember now, to draw her in the nude?

Maribel considered herself a free spirit but she wasn't; it was perfectly all right for her to sleep with Gerald at the same time that she was sleeping with Lipscomb, but unthinkable the other way around. And was it his fault that the girl had taken such a shine to him? She couldn't have been more than fifteen or sixteen, but she was already well developed and obviously in heat; and Villa Calpurnia was no place for a Catholic school-girl, with or without Lipscomb on board. Maribel prided herself on her nonconformity. She had spent the weekend with Lee Miller and Roland Penrose at Saint Martin d'Ardèche, she had been invited to Elsie de Wolfe's, but when you dig just a little below the surface all these Main Line women are exactly alike: solid citizens to the bone; it's the Quaker heritage. Lipscomb should know; he's painted more than his fair share of them, hasn't he?

Matisse said: I do not create a woman, I make a picture; and Lipscomb knows exactly what he means. What Lipscomb himself does as a painter is the opposite of creation—he doesn't copy nature stupidly, as he was taught to do at the Academy; instead he rubs away the surface until he uncovers what's hiding underneath and paints the face that they don't put forward, the one they don't want you to see: the true face hidden below the false one. That's why he could never do what Maribel wanted him to, and make the four-year-old Coby look sunnier and sweeter and merrier than he was. Coby might be too young to wear a mask, but a child that age already has his own little secrets and Coby's secret was that he knew there was something going on between his mother and the painter, and had not quite decided what it was or what to do about it when he did. Lipscomb painted the resentment and duplicity he saw in Coby's face, and Maribel wanted no part of that. Well, understandably.

Lipscomb remembers Maribel as he saw her last. The portrait, finished and framed, had been shipped to Maryland to please the adoring father in his old age; but Gerald had already begun to move out, and Coby was no longer underfoot. They had been lovers for five years by then but the impending divorce made Lipscomb nervous. He didn't believe her when she said she had no intention of ever marrying again, and she didn't believe him when he said he had no designs on the niece.

There's a statute of limitations on sexual love, alas; but let's be blunt, it's a law of nature, and things had come to the point between them where they had to resort to little tricks to bring themselves to the white heat of their earlier days together. Maribel's collection of erotic art was astonishing—stuff that she had sneaked out of Europe on the eve of war, with some silly Americana in the form of comic books thrown in; but what really moved him, what brought him back to the taste and texture of his original passion for her, were those drawings he made of her on the first day they ever made love. She kept them between the pages of a book in the tiffin box beside her bed and over the years they had accrued their own embellishments—a mirror here, a fig leaf there—everything subject to revision and erasure by either or both of them. They were a work in progress, and a collaborative one. Maribel said he had made her nose too long and her nipples too wide; they passed the pencil back and forth, correcting each other's misperceptions and adding afterthoughts of their own. Some lines were drawn and redrawn so often that they cut all the way through the paper and came out the other side. Until that last day, though, none of these redactions had been anything but a kind of joke and, as he remembers it, a long-playing and on the whole loving one.

Her jealousy was past the point of teasing by then, though; she had become remorseless, even if he can't remember exactly what it was that day that set her off. Was it something he had given Ninon, or something suggestive he might have said to the girl, and if so, what? Try as he may he can't dredge up any serviceable memory of his crime. It's true that the girl had sat for him, some quick sketches, nothing lurid, fully dressed; she had Maribel's hair but her own strange little face, and that adorable chin. The set of her head held a kind of challenging innocence that wouldn't last forever and that he was desperate to paint. Before she outgrew it; before she turned from a schoolgirl to a flirt into a case-hardened debutante before his very eyes.

Maribel accused him of besotment, but it was never that. It wasn't so much that he longed to put his hands on the girl as it was to put his picture of her down on paper, before she grew any older and wiser, before that look in her eye changed from unknowing to calculating, from true to false. Well, let's be honest, he was always drawing her. All that winter they had had long, ad hominem arguments about the relationship between the painter and the painted, and Lipscomb was amazed at her intransigence: after all, wasn't Maribel a painter too? Surely if anyone ought to have understood the cerebral quality of that connection between painter and painted it was Maribel.

That day—it was late afternoon, winter, they were in her bedroom drinking wine, straight from the bottle, taking turns. It was an old house and Maribel kept a cold bedroom; and now, with Gerald gone, the furnace was often on the blink or maybe simply out of fuel. He remembers feeling chilled, sick or about to be, not quite ready to face the music of undressing and making love. She fought him for his sweater but he hung on to it (was it that that set her off?). She was naked, he was fully dressed. The disparity between her nude body and his clothed one should have been seductive; but not today.

Not today. He was under the weather, and she was remorseless; she brought out the drawings, rested the book against her belly as an easel, and began drawing Ninon's face in place of her own. It didn't take all that much work, surprisingly. There was already a strong family resemblance, and the similarities didn't stop with that amazing hair. All she had to do was shorten the nose a bit, fill out the cheeks, and cut a deep dent into that tiny and perfect chin. She left the eyes alone and she didn't touch the body. It took her all of five minutes, ten at the very outside, and it was only when she lined the pages up at the edges and threatened to tear them apart that he came back to life, pried the papers out of her hand, and held them up to his chest like a shield. The likeness was extraordinary. She buried her face in her hands; it was the first time he had ever seen her cry. He remembers his last look at her, on her knees in the unmade bed, with her face in her hands and that nimbus of smoky hair astir with rage and grief.

YES, LIPSCOMB remembers the drawings; even with his eyes all but gone, all you would have to do is put them into his hands and he would read them out loud to you like Braille. He gave them back to her, finally, although he thought under the circumstances they'd be safer in his hands (what if Gerald found them and drew his own conclusions? what if someone got hold of them and tried to blackmail either of them or the girl?). But, after all, they were as much her property as his, and his investment in them was no longer sentimental. Or even erotic, if it came to that; because after that day it was all over but the shouting anyway. Her jealousy had become too much for him, and he thought it might be best for all concerned if he made himself scarce while she went through the last ugly rituals of divorce. He didn't need to be dragged through the mud as corespondent, did he? Let alone tarred with the brush of a portrait painter who made love to his married subjects and seduced their adolescent nieces and hangers-on. Nor, when it was all over, did he want to be the one designated to pick up the pieces. His mother was still alive in those days, and Maddie's husband, Roger, had just died and left her without a cent. It was no time to take on another woman, obviously. Especially a woman like Maribel.

Lipscomb cocks his knees at the ceiling, searching for a painless fit between the head of his right femur and his unyielding acetabula. He silently hums the old Piaf song: *Non, je ne regrette rien.* Strange that those drawings should have resurfaced finally in the fullness of time, though, isn't it? Now that Maribel's dead, Lipscomb is blind, and the girl who caused all the fuss has probably been happily married for years, with an adorable daughter or daughters of her own? If Maribel had had any sense she would have destroyed them after all. His fault, probably, for not letting her go through with it when she'd originally threatened to rip them down the middle, the day he'd walked out of Calpurnia for good. But they were much too beautiful to destroy; and he must have known she'd have held it against him if he'd let her have her way with them.

No, Lipscomb has no regrets; even now life is never as boring as he'd like it to be. Boring enough, however, that he'll have no problem going quietly when his time comes. To this day he's never married, his mother and sister have always been more than family enough and financial burden enough for him. But that's not to say he isn't leaving something behind him in the record, after all: his paintings, for better or for worse. Because although work like his has been out of favor since the sixties, he's lived long enough to know that everything comes back into fashion, given enough time and space. Look at the vogue for Victoriana in the last twenty years. Look at all that resurrected twenties kitsch. He may have to die to get it, but he'll have his crack at immortality yet.

As for Maribel, he wonders how she got on with her work in her declining years. Did she get handier at painting faces? Did she ever break out of that foggy, gray, mystery-making palette of hers? From time to time her name used to surface at certain dinner parties in certain houses he was regularly invited to, but never in the professional circles that he still frequented, and never at any of the local galleries, at least not as far as he knows, and of course Friedrichson's was just a joke. In truth, he'd known that she was sick; his sister Maddie had told him so; but by then it had become second nature to change the subject and shrug the information off.

As for that young woman who visited him yesterday, whatever it was she'd had in mind, she'd made for an interesting change of weather in this increasingly arid and seasonless social season. Because nobody ever visits him nowadays. It's the wages of longevity; all the people who used to see him are either dead or out of it; or else they have their own Miss Oxtobys, their own debt-ridden sisters and significant others who won't let them out of the house. And there's certainly not one of them under the age of sixty, God knows: unless you count the cleaning woman and the half-wits who deliver the weekly crate of booze.

It's interesting, isn't it, though, how much you can tell about a person without seeing them at all: age, for one thing, gender, of course, and the state of their health. As well as personality, obviously, and maybe even character, though that's the hardest; and always was, even with twenty-twenty vision or the aid of a seeing eye dog. Is it something in the way they smell, the timbre of their voices, the galvanic forces in the air that they set off as they go by?

Lipscomb eases his leg into its joint at an unlikely angle and waits for the return signal (yes?—no?) from his brain. It's a fit, a lucky strike, the pain is gone as suddenly as it's come. Out-side an ambulance whinnies its lugubrious hee-haw through the empty streets: but not for him, not tonight at least, thank God. Lipscomb yawns and sighs. He doesn't regret Maribel; he doesn't regret any of them. He doesn't regret those drawings; he doesn't regret not signing them; and he isn't even really dis-pleased that they've come back to haunt him at this late date. It's only the things you don't do that you end up regretting: the women not courted, the paintings not painted, the paths not taken. This is what he should have told that young woman yesterday afternoon. Whoever she was, whatever she looked like; whatever her real intentions finally turned out to be.

Tomorrow he'll sound out Miss Oxtoby on the visitor. He makes a mental note of it: Oxtoby's good at that kind of thing, as she ought to be; she's had good training at his hands. He'll ask her what color hair she had, how tall she was, whether she was fat or thin. He'll ask her whether she was good-looking, and if so, what famous movie star, past or present, she resem-bled most. Either way, in the long run you have to learn to make do with words. Not, he thinks, the ideal medium for describing the human face, but when you get right down to it there's not much choice. Once you go blind, unfortunately, words are all you've got

26

RIVING to Calpurnia for the last time, Elizabeth replays this morning's meeting with Ellios in her mind like someone revisiting the scene of an almost fatal traffic accident: happy to be alive and on the road again but not quite sure she's still intact, that there's nothing broken beyond repair. She doesn't think well on her feet, and never has; when he made his offer she was already halfway out the door with the shopping bag under her arm. Caught by surprise like that, with the car keys in her hands, it didn't occur to her to do anything but turn him down.

He'd offered her twelve thousand dollars for the drawings: a ridiculous sum after Verry's assurance that they were virtually unsalable, and her first reaction, absurd as it might seem, was to feel under personal attack: he was crazy if he thought she was going to let herself fall into his little trap. For the first time since Nina's message on her answering machine she'd felt almost grateful for bad news. "I'm sorry, but I'm afraid the sale's been called off," she said. "It just happened, some family crisis,

I don't know the details. But of course if they ever come back on the market again I'll certainly let you know."

She'd tried to keep her voice as blank as her face; but she doesn't owe him anything, does she? And now, with the drawings back in hand after a quick cup of coffee with him at Thirtieth Street Station, he doesn't owe her anything either: they're quits. He's on his way to Brussels on some mysterious mission having to do with computer chips; she can't remember how long he said he was staying away. "Well, I won't keep you," she'd said. She doesn't care if or when she ever sees him again, and had made it a point not to ask him when he was scheduled to get back. She'd only gone to New York with him, after all, accepted an invitation to lunch, let him pay for her train fare back and forth. But business is business, and they're both grown-ups, aren't they? She's still her own person, twelve thousand dollars or no.

Still: twelve thousand dollars. Looked at one way it's over ten months' worth of carrying charges on the apartment; or, alternatively, the first installment on Robin's tuition, due in September, with even a little left over to buy a new dress for David's visit in August: and twelve thousand dollars doesn't exactly grow on trees. Not in Elizabeth's life; at least not anymore. And surely every woman has her price?

Elizabeth closes the door behind her and tugs it to make sure it's locked. In hindsight she might have played the scene differently: stalled him, put him off. But faced with a choice Elizabeth defaults to virtue as if there were no other options available; it's an unthinking reflex, the paragon's easy way out. If she were a better businesswoman she would have told him she'd get back to him, buying time to work through all the possibilities in her head later when she's alone and undistracted by his face and the sound of his voice. Twelve thousand dollars would have gone at least part of the way toward restoring the lost bounty from the sale, and chances are no one would ever have been the wiser about the drawings anyway. What on earth would it have cost her to hand them over and hang the Carraccis back up on the powder-room wall without them, after all? How many people (if any, with Maribel gone) would even know the difference? In retrospect it's all too obvious. Anyone else in their right minds would have sold the drawings to Ellios for whatever the traffic would bear and gone their merry way.

Instead she's on her way to Calpurnia, drawings and Carraccis in hand; the final trip to Maribel's, the overdue farewell. She still has the key, so they can hardly accuse her of breaking and entering, and in any case she wants to say good-bye to Peg, tie up whatever loose ends Clemmie's left in the kitchen, hang the pictures back up where they belong, and leave with her integrity, at least, intact. Then worry about the sordid details later (Robin's vacation; David's visit; money in the bank).

Is it a trick of the light or have the magnolias at the river's edge begun to bloom a second time around in this ridiculously unseasonable heat? Elizabeth starts to think seriously of the months ahead, no longer mentally postponable. She had counted on rounding out Robin's fall tuition from her mother's money market account and the various hidden extras she foresaw from the sale: Maribel's trousseau lingerie, the little nineteenth-century Aubusson in the third-floor hall that no one but Elizabeth seems to have been even remotely aware was there.

Elizabeth hates asking Douglas for money. Will the day ever come when she doesn't have to worry about paying the bills, Robin's tuition, a year's worth of living expenses safely squirreled away? There are times when Elizabeth thinks everyone in the world is rich but her. She follows the hedges of Weavers Way past the by now familiar houses, all but hidden in their green stockades of privet and well-trimmed box, but the big stone urns on either side of Calpurnia's front door are full of last year's dead annuals and striped tropical grasses that have survived neither this winter nor the one before. On the evidence Maribel may have loved her garden, but only from a distance, and never enough to get down on her hands and knees and actually go to work in it. Like Elizabeth, it suddenly dawns on her, Maribel had struggled to make ends meet.

Elizabeth rounds the curve at Peg's tennis court and pulls in under the porte cochere: from the corner it's clear that she has the driveway to herself. Now that she has the hang of it the key turns easily, almost servilely, in the lock, and inside the house the silence is like a familiar tune; until she steps on a starburst of broken glass beside the telephone table, with a sound like a small explosion going off. Overhead the electrified gasolier hangs by a single wire. The rug has been wadded into an unkempt bundle by the front door, its waffled green underlay torn almost exactly down the center. Elizabeth comes to a halt just outside the living-room door, face-to-face with the large blank space above the couch. They've taken the portrait down, finally. It's as if the last living thing in the house is gone.

Everything else being equal it's always best to leave things shipshape. Clemmie took off in a great and understandable hurry on Tuesday, with most of the silver still unpolished and dishes still unwashed, and people judge you by the messes you make, not by the order you impose; but Calpurnia's not really Elizabeth's responsibility anymore: let the museum people deal with the minutiae, if and when they finally sort things out with the heirs.

In the powder room she yanks at the masking tape jamming

the strikebox, then inches her way in and down the steps. This is always the darkest room in the house and midway through this sunny morning it's still deep dusk down here under the stairs. For a moment Elizabeth mistakes the ghosts of the absent Carraccis on the wall for the real thing and feels her pulse start to race uncomfortably. It's as if the pictures have hung themselves back up on the walls at their own remembered distances to one another without any help from her, and it takes her another full moment to realize that the walls are really bare. She unpacks her fraying shopping bag and reinserts the Lipscomb drawings back to back with the Carraccis, then wipes what she thinks of as her fingerprints from the frames. One by one the pictures resume their rightful positions on the stair wall, self-effacing, black-and-white, safe in their dignified debauchery.

Elizabeth lowers the toilet lid and straightens the mirror above the sink. Shameless, she supposes, but she feels like a criminal reprieved. And good riddance: because she's turned down a rather small fortune for them and they're off her conscience now, back where they belong. Sweating in the aftermath of her tiny crime, she washes her hands at the chipped white oval sink and takes a last look at the powder room, reversed in the crazed Venetian glass. The mirror hangs at a slight angle from its little hook; Elizabeth tilts it a half inch to the left and even less to the right but it's still out of plumb, as if the hook itself is in some kind of perverse harmony with the spill of paper guest towels and stemless flower heads on the littered floor. From where she stands the Carraccis in their gilded frames form the only true verticals in the room and Deianira's face as she grips Hercules' erect member under its blue-black but not quite opaque banner is wide-eyed and serene.

She's done what she's come to do, and nobody's caught her

in the act, but at the last minute there's perhaps something too squared off and shipshape in the prints' progression up the stair wall compared to the mess underfoot. It's none of her business anymore, and she surely doesn't owe any of them anything, least of all Nina, but after all that's happened it doesn't seem quite right to simply hang them there the way she found them however many weeks ago and simply walk away. Instead, one by one, she takes each picture off the wall, loosens Lipscomb's drawings a little from the wooden backings, and pulls them up, ever so carefully, just a little past the top edge of the frames. It's her message to whoever finds them (Nina, presumably)—Caution: proceed at your own risk; these simple naughty antique pictures aren't exactly what they seem. It's the only way she can think of, when the chips are down, to give Nina a sporting chance.

In the kitchen, Elizabeth dries Clemmie's well-soaked china and puts it back in the cupboard over the stove. She tidies the counter and the tabletop and rescues one last silver serving dish and a pair of blackish salad tongs from the soapy sink. Polishing Maribel's meat platter for whoever comes after her and stacking her Meissen, Elizabeth tells herself she's gotten off easier than she had any right to expect. Tonight she'll call them all and deliver her official farewells: Nina, Roberto, Friedrichson, and Peg. She'll do what she has to do; deal with Clemmie and Clemmie's truck-driving brother-in-law, decide how to turn it all into an amusing story for David if and when he comes, leave the keys with Peachy and put in a call to Douglas in Sacramento; then figure out how to tighten her belt and survive the summer on whatever cash she can muster up. She'll find some way to get through the months ahead: call Mrs. Bright to see if she's ready to sell those nautical prints of hers, work up a flyer for the retirement homes, write something for one of the art and collectibles rags. She'll make ends meet; she always has; this isn't the end of the world. She has to stop thinking about the twelve thousand dollars on offer for Lipscomb's drawings. She'll put Calpurnia behind her and get on with things. She never has to see Ellios again.

27

THE SECRET of Peg's success as a gardener is that she loves to weed. There's something retributive in pulling up ragweed or shepherd's purse that appeals to the muckraking side of her nature and makes her feel that justice is being done. Even though she suspects she's getting much too old for it; her knees are worse every year and her back isn't what it used to be either. One of these days she's going to have the gardener plant hostas in all the flower beds: no more annuals, no more snapdragons and scarlet sage. As for the daffodils and peonies, next year they're on their own, and if and when she wants flowers she'll just go on down to Albrecht's and put in an order, like all those other old women in their pitiful two-bedroom condominiums up and down Montgomery Avenue, raising geraniums on their balconies in summertime and making do with fake grape ivy in winter to keep things green.

When it comes to flowers Peg has no real local competition now. Old Mrs. Archibald's death (was it forty years ago?) took the fun out of the bravura plantings women used to go in for in those days, and Maribel herself could take her mother's damn roses or leave them alone. As for Coby, he couldn't have cared less, now or then, so why knock herself out? It's enough of a job just looking after him till he gets back on his feet, forget about the flowers. And anyway, gardening is for the young; you need a strong back and sturdy knees, not to mention good eyes and a decent sense of smell: otherwise, what would be the point? Maribel never painted flowers: she couldn't be bothered with something that lived and died so fast. Maribel was an indoor person anyway, not made for sweat or child rearing or fresh air. Well, you can't be good at everything at once. And being a good mother was never high on Maribel's list of things to be.

Enough said. Coby's stirring in the kitchen, Peg hears the cabinet doors opening and closing: he's looking for something suitable to put his coffee in. Left to his own devices, drugs or no drugs (and isn't coffee a kind of drug?), he never gets up much before noon, and that's all right with Peg. Lunch is easier than breakfast anyway. You can get more meat into a person at lunch, and vegetables, solid stuff. Peg knows all about the care and feeding of substance abusers. Justin was a wonderful man but a serious drinker of the old school and Coby drinks beer for breakfast; Peg's a specialist on the nutrition of people who live on alcohol and thin air.

Coby appears to have found the coffee, and she's left the sugar out in its bright yellow box on the kitchen counter because the boy has a sweet tooth that would kill a lesser man. Peg takes what pleasure she can from knowing there's always something in the cookie jar for him; as long as he's here he must know he'll be fed, looked after, and sheltered in all the obvious ways. And sooner or later he's bound to get over this bad patch; his clothes will be cleaned and pressed, he'll get some meat back on his bones; the nightmares will subside.

Peg knows all about nightmares, her own and other people's

too. She and Maribel had burned the midnight oil, widow and grass widow, together or separately, for years. Maribel couldn't or wouldn't take the painkillers that the oncologist finally prescribed for her and sometimes instead got up in the wee hours and went upstairs to paint, while on a really bad night you'd see lights burning all over the house till she finally knocked herself out with drink and over-the-counter cough medicine. Until the night the lights stayed on all night, shining into Peg's bedroom window like the midnight sun. So that by now the darkness on the other side of the hedge is a kind of night blindness, or a sudden blackout like the onset of old age. She and Maribel have been through a lot together, and you can always make new friends, yes; but what about the old ones? Peg does her crying behind closed doors. When you get to be as old as Peg, there are no promises that tomorrow is necessarily going to be another day. Let alone a better one.

Turning right to weed her way back to the shed Peg sees Coby on the kitchen steps, naked to the waist, his chest as hairless as the day he was born, with that bright red coffee mug he likes so much in one hand and an unlit cigarette in the other. She waves her pruners at him and bumps her knee pads forward; he'd never offer to help in a million years, but she's glad for the company even so.

"They say all you need for a good garden is patience," she says, reaching for a clump of spotted spurge, "but don't let them fool you. Impatience is more like it, especially when it comes to the weeds."

Coby yawns. "Coffee's a little on the light side today, isn't it?" he says.

"If I drank as much coffee as you do I'd be a nervous wreck," says Peg. "Wait till you're as old as I am, and you'll see."

"Oh, great," says Coby. "I can't wait."

She's cleared a weed-free patch through the ivy to the juniper, throwing her harvest of wild grape and perfumed ragweed onto the drive where the gardener can sweep it up tomorrow when he comes. "Here, give me a hand up," she says, down on her knees just a yard or two from Coby's bare feet, "and tell me what you want for lunch."

Coby gets up, straightening his back, unkinking his legs, taking his own sweet time. He's about the same height as Mikey was but not as big in the shoulders; face-to-face with him that reedy body of his is always a surprise.

"I don't know. What's on the menu?" he says.

She dusts dirt from her knees and peels off her rubberized canvas gloves. He's bigger and healthier than she's seen him look in years, and she wishes Maribel were here to take a look: the peeling nose and brown forearms; the springy hair and sun-bleached beard; Peg's doing; her own personal work of art. She runs down the list of available items for him: hamburger (ground round) or creamed chipped beef on toast, or an omelette with shredded cheese; but knows better than to mention vegetables or fruit. As a child Coby was raised on spaghetti and peanut butter; even after she was divorced and the money ran out Maribel never learned how to cook.

Coby lifts his red mug and drains it. "Can we talk about this some other time?" he says. "I'm not sure I'm all that hungry now."

"You're never hungry," says Peg. "Go look at yourself in the mirror. Your mother would never forgive me if I let you starve."

He says, "I try not to look at myself in mirrors, and since when did Maribel care whether anyone starved or not?" It's supposed to be a joke, presumably. Peg watches him stir what's left of his coffee with his finger, like someone poking at tea leaves for omens. He stares at the dregs. "You were there the night she died, weren't you?" he says.

Peg sticks her pruners in the pocket of her overalls to anchor them. "Who told you that?" she says.

"I can't remember."

The pruners shift and stab her in the groin; she takes them out and puts them on the kitchen window ledge. "Well, whoever they were, they told you wrong," she says. Her voice is sharper than she means it to be (after all I've done for him? she thinks). "I only went over there to let Giles in," she says, "because Nina couldn't find her keys. And where were you that night, if you want to get personal about things?" It's the $64,000 question, and she regrets asking it the minute it's out of her mouth.

"At home in bed," Coby says. "Ask Nina. Ask Dr. Giles. At home asleep. Where the hell was I supposed to be?"

Peg says, "I'm right here. You don't have to yell."

They stand face-to-face across a yard and a half of flaking brick, looking at each other's feet. The silence is as thick as water, dense, unbreathable, and Coby's the first to break it. "Giles signed the death certificate, didn't he?" he says. "And everyone knows how sick she was. There'd have to have been an autopsy otherwise."

Peg takes two steps to the left and puts her hand on the railing. She's damned if she'll be browbeaten, and especially not by him. Acting as if he's not there she simply steps around him and mounts the kitchen stairs, careful of her knees. She remembers the night Maribel died with shriveling clarity. She'd let Giles in, then gone back outside, not wanting to be seen hovering ghoulishly at the bedside in case Maribel was still alive. She remembers standing on the terrace between those two urns in front of the house in a circle of pale daybreak, listening for sounds of life.

Coby follows her into the kitchen. "They say she died in her sleep," he says, in such a small tight voice that it sounds like a question or perhaps a wish.

"If she died in her sleep then why were all the lights blazing all over the house like that?" says Peg.

"Maybe she took a pill," he says. "And fell asleep before she could turn them off."

"Well, maybe she did," says Peg.

She retrieves her pruners from the ledge and hangs them up on the pegboard in the mud room, feeling blindly for the right hook between the big straw hat she never remembers to wear and the rawhide gauntlets she uses to prune the holly and roses with. The word *pills* hangs there between them like the echo of a pistol shot.

It's not even noon but Peg's tired and her knees are killing her; she takes off her rubber gardening clogs and lines them up to dry under the potting shelf, then folds back her sleeves and washes her hands and forearms under the faucet in the big square soapstone sink. There's poison ivy in that bed by the compost heap, but if you wash it off with soap and water within the hour they say you can ward off the itch. Peg doesn't know much about cancer but she knows that Maribel's had already gone to the bone; pills or no pills, the pain had to be pretty bad. She soaps meticulously around her wrists and under her rings. She's taking no chances; you can't help whether you get cancer or not, obviously, but poison ivy is preventable. Though either way there's no known cure. Once you've got it you've got it, and that's that.

"Giles wasn't looking for pills," she says, "at least not that I know of, anyway. Or if he was, he kept it under his hat." She takes a fresh dish towel from the top of the pile beside the sink and dries off her arms, like someone drying fine china, inside and out. She takes a deep breath. "And if you know anything whatsoever about it yourself, and I'm not saying you do, but if you were *my* son, anyway, I'd advise you to do the same."

He looks at her, and looks away; and then, instead of simply parking his mug on the drainboard the way he usually does, unrinsed, steps up to the sink, spurts dishwasher detergent into it, and goes through the motions of washing it out and rinsing it himself. He's not her son, but he was once one of her son Mikey's most faithful hangers-on, and must still know how any son of hers had been expected to behave. Peg doesn't want him to tell her what he was doing there that night. She tells herself she doesn't know and doesn't care whether Maribel killed herself or not. If she did that was Maribel's business, not Coby's; and certainly not Peg's.

"Don't be so hard on yourself," she says at last, handing him a dish towel, watching him ram it clumsily into the mug. "And stop asking people questions, me or anyone else. I look at it this way: you're young; you've got your whole life ahead of you." She takes the mug out of his hands and starts all over again with a dry dish towel, setting him a good example, showing him how to do it right. "Look, Coby, you're going to be fine," she says. "Just take my word for it. Everything is going to be all right."

28

ALL BY herself at Calpurnia for the first time in weeks, Nina feels mysteriously unalone; turning into the drive, unlocking the balky front door, raising the shades, turning on the fan, it feels as if Maribel were still alive in here somewhere. That intense quiet has a personal quality, not watchful so much as receptive, a house on standby for the sight of arriving guests. Nina can't begin to count the times she has driven up this driveway, rung this bell, or turned her key in this lock as Maribel's official protégée and grown-up daughter of the house. Her own mother never understood her, but Maribel had traveled in Europe; she owned a Schiaparelli evening dress and a Hermès bag; she had been on speaking terms with Misia Sert and Bakst.

Nina doesn't know artists and she has never aspired to be one herself, but it isn't true, as she used to tell Maribel, that she has no eye for art. On the contrary, as a child she spent hours with her head buried in picture books and, later, *Vogue* and *Harper's Bazaar*: and not just for the clothes. Nina can't draw a straight line and never pretended she could, but she has always known how to express herself—through her clothes, for example, and her decor, the things she buys for her shop, the way she sets her table, the colors she paints her walls. Because we can't all be artists, can we? Some of us have to live our art, make it up as we go along out of whatever we come across in the course of the day's work. Nina's spent the whole morning unpacking boxes from Alphabeta and Good Graces, logging in merchandise for processing, and hanging things up on the garment rack for steaming. None of this is exactly what you'd call fine art, and she's hopeless about the paperwork, but if she doesn't do it, let's face it, it just doesn't get done. Or, if and when it does get done, things tend to disappear. Which is of course the nature of the beast. You hire these great-looking women as salesgirls and then they fall in love with the stuff and start to help themselves.

Nina slides the big bracelet back on her wrist, its dozen keys jangling like enormous charms, conscious now that there will come a day soon when she won't have automatic access anymore, when her key will no longer necessarily fit Calpurnia's lock. She's resigned to that; she supposes she even looks forward to it in a way. Nina has her own house to come home to now, and it's much bigger and by many people's standards much better appointed than Maribel's ever was, at least within living memory. Though Maribel would have been the last person in the world to see it that way, probably; because, in all fairness, money never meant anything to Maribel. And why should it? Growing up she'd never had to go without. Once you're born to money you never stop feeling rich.

The house is a shambles now. Elizabeth's handiwork, partly, and Coby's delivered the coup de grâce. In the living room nothing is where it's supposed to be except the sofa with its little suite of encircling chairs: Elizabeth has moved all the prints and smaller artwork into the dining room to make room for whatever occasional furniture she deems to be of most interest to the dealers she's been parading through the house. For reasons of her own Elizabeth must have wanted all the furniture people in one room, the picture people in another; it's probably her scheme for keeping them out of each other's hair. And on the whole Nina has tried to stay out of her way, because the woman clearly knows her business, and far be it from Nina to tell her how to display a decrepit lampshade or showcase some bedraggled bibelot. Still, there's something doleful in this hodgepodge of things unrelated by custom or intent, where mirrors reflect empty mirrors and long-standing relationships between the tables and chairs have come to a sudden end. Disconnected from each other and taken out of context like that, they look unfamiliar and disowned; no longer Maribel's, they could be anyone's.

The living room is no place to go looking for lost objects anyway; much too formal and in its way too bare; Nina can't even remember seeing Maribel in here except at Christmas or interviewing maids or entertaining friends and pseudo-friends. By the last ten years of her life she practically lived in her studio at the top of the stairs; it was where she entertained guests, talked on the phone, ate her meals, and paid her bills. The library though, after all these weeks, still exerts its childish pull on Nina. It's where she once found a fifty-dollar bill in a volume of her grandfather's *Encyclopaedia Britannica,* and an unmailed, unaddressed love letter in Maribel's handwriting (to Lipscomb, probably) in the space between two drawers of Maribel's desk. An artist's letter, full of stuff about colors and light: there was a time, years ago (more years than she cares to remember), when Nina knew every line by heart. And it was here, even further back in time, that she found those drawings in the big black portfolio with its intricately knotted ties. The portfolio's still here, or one exactly like it, full of innocent Kathe Kollwitz prints now, waiting for a buyer at Elizabeth's called-off sale.

The library is lined with matching bookcases, oak brown, disemboweled of their books; Elizabeth has boxed the first editions and leather-bound volumes for auction and left the others unsorted on the floor, then rounded up what's left from Maribel's bedroom and elsewhere, and piled them two and three deep on the empty shelves. Nina shrugs her way out of the straps of her heavy shoulder bag and sits down to wait for the security people to arrive. She's given it her best shot, because she promised Hugh she would, but if there's still a hidden gold mine in here waiting to be found, too bad: someone else will have to dig it out. Because it's now or never; she's given herself this one last chance. Nina's finished at Calpurnia. Coby's rampage was the last straw. Enough is enough. Life must go on.

Nina puts her bag on the windowsill next to Maribel's paperbacks and back issues of *ARTnews* and *Vanity Fair,* with their antique dates and curling subscription labels. Composing herself on the window seat to catch her breath and watch for arriving cars is like stepping back in time; she remembers waiting here for Maribel to come downstairs, acutely but deliciously self-conscious in her navy blue schoolgirl's uniform with her legs pulled up to her chin, playing the part she thought had been assigned to her: golden girl, court favorite, Cinderella waiting for the ball. From the open window she can see the dense rhododendron thickets that will outlast them all, where she used to go looking for Coby until he got too old for hide-and-seek and went off through the hedge to Peg's for a game of catch or what have you with Mikey, leaving Nina alone with Maribel and all her noisy friends.

The security people are late, but Nina doesn't care; not yet, anyway: she actually likes it when people overstep as long as they don't go too far, because that way they know they're in the wrong and it makes them try harder the next time around. But it's hot in the window seat and Nina's restless; waiting for the sound of their car, she makes the rounds of the first floor from the library to the dining room, from the dining room to the hall. Someone has been at work out here, at least halfheartedly, sweeping broken glass into a little pile, scrubbing uselessly at the stains; and the pictures have all been stacked and tagged; there's even a sticker on the telephone, testament to Elizabeth's thoroughness. Another loose end to be tied up, because one way or another the woman will want to be paid for all the time she's put in so far. Hugh's been against the sale from day one, of course, and all the more so now with Coby running amok; he doesn't even have to say he told her so. Though on second thought, once the new alarms are installed, what's really the point of putting it off? There's nothing of real value left to break or steal, but what there is still has to be dealt with even so: you can't just leave it to Ibby's museum committee to throw it out. And knowing Julia Romaine, the brains behind the committee, it'll be in the contract somewhere anyway. But the last thing Nina wants, God knows, is to have Julia going through Maribel's things. Those ghastly pictures must still be here somewhere after all these years because Maribel never threw anything away and the idea of Julia's finding them is unthinkable. And just exactly how else does Hugh expect her to get rid of all this stuff?

The powder-room door looks closed but it isn't; the tape over the strikeplate has been peeled back—Coby's work, probably. Nina pokes her head in the door; she sees the cockeyed mirror, and the remains of her own ancient dried-flower arrangement. Whoever may have tried to straighten up in here must have stopped at the powder room, where everything's out of kilter and the only things that still line up properly are those three idiotic prints on the staircase wall: various gods and goddesses of Maribel's flaming youth in an assortment of roguish poses that Nina once knew by heart. She pauses at the top of the stairs: Is this something that would strike a stylish note in one of the dressing rooms at her shop? Or just the opposite, with everybody and their lawyers bringing her up on charges for obscenity and vice? Assuming Hugh would even let her hang them in the first place, which she doubts. Nina reaches for the last print in line to give it a closer look, and notices a quarter of an inch of ragged parchment paper sticking out at the top.

There's something familiar about the deckled edge of the paper, or so she will tell herself in retrospect, forever after: she pushes at the paper, trying to jam it back down behind the glass, then pulls at it instead; until the drawing below it comes crookedly out of the frame.

It's eighty-eight degrees in the shade outside, but Nina sits down hard on the powder-room steps with the gilt-framed Carracci in her lap, trembling, a little cold. She must have been in and out of the powder room at least three times since Maribel died, and God knows how many times in all the years before—checking to make sure the window is locked, the toilet working or not working, the lights on or off: she must have walked past these prints literally a hundred times without giving them a second glance. Not since adolescence, when she used to point them out to her girlfriends at parties and tennis matches, giggling, making them promise not to tell, has she even bothered to look at them close up; and wouldn't, probably, have looked at them today, except that they had seemed so unaccountably upright in the midst of all this chaos, so mysteriously and uniquely plumb.

And there they were. And here she is. These infamous and shameful forgeries! And, behind them, paydirt: the end of the treasure hunt. By some miracle she's stumbled across them, and without half looking, as she always knew she would: even after all these months. Those ancient tale-telling drawings, undestroyed, preserved for posterity by Maribel, who never threw anything away.

The powder room's a mess, but it doesn't matter: inside Nina's head there's a sense of sudden order, lost and found. She sits with the drawings in her lap, all three of them, shocking in their fidelity to her memory of them after all these years, back to back with the rakish Carraccis whose cockeyed classicism now seems like an ironic gloss on them, a detached and giddy aside. Nina believes in luck, her own as much as anyone's, but this is almost too lucky to be true, and she has to sit down to let it sink in. She's known in her heart of hearts all these years that Maribel would never destroy them, no matter what promises she made so many years ago. (Vanity, for one thing; and love for another: she must have kept every single scribble or pen stroke that Lipscomb had ever made.) Well, Nina's the same age now that Maribel was then; and Lipscomb's skill at getting a likeness didn't end, obviously, at the face and neck. Though a few more years and that body would no longer be worth recording: a few more years and she would have had to start undressing, as Nina does now, in the dark. But Lipscomb had spared her that: he'd caught her and put her down on paper in her prime, with maybe only a year or so to spare.

Nina mops her forehead with the last guest towel on the

rack; it must be a hundred degrees in here and she might as well be running a fever anyway. Outside the sun beats down on the skylight, cooking the wallpaper where it sags away from the plaster in the hall, and in broad daylight you can see every crack in the ceiling, every chip in the ancient paint. After the divorce Maribel never spent a dime on upkeep or even simple housekeeping at Calpurnia, but the house was built like a fortress and the neglect took years to show. People had stopped visiting in the daytime by then anyway, and after a while they stopped visiting altogether, period. Lipscomb had put an end to the so-called tea parties and tennis matches, but Maribel tired of the poets and millionaires and surrealists on her own. And the older she got the harder she worked, even though all she ever painted was the same thing over and over again, theme and variation, those mysteriously empty rooms that seemed to Nina to get emptier and emptier as time went on.

Nina loved Maribel. How could you not love someone who lavished so much time on you, took you anywhere and every-where she went, dressed you to the nines, turned day into night with possibility and suspense? Maribel was a dark fairy god-mother inviting you to an endless ball, and Nina saw Lipscomb as the price she had to pay for Maribel's company; until, in the end, there were just the three of them, up there on the third floor in Maribel's studio, eating take-out Chinese vegetables and drinking cheap champagne.

Lipscomb had no use for aesthetes and freeloaders; he liked people who paid their own way, as well as his—and with one or two exceptions he had a bad word to say for everybody; even Maribel was not exempt. Nina sat speechless as he told her to her face that her painting was unfocused, her colors muddy, her line slippery and unconvinced. Lipscomb challenged Maribel to paint her niece's face. You've known her from the day she was born, he said; if you couldn't paint Nina, how could you ever dream of painting anyone?

Nina's eye for pictures isn't that seasoned, it was never and will never be acute; looking at the drawings today she's still not sure which of those dueling draftsmen drew her face on Maribel's nude body, or why. Was it Lipscomb who performed this malicious trick, on a dare from Maribel? Or Maribel defending herself against his nastiness the only way she knew? Nina's not an artist but she's not a psychologist either. All she can do is guess.

Lipscomb must be an old man by now—assuming he's even still alive. Nina tries to picture him as he was then—already past his prime, that long elegant face with the mouth bowed upward in one corner in its permanent semi-sneer, offset by perfect manners and unpainterly spic and span. He had a handsome, bony head, long hands (artistic hands, she thought then) with, for a painter, unaccountably well-kept fingernails. At that age she couldn't see past his correctitude to his lechery; at least not until she found herself down on paper with her hand between her legs, some ugly old man's wish of his come true. He left the drawings unsigned, but did they really need a signature? It was one of those open secrets, and Gerald must have seen them too: it was said to be the reason he had finally asked Maribel for a divorce. And Nina, who had never in the fourteen years of her short life till then ever dared to touch herself like that, not even to wash down there or stick a tampon in, remembered the drawings in the middle of the night, and taught herself what everyone else already seemed to know about her body and its secrets without ever having to spell it out.

Of course Maribel hung on to the drawings; of course she

didn't destroy them; how could she? They were like love letters, with or without Nina's face on them, and Nina knows as well as anyone that no woman in her right mind ever throws old love letters away. Especially when, with a nasty divorce in the offing, Lipscomb had finally stopped coming to Weavers Way; then stopped calling her on the telephone; then stopped taking her around. Afraid of lawsuits, probably. Afraid of offending his rich relatives and richer friends; afraid of losing commissions once the husbands had heard about what went on behind their backs in Maribel's studio.

Well, Nina survived; the drawings stayed hidden and she married Hugh; things have a way of always turning out for the best, and she's back to normal now. Her heart has stopped racing, and her hands have stopped shaking; she feels as if she's begun to draw her first real lungfuls of fresh air since Maribel's death, and she wonders what gods and goddesses to thank for the fact that Coby missed these drawings on his rampage through the house. A close escape; but Nina has always been lucky: it's her secret weapon. Nina was raised in the church but it makes her nervous when people ask her if she believes in God; whereas luck is something that you either have or you don't, like twenty-twenty vision or perfect pitch, and Nina has always had it in spades. She was born that way. You have to be, her mother said, if you aren't born rich.

The powder room's a mess and Nina sets to work straightening the towels on their rods, refolding them in thirds at the creases, putting things back where they belong: the same straw flowers in the same basket under the sink; the same pink soap-buds in the soap dish; the same fruity potpourri in the cut-glass bowl on the étàgere. Little things like this can get to you; if you'd let them they could break your heart. The water in the toilet bowl is rusty and the potpourri has lost much of its smell;

she remembers standing at the little Venetian mirror washing rouge off her cheeks and mascara off her eyelashes at Maribel's command. She remembers arranging these flowers in this basket for Maribel to cheer her up the day some friend of hers almost died in a car crash in Berwyn. She remembers locking herself in the powder room with the dry heaves the day that Lipscomb asked her to pose for him privately at his studio in Franklin Square.

Nina remembers every inch of this house as if she has been born here: every lamp on every table, every picture on every wall; up to and including the naked gods and goddesses on the stairs behind her, and Maribel's raucous divorce, and all that nonsense in the papers about her collection of naughty books. Alone in this house where so much of her life, her real life, has been lived, Nina shuts the powder-room door behind her and takes one last look around the familiar living room. Lipscomb's portrait of Maribel is gone, and good riddance; presumably Coby's taken it, and so much the better. The painting is rightfully his and it never came close to doing Maribel justice anyway. Because with all his genius for faces, and his supposedly all-seeing eye, what did Lipscomb really see, either of Nina or of Maribel? At this late date she understands what she never did before: that he'd misread Maribel as profoundly as he'd misread Nina's schoolgirl crush on him. As a painter he might be famous for the likenesses he got, but when it came to the person inside the face you could see he was someone who would always get everything completely wrong.

OUTSIDE on the drive there's the sound of a car churning the gravel on the other side of the gate, heading for the porte cochere. Nina goes to the window; it's the security people at long last, three of them, men in gray suits with clipboards and briefcases under their arms. She should go to the door and let them in, but they've already started walking up and down around the front of the house, looking up at the third-floor windows, taking notes, getting the lay of the land.

For a moment she feels like a princess locked in a tower, primed for rescue but not quite ready yet. Because there's still all this unfinished business at Calpurnia: Coby's blood; the broken glass in the hall, the studio, the books, the sale. And once the security system is back up and running again, does it still make much sense to call off the sale? Either way the furniture has got to go; she'll have Ibby and Julia Romaine on her back from now till doomsday otherwise. Not to mention the trash, the papers, the pots and pans. Elizabeth Oliver's owed money for the time she's already put in anyway; and now that the drawings are back in Nina's hands, what earthly difference does it make who goes poking through what's left of Maribel's life, or anyone else's, in her dusty closet shelves and balky bureau drawers?

29

OBY LIES with his head to the wall in Peg's best guest room. It's as dark as he can make it in here; the heavy white moiré shades, pulled down to their full length and weighted with books and knickknacks at the bottom, hide a view of the tennis courts and Calpurnia's back terrace, still in pale shadow till the sun crosses the roofline at noon. He faces away from the view and away from the even more intimate reproach of Lipscomb's portrait, which Peg has kindly (or otherwise?) had carried up to the guest room for his sake. Where, if he's not careful, it's the first thing Coby sees when he opens his eyes in the morning, and the last thing he's likely to look at before he turns out the light at night. The painting takes up the better part of the facing wall, poised at an awkward angle on the huge double dresser, hiding the matching mirror and several lithographs of exotic species of monkeys and apes in their native habitats on either side.

Coby can't stand the sight of it; has never been able to stand the sight of it. For years he refused to bring friends home from school because of it. Long before he caught on to the stories about Maribel and Lipscomb he hated the painting, starting with his own four-year-old baby face in the left-hand corner and ending with the reflection of Maribel's silly smile in the center of the shield on the right. People say Lipscomb's likenesses are uncanny but to Coby's eye there's little or nothing in that painting of the Maribel he knew, and he can't understand why the damn thing is so widely admired. Not that he cares at this late date: why should he? The painting means nothing to him anymore; it's just something to put on the market and sell. Something expensive and disposable: a windfall waiting to ripen and drop. One of these days he'll get his ass in gear, go downtown, and start scouting out galleries, get estimates, figure out how to put out the word that it's for sale. He can't stay here at Peg's forever. Even Coby's capable of seeing that.

Nina knows something about the missing pictures in the powder room, Coby's sure of it. Last night she phoned him to tell him the sale's back on again, in that fruity voice of hers, and, more important, he supposes, to make sure he knows that she's having a new security system installed: a word to the wise.

"I put in a call to Elizabeth Oliver last night," she said. "The estate lady, you met her; the blonde. Hugh's reconsidered and Conrad seems to agree; the Sotheby's auction isn't until November, this way there'll be at least a little cash flowing almost immediately, and I know you can use the money. Well, of course; I mean, can't we all? There's a new alarm system, infrared, state of the art, they're coming tomorrow; the least little thing will set it off. So do be sure to let me know if there's anything you still want up there, because it's now or never, Coby, and I'll have someone put it aside for you. It rings at police headquarters in Ardmore. You wouldn't want to set all those bells and whistles off."

"Put aside what?" said Coby.

He'd had one ear cocked to what Nina was telling him and one to the replays of the day's events at Wimbledon: the roar of the polite British crowd as Lendl battered the top-seeded French hotshot into the left corner of the court. He's always hated that tone in Nina's voice (fussy and reasonable, mother knows best) but he'd gotten her message loud and clear: don't try to get past the new security system or there'll be hell to pay. Hugh's idea, probably, but so what. There's nothing left at Calpurnia that Coby wants anyway.

"How on earth should I know what?" Nina had said. "Some token, or whatever; some remembrance of things past? Unless of course you've already taken whatever it is you wanted, without signing for it with Hugh, the way we all agreed."

"I haven't taken shit," Coby said, and cringed at the sound of his own voice; Nina always brings out the worst in him.

"Well, just let me know either way," she said, "and I'll make sure there's someone there to let you in."

It was her parting shot: Nina will call somebody to let him into his own house, the house where he was born and raised. From Peg's guest-room window he watches the slightly crooked line drawn by the sun on Calpurnia's northern wall, white on white. No, this time Coby is calling it quits. He's been in and out of the villa at least eight times since the funeral, not including his first panicky search the day after the night she died. Since then he's combed through the second-floor bathroom cabinets four times, the powder room twice; he's checked every pocket in every jacket, dress, sweater, shirt, or coat of Maribel's he could find, and there isn't a closet he hasn't gone through at least once, alone at night or even in broad daylight, with or without the estate liquidator, Liz (Elizabeth), bustling around somewhere downstairs. In her presence he's always tried to look self-effacing, plausible, the son of the house, and Elizabeth is always polite, but he can tell from the look in her eye that at the very least she must think he's some kind of nut. Not that there aren't a lot of people out there who wouldn't agree with her on that, and not that he totally disagrees with her himself.

Coby knows what people say about him: the fuckup, the bad boy, the dreamer, the schemer: someone who knows someone who can get you anything you want. Including, if you want out, the pills to make a painless end of it if and when you decide the time has come. Not a bad rap to have, he'd have thought once upon a time. Because who wouldn't like to make people happy, bring them together either to party or to put them out of their misery, whichever their hearts desire?

Coby knows people from every walk of life and some of them owe him favors, he could call in his chips whenever he wants, and someday he will, but right now he doesn't have the energy. His mother's death has left him hanging in a way that vaguely threatens to become permanent. It's not that he misses her or even remembers what it was they talked about, if anything, because unless you could talk painting and painters to Maribel she never had much to say to you at all. Still, their silences were companionable, and even Maribel liked a little company at the end of the day. Drinking company, driving company, dinner company; and she always picked up the tab. People seeing them together on the road would have said she was a loving mother, Coby a loving son.

Peg's big-screen TV is a treat to watch tennis on, and Coby drinks up and waits for the beer to buzz him. Trying to bring Maribel back into focus he counts the qualities that he loved in her, carefully, like someone counting the last coins in the bottom of a jar. Her generosity with money, when she had it. Her fearlessness about bugs and bills. Her laissez-faire about Coby's drinking and, later on, his drugs. Her cigarette voice;

her throaty, prewar debutante's drawl. Her ability to shrug off insults and turn them into jokes. Her hundred- or hundred-and-fifty-decibel laugh.

He won't go into the things he hated, not even to himself. (Her indifference. Her relentlessness. Her contempt.)

It would have been wonderful to find the pills, either intact or with just one or two at the most missing, he'd settle for that. She begged him for them for months; starting last year, joking at first, then more and more seriously as her illness took its toll. After she'd had a bad night, especially; and they both knew there were more and more bad nights to come. He'd put her off, and days later she started in again. It became a kind of tease, a running comedy riff.

"I don't understand you, Coby," she said. "After everything I've done for you?" She had taken to whispering in broad daylight with only the two of them in the house. "Look at it this way," she said. "You've got to die of something; everyone does. So why not die of guilt?"

Till now she'd never accused him of not being able to take a joke, but there's always a first time for everything. "Look, Ma, I can't do it," he said. "Don't ask me. You know I can't."

They were in her studio; it was late afternoon; she was painting a collection of little brown pill bottles on a tabletop under a circle of silvery lamplight, because, as she told him, you can only paint the things you love. "It's for you," she said. "I want you to have it when I die." She waved her loaded paintbrush at him like a gun (just kidding!), then sketched a broad arc in the shape of a smile in the air between them. "Coby darling, it's an eye for an eye," she said. "Who gave you life? Don't you think it's time to return the favor and give me a nice little easy death?" She laughed uproariously, senselessly, too loud and much too long; God only knows what stuff they were giving her to kill the pain.

"Right, Ma. Very funny," Coby said.

COBY'S sick of the sight of Calpurnia. He used to love that first glimpse of it from the road at the end of the driveway coming home from school in springtime with the linden trees in leaf and all six windows reflecting the western sun, but now he sees it as a mausoleum: the house of the dead, just sitting there waiting for its final occupant. Though to be a murderer, do you actually have to take a weapon in your hands and fire it off? Coby knows Nina thinks he killed his mother; it's in her eyes, the way she talks to him, as well as all the things she doesn't say. What he isn't totally clear about is whether she's right or wrong.

Coby uncaps the last bottle from the last six-pack of Peg's rather elderly beer and his heart sinks in a familiar way. Maribel was always good for the odd twenty, fifty if she was flush; but he can't live on Peg's largesse forever and wouldn't want to if he could. In his short life to date Coby has always tended to rely on the kindness of family friends and other relative strangers; because, as Maribel Archibald Davies' son, when you get right down to it, what other choices did he have?

He closes his eyes and tries not to think about the future. Conrad believes there's buried treasure in some obscure bank account or stock portfolio of hers somewhere but Coby knows better; Maribel was living on capital, the slowly decaying corpse of his great-grandmother's estate. Maribel embraced her poverty and flaunted it; she had always hated being called rich and thought it would stiffen Coby's spine to be poor, but it never did. On the contrary, it just scared him shitless and brought out the lowdown and craven fatalist in him. Coby believes in kismet, predestination. Life is not a game of tennis, where by definition alone the best man always wins.

At Wimbledon Lendl stretches for the other fellow's ball and hits a slow return. His return bounces into midcourt and hangs there for a minute amiably, seductively, like a pet dog looking for a pat on the head, and the crowd holds its breath; even the pennants take a second or two to catch the breeze. Whereupon the Frenchman winds up his forehand and smashes the ball into the opposite corner of the court. But Lendl's ready; he's seen it coming; it's almost as if he'd ordered it up at just that angle and that split second in time and space so that he could be sure to get himself ready for it and send it soaring back.

Coby sits up and puts his bare feet on the bare wood floor, kicking Peg's little flowered rug out of the way. He likes Ivan Lendl but he likes the other guy too; the truth is he likes them all; you could say he wants them all to win. Coby's not a killer and never was; you could even argue that that's one of the reasons he's never made it into the big time, either in tennis or PR or incentives and fulfillment or anything else he ever tried to do. He doesn't have that kind of energy; he lacks the winner's taste for blood. He loved his mother and in his most honest moments, face facts, he needed her, and wanted her to live forever: you could almost say his life depended on it. Though for just a few bad days and hours, especially there at the end, with her hand on her side to hold the pain in place and keep it from spreading around, it had seemed an utterly childish and dishonorable thing to wish.

Coby stands and stretches, then walks to the window to see how the day is developing weatherwise. Beer for breakfast; how low can anyone sink? But although he may be down he isn't completely out; he'll take a cold shower in Peg's immaculate guest bathroom, then march downstairs and offer to give her a hand with the shopping when she goes to the store. Maribel's in her grave and he's down to his last ten bucks but he isn't dead yet, and the world hasn't come to an end yet either. The villa's still standing, Maribel's little secrets are still under cover, and he's still the acknowledged son and heir of whatever's left to inherit at Calpurnia: he's still his mother's child. And make no mistake: if to know someone is to love them, Coby loved Maribel and Maribel loved him. Dead or alive; and for the moment, anyway, Coby, at least, is still alive.

30

PEG SITS in the north bedroom window folding slips and nightgowns, sweaters she hasn't worn in years. From here it's easy to keep watch on Nina's visitors, a committee of gray jacketed men on the other side of the hedge below—measuring windows, testing doors, taking notes, getting in each other's way. She'll wait till they've gone, whoever they are, then make a beeline for Calpurnia before Nina leaves the house. She's been meaning to sort out these cabinets for months anyway, and the window seat happens to make a convenient perch while she's doing it, but even so she's careful to stay well behind the dip in the curtains, out of mind and out of sight. She knows what Nina thinks of her, but keeping watch on Calpurnia has become second nature after all these years. And there are times, whether they know it or not, when the whole family has had cause to thank her for it.

Down the hall Coby's watching tennis on the big TV in Mikey's old bedroom. She can hear the measured, gentlemanly singsong of the English sportscaster's voice as he calls the shots against the air conditioner's soothing background buzz. Surely there must be worse things for him to do than lie in bed in a cool dark room looking at television on a murderously hot day in June? She's offered him lunch but he's still working on breakfast: a bottle of beer and a deviled egg, though just eating breakfast and watching tennis on TV seem to take more out of Coby than a day's honest work would take out of anyone else. Peg's better than forty years older than Coby but she's got twice the stamina and more than twice the get-up-and-go.

She's more than forty years older than Coby and she was a good seven years older than Maribel, with a secret list of aches and pains and midnight terrors of her own, so she used to trade on the difference in their ages to make fun of Maribel's fear of dying. But it didn't work; by this time last year they both knew that of the two of them Maribel was closer to the finish line. Not an unmixed blessing, if you get right down to it; because who wants to be the one left crying on the dock, the last of the Mohicans on Weavers Way with no one left on either side of the hedge to turn to you when your own time comes? Peg has lived here for fifty-three years and for most of those years she knew every family on the block, but one by one the others all died or moved away, and in the long run the only friend or friendship that survived was hers with Maribel. Peg moved in at the bottom of the market in the thirties, when Justin's father died and left them all that money from the roofing business and Maribel's mother was still in residence. The tennis courts were still on Calpurnia's side of the lot line in those days and the Callery pears still went marching down the hill as far as the eye could see. These were the only two houses on this side of the street back then, and old Mrs. Archibald made it clear that Peg and Justin's was one too many. Mrs. Archibald hated the Irish in the way other people still hate the blacks and Jews, and died of a stroke the same year that Justin bought the famous tennis courts; which became a family joke. But by that time Peg and Maribel were friends, and Mikey and Coby were practically inseparable.

Peg's an old woman now, as she'd be the first to tell you, and she's already outlived all of them but Coby, though at the rate he's going she wouldn't be surprised to outlive him too. This in spite of the pain in her gut, the vertigo, and the bloody noses she no longer even bothers to call the doctor about. It's not that she considers herself indestructible—not at all: on the contrary, she's acutely aware of her own fragility, and more and more so with every passing year. It's only that after Mikey died it dawned on her, once and for all, that it didn't really matter, because nothing did. Mikey's death is her secret weapon. With Mikey dead Peg doesn't really care anymore whether she lives or dies herself.

Like Peg, Maribel didn't care whether she lived or died, or said she didn't: and maybe it was true. Though artists are a special case—they've got something to leave behind them when they go—whereas your average gardener's work is gone in a matter of months or years, wiped out, erased from the face of the earth as if it never happened at all. As witness old lady Archibald's roses, and those hybrid irises she loved so much. Even so, Maribel wasn't happy with the actual business of dying, not even after she finally admitted to herself that that's what it had come to; and even then she meant to put it off as long as she could. Though who knows where or when she intended to draw the line?

"I'll know when I get there, I suppose," she said.

"And then what?" said Peg.

"And then take something or other to get it over with," she said.

Well, don't look at me, thought Peg. Though she had her

own little stash of something or other, dished out to her by a bearded ship's doctor on a cruise, after a bout of diverticulitis in the middle of the Aegean Sea one agonizing August night last year. Peg came home from her trip to watch Maribel die like someone following someone else up a cliff, taking lessons from a novice in a difficult sport, the blind leading the blind. And wondered if, when her time came, she'd have the same grit and the willpower to wait things out till the last bearable moment, then close in rationally for the kill. Whatever she's learned from Maribel (no painkiller without its unbearable side effects; never let the doctors know that you know you're dying; never show your hand) are not lessons she would have come to easily by herself. And that's not all, because what about all the stuff you can't help leaving behind: houses, furniture, documents, photographs, pictures on the wall? For weeks she's been watching Elizabeth come and go at Calpurnia, chatting with her across the cutting-garden fence, getting to know her, sizing her up for the time when Peg may need her services herself.

Elizabeth had seemed starchy at first, one of those thwarted-looking blondes too well brought up to pick her nose even in the privacy of her own home, let alone go out and get herself a regular job in a regular office like everyone else. But once you got to know her she loosened up a bit, and by the end of the second week it became clear that she was more approachable than not. She'd endeared herself to Peg by befriending Coby; and, in some strange way, dead or alive (hard to explain), the absent Maribel. Peg had had her over for a drink the week before Coby ran amok, and bent her ear (but hadn't she asked for it?) about old Mrs. Archibald and the rich and famous Aubrey clan. But Elizabeth was a good listener, a history buff, and Peg told her things she hadn't thought of or talked to anyone else about for years.

Peg folds and refolds the yellow cashmere sweater set that Justin bought her for Christmas the year he sold the business. It's a color she never wears, would never wear in a million years: expensive and expiatory, he refused to tell her how much the sweaters cost, interpreting all her arguments about pricey presents and the dead dealership as pleas for money in the bank. Retirement will be the death of you, she said, and it was, but Justin would never admit it and maybe he was right. If you live long enough, isn't anything the death of you anyway, after all? For the third time in at least as many years Peg debates throwing the sweater set in with her annual carload to Goodwill, and for the third time decides it's probably too fine to give to the genuinely poor.

Downstairs on Calpurnia's terrace Nina is holding forth in black and white, shaking hands with the men in gray and giving them directions uphill and left to the pike. As the men pack and repack their briefcases and say good-bye, Peg shoves her yellow sweater set back into the plastic bag and heads for the stairs. She's got the keys in her pocket; all she has to do is work Maribel's off the ring, hand it to Nina, and say good-bye.

"I WANTED to catch you before you left," she says. It's an admission that she's been keeping an eye on things from the other side of the hedge, as she only realizes once the words are out of her mouth; but who's fooling who? The look on Nina's face is a mixture of exasperation and surprise. Peg has caught her in the act of reaching for the car key, about to get under way; her diaphanous sleeves stir and resettle like birds lighting down. She's got an armful of books and papers in one hand, her bracelet of jangling keys in the other, and anyway Peg's gesture is merely symbolic, as they both know. Hugh changed the locks the day after Maribel died, and it must be obvious by now that Coby's more than capable of getting in and out of the house without benefit of locks and keys whenever he jolly well chooses to.

"Peg, you look great. How marvelous to see you," Nina says.

"You're looking grand yourself, as usual," says Peg. "And isn't that a pretty dress!"

"Oh, this?—it's as old as the hills," says Nina, but Peg seriously doubts it. Like everything Nina puts on her back, it looks like tomorrow's news. Peg has reached the age where she doesn't so much buy clothes as seek out replacements for things they don't even make anymore, her sense of what looks right with what having atrophied sometime in the early seventies at the height of the so-called sexual revolution, like a kind of hearing loss or an inability to smell certain cooking odors and strong perfumes. Whereas Nina's been a fashion horse since the day she was born: aided and abetted by Maribel as long as she had the money to keep up with the department-store bills and subscribe to the fancy fashion magazines.

"I wanted to give you back the key," says Peg, as if she didn't know that the locks have been changed and may be about to be changed again. "They make these damn things so stiff nowadays, don't they? You have to be Hercules to get anything off or on."

"Here, let me do it," says Nina. "I've got strong hands. It comes from opening all those packing-case seals."

Peg hands her the key ring with its three old and almost identical keys, a sad sight next to the arsenal on Nina's bracelet with its jangling array like a jailer's or a chatelaine's. Nina puts her papers and books on the top of the car and anchors them with her bag. She's making it a point to humor Peg: let the record show that she was unfailingly polite to her aunt Maribel's ancient neighbor and old friend when she came to return the key. Though even from the first there'd never been much warmth between them, going all the way back to the days when Nina was still a child. Peg never quite knew how to talk to little girls, having none of her own, and Coby, who was always running through a break in the hedge to play with Mikey in those days, became Peg's favorite by default. Leaving Nina to Maribel's undivided attention, which was probably what they both wanted anyway.

It's much too late in the day to revise this status quo but age has its privileges, and Peg says: "In case you're worried about Coby, I just thought I'd tell you he's been staying with me; he's doing pretty well."

"Oh, great. That's marvelous," says Nina. "We've all been so worried. Well, you can imagine. I can't tell you what a relief it is to know somebody's looking out for him."

Peg warns herself to leave well enough alone, then disregards her own warning and bulls on through. "Well, I'm happy to hear it," she says, "because I kept telling him to call you and let you know he was alive and well. I mean when I hadn't heard from anyone, after the big ruckus over here last week."

Nina's having trouble working Maribel's key around the second, outer bend in the ring. "Look, Peg," she says, "Hugh and I have always done whatever we could for Coby, including keeping him away from the long arm of the law when it came to that, but he's his own worst enemy. As who should know better than you?"

Peg keeps her eyes on Nina's hands. She's waiting for one of those perfect pink fingernails to break. "And what exactly is that supposed to mean?" she says.

"Please, Peg, let's not play these little games."

It's hot out here in the driveway and Peg's hungry, her blood sugar is running low; she knows the signs. "Coby didn't kill Maribel," she says.

Nina says, "Of course he didn't. Nobody ever said he did."

Peg says: "He didn't kill her. He might have given her some pills; but if he had it would have been her choice. She wouldn't have had to go and take them, after all."

"Then why on earth would he have given them to her in the first place?" Nina asks.

Peg says, "Because she might have asked for them. Did you ever think of that?"

Nina jams the key through the last half inch of stubborn metal with the unbroken nail on her right forefinger, then hands the key ring back to Peg. "Yes, I did think of that," she says. "Believe it or not, I've just about thought of everything. But Hugh's a lawyer; he says that defense would never stand up in any court of law. Assuming it ever came to that, which it won't."

Peg pockets the key ring with its two remaining keys. "He's your own flesh and blood, Nina: so don't let it," she says. "You know how he lives as well as I do; how can anyone blame him for breaking in? If you can even call it that, considering that you're the ones who went and changed the locks. Coby's flat broke. He was looking for whatever he could find to sell."

"Then he just shot himself right in the foot, didn't he?" says Nina, "because if he hadn't trashed the place like that no one would ever have had to call off the sale."

"Maybe you should think of calling it back on again, then," says Peg. "Before he decides life isn't worth living, and you've got two suicides on your hands instead of one."

Nina shuts her mouth hard, like someone biting off thread, and Peg can suddenly see exactly what she's going to look like as an old woman. That thin mouth will only get thinner; the dimpled chin will lengthen and sag.

"I won't be bullied, Peg," Nina says. "Not after all I've done for him. Not after I've gone way far out on a limb to keep the police off his trail."

They stand sweating quietly under the humid sun, careful to keep their voices low, seared by the same hot draft off the hood of Nina's car. Inside her pocket the depleted key ring with its two remaining keys carves out a bite-sized zigzag in the center of Peg's palm.

"Well, I won't be bullied either," she says, "so that makes two of us. And nobody's asking you to go out on any limbs for anyone. It isn't necessary; it never was. Coby didn't give Maribel those pills she took anyway. I did. It was me."

Nina looks blankly at Peg as the sounds of summer silence ring in both their ears: a stir of squirrels in the hedges, Peg's shoes in the gravel as she shifts her weight from her right leg to her left.

Peg spells it out. "Those were my pills she took, not his," she says. "I got them last summer on that cruise I took to Greece. I'd had a bad stomach and the ship's doctor didn't trust the Turkish doctors where we were due to land, so he gave me the pills in case I had another bout. Which, thank God, I didn't. It was some sort of giveaway sample, the bottle had never been opened, and I was saving it for a rainy day. But those things don't last forever; and I thought that night, the night she died, well, by the time I need them they won't even work anymore anyway, so what am I waiting for? I made her throw away the pills Coby gave her. They weren't even marked. I said, How do you know what's even in that stuff? You'd be crazy to put them in your mouth; you could end up worse than you began."

She takes her hand out of her skirt pocket like someone

with nothing to hide. "You don't have to look at me like that, Nina," she says. "It's nothing to be ashamed of. I just happened to think my pills were better than Coby's, and what she did with them was her business anyway, not mine. Or yours either; or his, or anyone's."

Nina looks at the key in the palm of her hand as if she can't remember how she got it, what door it unlocks, who gave it to her, what it's doing there.

"So now you can climb down off that great big limb of yours you're hanging from and tell everyone to stop spreading rumors," says Peg. "Because Coby didn't kill Maribel. I wouldn't let him. I wouldn't let her let him. Now you know."

31

THE BIG day, as Elizabeth thinks of it (but only in quotation marks, straining for irony), is going to set records for heat and humidity. It's been announced on every local weather service forecast and at least one national one for the last two days: a scorcher, with the sun not due to set till almost nine. And who in their right mind is going to leave the comfort of an air-conditioned house on a day like this to come to her hastily advertised sale? It's been a week and a half of scramble and commotion, trying to put things back together, renew broken promises, and scare up a working staff from the people she'd already just let go; Nina's reprieve has created as many problems as it's solved. Elizabeth's going into this with her eyes wide open. It's a foregone conclusion that things will be overlooked, lost in the shuffle, or simply left undone.

And yet, coming around the corner into Weavers Way an hour before the scheduled opening, it's clear at a glance that the sale isn't going to go unattended. There are cars parked in long lines both ways from Maribel's front door as far as the eye can see, snaking downhill through the red roofs of Weavers Circle and uphill toward Gladwyne out of sight. All these people have braved the heat and gotten up at the crack of dawn, eager to stake out a position as close to the house as possible, first come first served.

She knows them, collectively if not by name or by face: they're the small dealers, the professional scouts and pickers, the flea-market buyers, and the simple out-and-out fanatics—with, on Maribel's behalf, no doubt, a sprinkling of local history buffs, part-time artists, and neighborhood hero worshipers thrown in. Maribel may have been reclusive, but for a painter who rarely sold a painting she obviously had and still has a following. There will be souvenir hunters and sensation-seekers among the fans and dealers, a nightmare in terms of security and crowd control. Meanwhile, the new alarm system Nina had installed last week is so complicated you can never be quite sure it's armed. If Henry shows up ahead of time she'll post him at the French doors to the side garden where she's set up her card table and her cash box; if not she'll have to wing it. Elizabeth tries not to think about the day ahead as she pulls in under Calpurnia's porte cochere. At least she's had the presence of mind to get Peg's go-ahead on this, and warn her about the parking in advance.

Parking the car, Elizabeth feels the dry heat of stage fright. It's always a command performance, the obligatory grand finale, the sink or swim. She works the car into its berth of stringy shade, puts on her sunglasses like a movie star ducking paparazzi, and threads her way to the back door, then taps out the new security code and hopes for the best; but it works like a charm. Inside, the house is almost supernaturally cool and she has a sense of herself as a ghost at her own funeral: Maribel's surrogate among the grieving mirrors, the familial tables and chairs.

On her way to the powder room to stash her purse, she takes off her sunglasses and puts them in her pocket like someone shedding a disguise. The house is already becoming unfamiliar in minute unremarkable ways: since yesterday everything seems different, older, dustier, and less recognizable than it was before. Elizabeth hides her bag in the basket under the sink and notices at once that the doctored Carraccis are gone; ransomed, she hopes, as intended, by Nina, their small square ghosts left to fight it out with other shades of gray on the lumpy staircase wall. It's not her problem anymore, thank God. Outside the buyers are waiting, ready to swarm. The thought of all those people out there on all their separate quests and warpaths makes Elizabeth hot.

In what may be her last few moments alone in Maribel's house Elizabeth sets the cash box down on the card table in the dining room, then checks to make sure that the French doors to the library are securely locked, the kitchen door secured. Henry and Clemmie aren't due for another five minutes and they've promised to be on time, but both are notoriously tardy and she isn't sure she can wait for them to get here before she unlocks the door and steps aside for the stampede. The kitchen window flares with the eastern sun, and Elizabeth rolls up her sleeves and fans herself with a paper plate. Whatever way you look at it, it's going to be a long, hot day.

FRIEDRICHSON is, literally, the first one in the door, but she doesn't recognize him till some moments later, when he bends to examine a gilt lion's-head umbrella in a stand and she sees the giveaway sideburns below the thinning hair. He's dressed like a golf player today in a white rugby shirt and cuffed beige slacks.

"I couldn't resist," he says. "I saw your ad, so totally unexpected, because I'd heard the sale was off; or did I get that wrong?"

"No, not at all, but we've had security problems, I'm afraid. I'm sorry," says Elizabeth. "I should have gotten back to you." One more detail left undone; or is it too late to interest him in the paintings upstairs after all? If he takes them off her hands she'll be glad to sweeten the deal with a small memento of his own choosing: a sketch, if she can find one, or a gouache.

"Oh, security, of course," says Friedrichson, "and believe me, I know whereof you speak. Can't be too careful these days, can you, even out here, so knee-deep in the Garden of Eden, ha ha ha?" He's charming and exculpatory; he's in the business; he knows how these things go. Elizabeth points him up the stairs to Maribel's studio, then turns to face the threesome at the garden door—two middle-aged women in almost identical denim dresses with their purchases already picked out after a bare five minutes inside the house.

The crowd is thicker than it looks; fanned out through the downstairs rooms they're like people at a museum opening, respectful but avid, many of them with her belated ad in hand. There are women in tennis clothes (white, immaculate, children in tow, exclaiming at the view); young couples in jeans or shorts, picking things up and putting them down and picking them back up again; and then the solitaries, dealers or runners in their anonymous khakis and seersucker suits. The pros are not in awe of the architecture, and they haven't come for the atmosphere or the auld lang syne; their single-mindedness gives them away. You can tell who they are by the way they move, the beeline they make for the object of desire.

Deep in this shifting sea of known and unknown faces, ten minutes later, Elizabeth finally sees Henry's, and she's much too relieved at the sight to read him the riot act for being late. She sets him up with the cash box and the receipts pad at the garden door and leaves him on his own. He's done it before; Henry knows the drill. "Don't let them open those French doors in the dining room, whatever you do," she says. "I don't care how hot it gets. We're horribly shorthanded—it's just you, me, and Clemmie till ten." At ten she's got reinforcements coming: old Mrs. Snow from the salesroom at Uxley's, and Dorrie McNulty, a vintage linens dealer from one of the New Jersey flea markets whom Elizabeth finally tracked down at the last minute yesterday and who has promised—not altogether convincingly—to pitch in.

The ad went in belatedly last Thursday for its single run, by which time Elizabeth would have assumed that most people were already at the shore, but it's barely eight-thirty and Calpurnia is already overrun. Elizabeth feels like the invisible hostess at a monstrous party, adrift in the ocean of her own hospitality. Well, it's a historic site, and everyone wants a look; though with luck the early birds will clear out by midmorning and the latecomers will be few and far between. When she finds her in the potting shed Elizabeth sends Clemmie upstairs to monitor the second floor, then makes her way back toward the kitchen through the crowded dining room and the busy pantry, trying to be everywhere at once. For a moment she thinks she sees Roberto's face in the front hall, but someone calls her from the stairs where the otherwise undistinguished silhouette collection (left-facing Aubreys, all with the family nose and chin) now hangs in ascending order from the eighteenth century to the gilded age, and when she turns to look again he's gone. And who would have told him, anyway? Elizabeth supposes she's come to think of Roberto as her special responsibility, a human legacy from Maribel. She meant to call him yesterday but under the circumstances it was just one of the twenty or so things she never got around to in the end.

It's ten o'clock. The Eastlake overmantel has already gone for five hundred dollars, Maribel's mother's doll collection for seven-fifty, but Admiral Archibald's mezzotints of Roman senators are still hanging in a tipsy row on the library's south wall and the little breakfast-room Aubusson is rolled up in a corner of the studio where she carefully tucked it weeks ago. Elizabeth turns back the way she's come; she's wanted in the dining room to confirm the price on a pewter soup tureen. "My mother had one exactly like it," the would-be buyer says, a razor-thin blonde in a designer jumpsuit who can't believe her luck: two of the three initials in the engraved monogram are an actual match and the other's illegible anyway. Elizabeth smiles and breaks away; only someone whose mother had the same initials as old Mrs. Archibald's would pay the price she's put on it: the Calpurnia connection is money in the bank. Maribel's dullest steak knives and most frayed straw place mats will go for a premium today, if only so that the buyers can boast about their antecedents when they get them home.

Dorrie McNulty, the linens dealer, a pink-faced woman in a graying ponytail and an ancient Dacron blazer, is suddenly at Elizabeth's elbow, ten minutes early and ready for action. "Am I late?" she asks. Elizabeth sends her to the kitchen to keep an eye on the collectibles and cutlery—things small enough to put in your pocket and walk out the door with, if you're so inclined. The good silver is already gone, thank God, sold three days ago to Byrne and Smith for what Elizabeth thinks of as a pittance. Still, who wants the responsibility of monitoring all that stuff while twelve hours' worth of unaccredited strangers roam through Maribel's swiftly emptying rooms? Getting rid of the silver at giveaway prices seems a small price to pay for all the indecisions and reversals of the last three weeks.

At the terrace door Henry is collecting money from a queue of would-be buyers in slow motion. Elizabeth sees the edge of a rococco mirror, an armful of art books, a trio of nested brass betel boxes waiting for their turn to pay and go. It's almost ten, and already the rooms seem barer, like forest thinned of its leaves by the first autumn winds, some fleeting premonition of winter and hard times. Time to track down Friedrichson in Maribel's studio and see what kind of deal she can make with him on the paintings, as long as everything's more or less under control down here.

The ribbon she's tied across the third-floor landing to keep people out lies trailing on the floor, but the door is blocked: stepping into the hall Elizabeth sees Roberto standing with his back to the studio door, deep in conversation with Friedrichson. "She had this affection for terra verte," she hears him say. "A color Dewing was also partial to. Semitransparent and a bit gritty; not that Giorgione green that you see in so many of the Venetian paintings, not at all."

"Ah, Dewing, yes, of course," says Friedrichson.

Roberto shakes Elizabeth's hand as formally as if they'd just met; he feels sorry for her, a decent woman with a tough job, and hopes there's no trouble about the painting of the pill bottles once the lawyers and accountants get wind of it. Friedrichson's a fool, of course, but you can see he's an admirer, and Roberto will talk about Maribel to anyone who lets him these days. "She was surrounded by painters, growing up," he says.

"Her grandmother could do a perfect Redoute rose; she turned them out like little cakes for all her friends and relatives on request. A kind of mass production; you could trace it back to the founding father, probably, the one who made false teeth so perfect they could almost be taken for the real thing." Roberto's of two minds about this museum the family's promoting, and wonders where Friedrichson fits into the scheme of things. For his own part he honestly doesn't care. He's the curator of his own memories of this house, and that's enough for him.

Friedrichson laughs at Roberto's little joke and Elizabeth nods; though he should have called her, put in his bid for his favorites, and allowed her to get them out of the way before Friedrichson saw them and made his pick. "It's a shame that we've come down to the wire like this with the paintings still not really inventoried yet," she says. It's a lie; she has her own list with her own titles, rather hit or miss, but she wants Friedrichson to think he's still in the running for the whole collection, in case it should come to that. Elizabeth walks to the window and fiddles with the shades. Up here the familiar heat is already intolerable; there's a glaze of sweat on Friedrichson's forehead and Roberto has started working discreetly at the knot of his tie; any minute now she half expects the paint on Maribel's canvases to start melting off in bluish arabesques onto the gummy floor. She looks back at Roberto and flashes him a smile. "Dr. Leal has promised to help with the catalog," she says to Friedrichson, "once we get the retrospective under way."

Elizabeth watches Friedrichson's face. The man's no fool; he's obviously interested; she can almost feel his temptation as a sort of electrical impulse in her bones: some spark of connection, the split second between off and on. Roberto's imprimatur on the catalog as an art historian and the last lover of record is probably worth its weight in gold, which Friedrichson will surely realize as soon as he gives it any thought.

Roberto wipes his forehead with one of his enormous handkerchiefs and waves a regretful hand at Friedrichson; he needs a glass of water; he needs to sit down; he's too old, too hot, and too easily moved to tears to stay up here so long. He follows Elizabeth down the stairs past the admiral's scenes of old Cathay: a quartet of improbable mountains, wispy pagodas, and junks at anchor in a wavy bay. Nina is nowhere to be seen and neither is Coby. Elizabeth might have known they'd back out of this chaos at the last minute, and in a way she doesn't blame them. Except for Roberto, and she's not even sure he really counts as family, she's obviously on her own.

Downstairs the mob scene is slowly sorting itself out into curiosity seekers and serious buyers. There's a queue in front of Clemmie's table waiting to pay and run and a couple arguing in the dining-room doorway; a young man in green pants heads her off on her way to the living room, crossing the hall. His wife has sent him over to bid on Maribel's dressing table, a heavy, kidney-shaped piece with Chippendale legs and glued-on Adams trim, and he's holding one of its side drawers in one hand and a piece of unfired red clay, misshapen but roundish, in the other. He's found it inside the apron, he says, on the little shelf between the drawer glides and the outer curve of the tabletop, and he wants Elizabeth to look at it before he throws it away. "Somebody's kid's handprint; I didn't want to just toss it," he says.

Elizabeth stops for a moment, confused. She has one almost exactly like this at home: an impression of Pen's hand made long ago in kindergarten or nursery school. She keeps it in her underwear drawer, in the old divided silk pouch her mother used as a jewelry case; it's one of those things you carry around with you from house to house and life to life: too personal to set out on display but too loaded with memories to throw away.

Elizabeth takes the disk of red clay and turns it over as the crowd closes in around her, full of faces and voices on every side. Scratched into the back in clumsy block letters there's the name COBY and the date 1951. "I'm so grateful to you," she says, "how kind," as if it were Pen's four-year-old hand, not Coby's, that the young man has so unexpectedly handed her. She wraps it carefully in a square of old newspaper and starts working her way to the foot of the stairs. From where, on the threshold of Maribel's locked powder room, she sees the shape of a familiar head in the knot of people at the door, and freezes with her hand on the stairpost finial, just seconds too late to avoid coming face-to-face with Ellios.

ELLIOS has been up since four; he's jet-lagged; he's been in Belgium talking to a pair of excited Greeks about a revolutionary new way to identify works of art by embedding invisible chips impregnated with chemical markers in their underlayers, like lost pets. The inventors are young and absurdly unbusinesslike but it's an interesting concept and one that Ellios thinks might be profitable. He wants to explore the idea of running an American franchise, but so far they're playing their cards much too close to their chests for him to know whether it pays to do business with them or not.

Calpurnia looks different to him in daylight with all its fissures and fractures and empty spaces showing. The old girl must have been living in reduced circumstances for a long time; you don't get scars on the parquet or serious cracks in the plaster like that overnight. It's the old story: the ancestral fortune never outlasts the third or fourth or fifth generation, not even here in the so-called birthplace of the nation where the money is so much older than most. Ellios remembers a portrait in the living room (gone now) over the couch: the *maitresse de maison,* according to Elizabeth. He liked the look in the painting's eyes, as well as its play on the classics, some jokey reference to an unforgiving god. Has she sold it already, and if so to whom? Not that he ever had any really serious intention of buying it for his own collection, because Ellios can hardly afford to tie up serious capital right now in something that would be, at best, a very risky investment, and one with appeal only to a very special taste: the gay market, subspecies nostalgia buff, subsubspecies postwar forties society grande dame. But Ellios's life is about to change. He's got lots of new irons in the fire: including Elizabeth, if she's game.

He's broken his neck to get here on time because these cool blondes with their dismissive chins and elegant teeth are always impressed by punctuality, and he has already begun to think of her as someone to be propitiated, or even honored; like a wife or a blood relative (is this what they mean by love?). He's had two weeks of relative celibacy and rain and solitary dining in Brussels to think it all through in detail. Because love is love, yes; but he knows from experience, or ought to, God knows, by now, that it's always best to make these decisions fully clothed, standing up, without distractions, and all alone.

Ellios makes his way into the library, past the avid-eyed book lovers with their first-edition whodunits and coffee table tomes; he's looking for good value, as he always is, but that isn't the whole of it: he wants to pick out something that will not so much remind him of her as remind her of him when she sees it next: of Calpurnia and the drawings behind the Carracci prints. Something with or without any intrinsic value of its own, and damn the expense. In fact, the more expensive the better; because the twelve thousand dollars she refused to take for those drawings has left him feeling strangely enriched: one way or the other he means to spend money on her, and he might as well start here and now. How else, when you get right down to it, can he make her understand that he's really serious? How else does a woman ever know what value a man stands ready to place on her?

Watching her come and go in the doorway, across the hall, Ellios sees himself with Elizabeth at his side: his Fiammino Venus, his Aphrodite with mirror and pearls. Is it love, by definition, when you can't stop looking at a woman's face? He's jet-lagged, sleepless, and ready to stake his claim when he catches sight of her, finally, halfway up the stairs, her pale hair backlit by sun, bare-armed but with that odd ritziness these women always have; to the manor born. He wants to possess her but he would settle for possessing a picture of her: something enduring; something that can't darken or decay or be taken back. He thinks of the clothes he'll buy her, Edwardian linens and Oriental silks; and eight-millimeter pearls instead of those undersized things she's always wearing, so small they're almost child-sized, ridiculously out of scale with her perfectly grown-up shoulders and handsome neck.

The idea of the money he means to spend on Elizabeth pleases Ellios profoundly. He hasn't seen her for weeks and she hasn't returned his call from Brussels, but he tells himself he wasn't really expecting her to, that he'll know how to get back to the place where they left off when the time is ripe. And then, weeks or months later, when they've reached some sort of understanding, set her up in business, bankroll her to an office and a small collection of her own, or put her in charge of the embedded chips, if and when that deal becomes a viable reality.

Something clever, something chic; something that will establish her credentials in a wider world than this. It doesn't matter that Calpurnia has seen better days. He'll find her other, bigger, better mansions to dismantle; other collections to curate; other entrances to make. One way or another, he'll put her on the map. If it means he has to marry her, he will.

She sees him, finally, locks eyes with him, and takes a small step backward; then stands stock-still and reminds herself to smile and wave. He's got her dead to rights, like a bird hypnotized by a snake. A shifting swarm of buyers and browsers crosses the sight lines between them, and from the extreme stillness with which she holds her pose he knows he's managed to stamp his image on her eye: at least for now.

COBY'S disgusted with himself; he wasn't going to go, dead horses couldn't have dragged him, especially after the dustup with Nina two weeks ago, but Conrad has asked him to get the metal plaque on the pillar to the left of the porte cochere— Villa Calpurnia, a flat bronze square so weather-beaten it's the same color as the stone, buried in ivy from one of the twin rococco urns: if you didn't remember every inch of the place from childhood you'd never even know it was there. But just how is Coby supposed to get it for him? For obvious reasons, Coby has no desire to be seen down on his hands and knees trying to pry things off of walls, though if that's what it takes, it's probably better to do it in broad daylight with a hundred sightseers and curio hunters looking on than all alone by flashlight like a thief in the goddamn night. And Conrad's his only uncle, his last remaining defender in a family of finger pointers and naysayers. Under the circumstances, how could he say no?

It's a madhouse at Weavers Way, starting at the bottom of

the hill; there are cars parked for miles in both directions as far as the eye can see. Well, talk about humbling experiences, and he's had plenty of those in his life, but this beats most. Coby puts his hands in his pockets and pretends to be whistling a little tune as he cuts through the hedge to the house, half lord of the manor, half long-lost and prodigal son. His last time, ever, at Calpurnia: a promise he makes to himself like someone swearing off liquor or dope. The heat is an embarrassment, but he hates to take off his jacket; there's an ink stain on his shirt pocket and his sneakers have seen better days. After all, he's still family, son of the house, the last of a long, long line.

On his way in he locates Conrad's plaque, all but illegible, hoary with bird shit and garden dirt under a scrim of English ivy as thick as anchor rope. It's screwed into the stone with four decorative bollards in the shape of little starbursts; in his grandmother's day the whole thing would have been polished to a fare-thee-well at least once a week. Amazing that Conrad should have remembered it, and proof that the old guy's not as soulless as he seems.

Inside the house the rugs have been rolled up, doubled, and tied with baling twine; footsteps and the sound of furniture being moved echo off the bare floors and there's a strange low-level murmur like the sound of voices at a cocktail party or a wake: uninflected, whispery, all vowels and no consonants. Coby sees Elizabeth the minute he walks in; she's standing in a knot of people in the dining room adjudicating some misunderstanding about a chair. With the light from the garden behind her, she looks bright and otherworldly: an avenging angel, sent to administer the last days of Calpurnia and divide the spoils. He crosses the hall to the living room and stands in the doorway, bowled over by the absence of Maribel's portrait on the wall above the couch: the empty space is like a photographic negative, much more powerful in some strange way than the real portrait with its official version of her face. Does Elizabeth know he has the Lipscomb portrait, Coby wonders, and if so does she mind? More important, will she be helpful about marketing it when the time comes?

But there's no point bothering her about it now; he'll wait till the crowd thins out, then make his little pitch for Conrad's plaque. Find out who has official title to it, cross all the little t's and dot all the little i's, law-abiding citizen that he's at last become; then bring up the painting as a by-the-way. He's taking no chances, because God forbid there's any damage to the stone and he's hauled off to court for vandalism and loitering with intent. But Elizabeth is still a long way off, sorting things out about the chair, and the dining room is full of women he mercifully doesn't know banging spoons against lead crystal to test the ping. Meanwhile who's to say he shouldn't just have one last look around?

And why not?—he's here, isn't he? He hasn't picked any locks or broken any windows to get in; until the house gets sold out from under them doesn't he have exactly as much right to be here as anyone else? Coby tells himself that he quit looking, called off the whole search weeks ago, and he has; but something might still show up at this late date, you never know. You can never tell, that is, what will happen in the chaos of dismantling a room, rolling up the rugs, shoving the furniture around. Something might fall out of a pocket somewhere, or come to light behind a bureau or under a rug. Years later the missing brooch might still be found in the dying pachysandra, for example, or the lost diary squashed behind the books in the bookcase. These things happen; you read about them all the time.

Coby weaves his way through the treasure hunters in the

doorway to the living room, where someone is in the process of loading the couch cushions into a towering pile. The last standing lamp lists in the window well with its electric cord wrapped umbilically around its neck. Without Maribel's portrait to supervise the room and distract the eye, it's suddenly open season on chipped dadoes, exploded wallpaper seams, undusted picture rails. Sun blazes in from the three French windows on the east-facing wall, throwing a series of disjointed parallelograms onto the parquet at odd angles to the prevailing inlay, a modernist mirage. His grandmother's famous Hiraz rug is gone; without it the room looks the way it always did in the days before the family packed up for two months in June and headed for Gerald's mother's house in Penobscot Bay. Coby flinches from the light; his grandmother was a fanatic about curtains and shade. The couch cushions leave the room in a precarious tower, streaming dust, and Coby watches them go. He feels like a sightseer in some decaying castle close, on the lookout for vanished masterpieces and proofs of happier times.

"Let me help you with that," says Elizabeth, as he starts wrestling one of the window shades to the sill.

He turns to face her; it's the first time they've met since the fiasco two weeks ago and he has no idea how much she knows about his role in it. "My grandmother had a thing about sunlight," he says. "She said it fades the rugs."

"I know how she felt," says Elizabeth. "People want rooms with all the light they can get, and then they spend the rest of their lives trying to save the rugs and furniture from bleaching out."

Coby looks over his shoulder. "I'm glad I caught you," he says. "There's a plaque on one of the front door pillars that my uncle Conrad seems to want. He's asked me to pry it off. Is that all right with you?"

"I'm afraid I don't have jurisdiction," says Elizabeth. "Shouldn't you ask your cousin Nina about it?" With everything else that's going on she isn't eager to face any additional complications than the ones she's already contracted to deal with. "Not to change the subject," she says, "but I wasn't sure you'd be by today, and there's something that came to light a little earlier this morning—I've been saving it for you. That's the thing about this awful business: you think you've unearthed every single last thing, every last paper clip and old sock, but something always turns up at the very end; I've never known it to fail. I've put it aside for you; I'm just so glad you managed to come by."

For a moment Coby's heart is in his mouth. She's found the pills or the pill bottle; it so exactly matches his obsession of the past two months that for a moment it's as if she'd uttered the words he wants to hear out loud. Elizabeth looks suddenly radiant to him, blond and perfect, riding a single beam of light from the unshaded window behind her like something from outer space: he's known from the beginning that she would bring him luck. Where is this treasure she's unearthed for him? His life is in her hands.

So much so that when she holds out the little terra-cotta slab with the child's handprint on it he doesn't get it at first, at all. What is this shapeless piece of lumpy unfired clay? Coby looks at it uncomprehendingly, unlovingly. It's one of those idiotic casts of their own hands that kids make in kindergarten, red plasticine, four little dimpled fingers and a sturdy thumb, adorable, the standard fare. Elizabeth turns it over and points out the ragged capital letters of his own name with its backward C and rakish B as if she's discovered gold. Through a fog of disappointment he hears her say: "Isn't it amazing? The man who bought the dressing table found it in the dead space beside one of the drawers; it must have been one of her little hiding places. He was kind enough to salvage it and give it to me for safekeeping. I knew you'd want to have it."

"Oh, yeah, of course, absolutely," says Coby. "Thanks." He feels like a moron standing there beside her on the threshold to the tiled powder room holding this stupid facsimile of his own hand at the age of four or five. What's he supposed to do with this lump of worthless clay? Does she think she's handed him a pearl of rare price? Coby turns the handprint back to front and tries to look happy with it, then has second thoughts. "You say someone bought the dressing table?" he says. "Have they already paid for it? Is it still around?"

He knows the dressing table well (how could he have forgotten it?) and is full of a poisonous self-disgust for not thinking of it first. She kept all the little pieces of paper she couldn't afford to lose sight of stuck facedown under the thin marble top: tickets, lawyers' letters, canceled receipts for disputed bills, angry letters from his father's lawyers. Who would have thought to pull out the drawers themselves and check around inside?

He takes the stairs two steps at a time. In the bedroom a pair of elderly women in pastel dresses are helping each other sort through the tangle of unmatched blankets on the bed. The dressing table is still there, pulled out at a slight angle from the corner, its drawers closed and neatly aligned under the marble lid, a crude SOLD sign on shirt cardboard propped on its top. It's over ninety degrees in here, at a guess; Elizabeth's bargain-basement fan cuts its slow steady diagonal from the door to the dresser and back again, and the fronds of a Boston fern inflate and deflate in its aftermath like lungs. Carefully, as if he's inspecting the piece for signs of wear and tear, Coby eases out the two side drawers of the dressing table and lays them on top of each other, then gets down on his hands and knees and inserts first one, then the other hand deep into the oval recesses on either side of the drawer guides. It's like reaching into his mother's entrails and the dust under his hands is as revolting to him as living flesh; but there's nothing there: he comes up empty on both sides.

Coby sits on the bare box spring at the end of Maribel's bed, just an inch or two outside the trajectory of Elizabeth's fan, but he hasn't got the strength to move. Did she or did she not take the pills he gave her, and, if so, did she take all of them? Enough to kill her, say? Or if not, did she have a last-minute change of heart and throw them all away? And faces the unfaceable reality that he could spend every night of his life at Calpurnia for the next hundred years looking for answers and come up empty-handed every time.

He leans his head on the bedpost and the two women refolding sheets behind him give him an outraged look, as if he's moved in on territory to which they have a prior claim. Around their look the room comes back into focus in its present incarnation as a marketplace: the rubber plant, the fan, the iron lamp with its shepherd staff crook from which his mother used to hang her store-bought reading glasses and her pearls. The kidney-shaped dressing table on the wall opposite the bed is no longer his mother's dressing table at all, but simply an antique throwback to an even older style: a piece of furniture, merely; something capable of being bought and sold.

The two women back away from each other silently with their sheets, ostentatious in their disregard, but they might as well be invisible to him: the scene in which they're embedded is like a painting of itself, familiar at the surface but jarring and unfamiliar at some other and truer level of vision deeper down. And it's here, at the foot of this bed that is no longer Maribel's bed, in this new room that may once have been Maribel's bedroom but never will be again, facing away from the little hexagonal table she used as her bedside table, that Coby remembers the picture she had on her easel the day before she died: a picture of this table itself, with its square of embroidered white linen and its drinking glass with a single stick of willow branch, its clumsy lineup of little pill bottles. Three of them (or was it four?) with one knocked over and lying on its side, precisely that little anonymous brown bottle, uncapped, that might have been the one he gave her finally; though, on second thought, how could she ever have had time enough to paint it in?

Confused, Coby tries to reconstruct that last awful week, but it's all a blur to him now. He remembers her jokey request for the pills and his last trip to the badlands to get them for her, and although he remembers throwing the pills onto the foot of her half-made bed he doesn't remember buying them and doesn't remember the day of the week or the hour of the day that the trip took place, or whether she was in the bed or not when he threw them at her. Had all this happened the day before she died, or days, or even a whole week earlier? Was she still even painting then? His memory's shot; he'd have to see the painting to be sure.

He'd have to see the painting. Not like this, in his mind's eye, but live and in the flesh. Because the painting will tell the truth. Unlike the rest of them, his mother painted only what she saw. And, by her own say-so, only what she loved.

Coby gets up, relinquishes the bed to the sheet folders, and leaves this room that is not a real room to him anymore. Maribel, who never threw anything away, may have thrown away the pill bottle; but, unlike the pills and the bottle itself, the painting still has to be around here somewhere. It's too big and too unmysterious to get lost, and Elizabeth's too organized to lose anything anyway. She'll have it named and numbered and inventoried somewhere; he's seen that clipboard of hers; he's read those lists. Coby ducks through the knot of arguing newlyweds in the hall and heads for the third floor. He'll find it in the studio, with all the other paintings: or even, if he's lucky, right up there on the easel where he saw it last. Maribel's last message to him; her own little joke. The truth, the whole truth, and nothing but the truth.

N I N A ' S not sure till the last minute if she's going to be able to make it across the river or not. She's got a good excuse, an unexpected UPS delivery that needs immediate unpacking and no one downstairs to do the job; she needs every last pair of hands up on the shop floor selling, it's the last of the really strong Saturday crowds, her only chance to clear out what's left of the summer sale merchandise before everyone packs up and heads to the shore. Unpacking, checklisting, she's busy composing various excuses to Roberto in her mind (the shop, the traffic, the heat), but in her heart of hearts she knows it's no good: it's either this or meet him in New York. And she's not up for that; when she goes to New York it's to visit the showrooms, check her sources, make the rounds; she doesn't have time for Roberto and his everlasting grief. She's promised herself to give him Maribel's lion's eye pendant; it's little enough and God knows he deserves it, but she must have been crazy for saying she'd meet him at the sale. Peachy Carmichael advised her a long time ago to stay away, let Elizabeth handle everything ("Leave it to the pros, that's my advice; isn't that the point?"), and she's right; Calpurnia is the last place in the world Nina wants to be on this hot Saturday afternoon. Besides, in the back of her mind she keeps thinking of how that big beautiful yellow agate would look on the art deco hat-stand beside the cash register just inside the door to the shop.

Annoyed with herself for getting into this pickle, Nina takes her time over the receivables check-in sheets, goes over her bill of lading twice, and for a moment even flirts with the idea of steaming the clothes by hand. At least that way Elizabeth's sale will be winding down, if not as good as over, by the time she finally gets there. And Roberto will be worn out, ready to be driven to the station and headed kindly back to New York with, at most, a quick scotch on the rocks and a sandwich somewhere along the way for old times' sake. Not that, in the back of her mind, she doesn't have a small flicker of curiosity about the total take from the sale, because who wouldn't? Nina's only human; she's never exactly broke but she can always use the money, God knows: Can't anyone? Can't everyone?

Time to get going, if she's ever going to go. She knows what these estate sales are like—utter madhouses, if they're any good at all. She's been to enough of them herself, looking for the odd item—a marble egg for her collection, old dolls, a set of matched leather law books for Hugh's office, old costume jewelry for the shop; but Calpurnia's another kettle of fish. And not just because of the nostalgia factor, the trip down memory lane. It's more that she doesn't want to be seen there, either by Elizabeth or anyone else, including, for all she knows, the press, counting the pennies, sizing up the take. Even though, when all's said and done, it may be the only cold hard cash that she or any of them stands to realize from what's left of their grand-mother's once legendary estate; excluding whatever Maribel's Dewings and the one Sargent and Augustus John end up pulling at Sotheby's, split three ways. Because the house itself won't fetch top dollar, as Peachy has been kind enough to point out more than once. It's a white elephant: much too big for its shrunken three-quarter-acre lot, a zoning nightmare, impossible to heat. Nina has been careful not to mention the museum to Peachy, and she hopes Julia knows what she's getting into if that's what it comes to in the end. Either way, she'll breathe easier when it's all over, signed and sealed.

Nina drives fast but carefully; if she goes too slow her mind is apt to wander: she's capable of misreading traffic signs and running lights. But traffic is light on this hot Saturday afternoon and she's across the river and up the hill within ten minutes of leaving the shop. Turning into Weavers Way, she sees the tail end of the day's unexpected traffic jam: cars parked bumper to bumper up and down the rise, just the way they used to be for Maribel's cocktail parties in the days before the divorce, when there was still money for champagne and at least one maid to carry the canapés around. Nina was in full flight from her mother's panicked widowhood in those days and much too young to see the signs of decay that had already set in at Calpurnia. Or to have foreseen that Maribel's divorce was about to change everything: the flow of money in and out of the house, the vacations and the quick trips to New York, the surge of callers and house guests up and down the stairs.

Nina circles the block twice before pulling in behind a departing car with a section of standing lamp wedged perilously out its rear right window and a brace of old sofa pillows lashed to the luggage rack on the roof. She puts her Lexus in neutral and switches it off. Nina hates parking on the street; the neighborhood isn't what it used to be at all and the car is only three months old, a wild extravagance, Hugh's forty-third birthday present to her.

She hopes she's missed Roberto, although in all honesty she's grown quite fond of him over the years. They all have, she supposes, especially when you think of the people Maribel might have taken up with, let's be frank, and almost did, in her declining years. Even so, Roberto's grief has a reproachful, irreversible quality that makes her wonder, somehow, about her own. But never mind: one of these days she's going to come here all by herself and have a good long cry, her own little private memorial service: just the two of them, Nina and Maribel. Well, Nina and Maribel's ghost. Now that she's found the pictures, she can finally afford to grieve in peace. Finding them like that, finally, after all these years, was the stuff of miracles; tonight she'll go home and burn them. But not without showing them, at least one last time, to Hugh.

Nina ties a scarf around her head and puts on her outsize sunglasses with their aggressive bridge and wraparounds. It's just five days past the longest day of the year, and the light in the western sky is still white-hot. It's not that she expects to go unrecognized, God knows, or that she has any reason to mistrust Elizabeth or any member of her staff, but it's always a good idea to put in an appearance, assert the family presence, show the flag. And sunglasses are more than mere disguise; she likes the green underwater light they cast on things, turning Calpurnia into a kind of dream house with its crowd of bargain hunters and sightseers only half-visible through the phony dark. Besides, her eyes have been giving her some trouble lately and she finds herself tearing up for no good reason, ready to cry at the drop of a hat. Though Maribel's been dead for two months, going on three: it isn't as if she died yesterday. It isn't as if Calpurnia's anything but a giant albatross around all their necks.

ELIZABETH is exhausted; she's come to the end of her strength and no longer has the energy to duck the reporter from the *Main Line Times*. The woman had called her last week and wouldn't take no for an answer: but since when has Elizabeth become the sole living repository of Calpurnia lore and the Archibald and Aubrey family histories? "I understand the parking situation is the sticking point," she says. "The township is very conscious of the neighbors' concerns, and who wouldn't be? I mean, look at the Barnes. There are always problems with a museum, or even some sort of arts foundation, say."

The young woman from the paper is dressed much too formally for the weather or the time of day; there's a beading of sweat like seed pearls at her hairline, and they both struggle to overlook her wretchedness as she flicks back the cover of her little stenographer's notebook and uncaps her pen. "How much do the heirs expect to clear on the sale?" she says.

Elizabeth laughs. "Lord, who knows?" she says. "At this point your guess is as good as mine." Or at least it is until she consults with the family after the final tally, as she doesn't add. Oscar was always so good at the required double-talk with the press, drowning them in artful chatter without ever releasing a quotable opinion, let alone a fact; but for all the years she worked with him Elizabeth never quite got the hang of it.

Besides, it's getting late. Time to wrap things up. Henry has been buzzing around her for the last half hour, wanting to know what goes where, and Clemmie may be out of her depth at the garden door, trying to register the odds and ends of kitchen stuff that never seem to go till the bitter end. The security contingent is probably ready to go home by now, and she'll have to do a last-minute flyby to see if there's anything left worth securing in view of the overtime it will cost her if they stay. She smiles at the young woman from the *Times* and makes no move to go. If Oscar taught her anything, it was that it never pays to get on the bad side of the press.

"What price did the Empire fainting couch finally go for, assuming it sold?" the reporter asks. She's small, intense, and determined to tough out the heat in her high-buttoned linen suit; she reminds Elizabeth of Robin in her single-mindedness and unstrategic charm.

"I'd have to look it up," she says.

They're standing at the foot of the stairs, and it's Elizabeth's instinct to keep moving but she can't; inside her some crucial line of supply seems suddenly to have given out. "Do you mind if I sit down?" she says. She hasn't eaten all day and the afternoon's accumulated heat has gone to her head like alcohol. She leans her shoulders back against the peeling red wall and fans herself with the papers on her clipboard, waiting for her strength to return. "Are you all right?" the young reporter asks.

For a moment Elizabeth misses Robin viscerally. She smiles and touches the young woman's hand. "It's been a long day," she says; or is even that saying too much? From here she can see Ellios waiting for her in the bay window beside the garden door; she's been aware of him for the last half hour, pivoting aimlessly in a small tight circle of bare parquet between the library, the dining room, and the hall. From what she can see of him from here he has an armful of outsize books in the crook of one elbow but appears to be in no great hurry to pay for them. Elizabeth is careful not to catch his eye, but she's conscious of him in a way that bypasses direct vision. She can feel his presence in her skin like electricity, or heat.

Slowly, one by one, the sale staff drifts in from the far corners of the house: Henry; Clemmie; the St. Joseph's boys Elizabeth has hired as security; and the two long-haired pickup drivers who have promised to pinch-hit with the hauling on request. It's time to chase the last stragglers down from the second floor, flush out the buyers from the deadbeats and merely undecideds, lock up the cash box, collect the receipts, and, if she's lucky, start to think about calling it a day.

Elizabeth pulls herself together and begins directing traffic—to the kitchen, to the library, to the garden, up the stairs. She says good-bye to the young reporter and shakes her hand. "A house like this is one of a kind," she says, and waits for the girl to write it down as if it were some kind of scoop or secret revealed. Ellios is no longer in sight, and for a moment she's almost disappointed; seconds later, though, she sees him just outside the dining-room window bay, leaning against one of two stone parapets on either side of the rose garden. It's been a long, grueling day; she hasn't eaten since breakfast and he'll probably insist on taking her out for a drink. She looks at him helplessly, too tired to think up a passable excuse.

Elizabeth gives Clemmie the high sign, and seconds later the last customer comes slowly down the stairs from the second floor carrying a vaseful of artificial roses from Maribel's bedroom windowsill, and makes what must be the last purchase of the day as Elizabeth goes to retrieve her purse from the locked powder room so that she can pay the St. Joseph's boys before they leave; she'll settle up with the others tomorrow, as agreed. Hooking the door behind her, she picks her way past the gray spaces where the vanished Carraccis once hung, takes up a position at the mirror, and tries to salvage what she can.

Her hair may still be retrievable with a little work, though her face is a mess and her white linen shirt is completely limp; but her pearls always give her courage and her skirt's still miraculously uncreased: she'll have to do what she can with what she has. Elizabeth retrieves her bag and gropes her way to the bottom of it for powder and blush. The south light is already fading as she draws a new line around her mouth and uses the same pencil to reshape the outer corner of her eyes, then spreads another layer of powder like a second skin. Squinting at the mirror, she tries to draw herself as a young woman, a little more mysterious than she ever really was and very slightly more wanton; down to and including the ironically arched eyebrow, the fake cheekbones with their brownish blush, and that morning's renewable pink smile.

She's grateful for the south light and the soft focus of Maribel's Venetian mirror (uncleaned, as far as she can tell, for years) erasing all lines and fudging any noticeable asymmetries. She's forty-five, her own work in progress, and no longer game for full dress inspection under a strong light, but probably otherwise still passable, as Ellios's persistence suggests. By her own standards she's better-looking now than she was when she first started painting this portrait, or at least better at faking what passes for beauty at a distance of at least three feet and in any halfway accommodating light. Her face is thinner and more definite now than it was then, she's a finer colorist with a lighter hand on the brush, and she's drawn this same likeness so many times by now that she could do it in her sleep; she knows its hills and valleys, its ins and outs, its excesses and deficits by heart. And when you get right down to it, what else is there to work with? Your face is your signature: it's what you hold out ahead of yourself to show at all the frontier crossings and checkpoints along the way: a kind of passport, your *carte d'identité.*

Elizabeth closes the compact, caps the lip liner, and puts it away. Outside in the hall there's the sound of a door slamming, chairs scraping; someone's voice raised in mock surprise. Elizabeth runs her wrists under the cold water to cool her arms, then checks the mirror one last time and makes a little tragicomic face at her reflection in it. She's looked better and she's looked worse, but it's much too late now for any major repairs. Skin isn't canvas; there are limits to what paint and pencils and brushes can do. My work of art, she thinks, such as it is: but it will have to do.

A NOTE ON THE TYPE

This book was set in Adobe Garamond. Designed for the Adobe Corporation by Robert Slimbach, the fonts are based on types first cut by Claude Garamond (c. 1480–1561). Garamond was a pupil of Geoffroy Tory and is believed to have followed the Venetian models, although he introduced a number of important differences, and it is to him that we owe the letter we now know as "old style." He gave to his letters a certain elegance and feeling of movement that won their creator an immediate reputation and the patronage of Francis I of France.

Composed by Creative Graphics,
Allentown, Pennsylvania
Printed and bound by R. R. Donnelley and Sons,
Harrisonburg, Virginia
Designed by Virginia Tan